SORCE

BIRTH OF ECHO

CASEY TRULY

Encyclopocalypse Publications
www.encyclopocalypse.com

CONTENTS

Acknowledgments

I want to firstly thank God for giving me the courage to write this book, and praying that He gets this book into the hands of those who need it. I also want to thank everyone who has encouraged me through this process and those who've been anticipating this book for a long time. I'd like to thank a few names in particular for making this possible.

Ray my mother
Eugene my father
Gen
Foster
Thomas
Johnny
Ryan
Mark Alan Miller
Dr. Linda Dove
Mike Sonksen
Dr. Mathew Bridgewater

Thank you.

SORCE

BIRTH OF ECHO

I

"That's it then?" I say, sitting on my bed watching Laurie walk to the door.

She's wearing one of her regular outfits; a white shirt, the collar cut into a v, black jeans that hug her legs, a pair of blue sneakers, and her auburn hair tied in a loose ponytail.

"Yeah, that's it I guess…" Laurie replies.

"Am I allowed to talk to you?"

"Charlie, look, I know this isn't going to be easy for you, but I think you should distance yourself for a minute," Laurie says, letting out a sigh.

"You're the only person I know here," I plead.

"You have Mat. And Zach."

"We haven't seen each other in over a year. We're not in the same caste," I say.

"Maybe, you should fix that." Laurie turns to the door and cracks it open slowly.

The sound of people rushes in, the students who haven't fully moved into their dorms during the early move-in times are getting ready for the semester. Laurie turns back to look at me.

"Don't take this personally, please. I'll miss you." Laurie closes the door behind her.

Laurie and I were dating for three years, eight months, and twenty-four days. Now, we've been broken up for ten minutes. She couldn't have picked a better time, a day before the semester at Sirrus starts. Laurie and I decided to go to Sirrus together to pursue a career in the Sorce caste. Laurie always wanted to make a difference in the world, always talked about the travesties happening in our city, New Shelltar, or other countries around the world. I never really cared about the world the way she did, but I did like the idea of being a famous Sorce Master, or is it Master of Sorce? I'm not sure.

I want to do the right thing…and I also want the glory. Saving people from natural disasters, criminals, or monsters. I wanted to make my mark on history in some way, she wanted it more for the altruism of it. So, we both decided we'd join the Sorces; a caste of people who specialized in raw sorce manipulation.

> Sorce: The power or essence or ability used to influence/manipulate events, outcomes, course of nature, or otherworldly aspects. Whether illusions, elements, animals, spirits, minds, or creatures, sorce is present and can be controlled through different means.

At least that's how the text books describe it. I remember that much, but nothing else. At the age of twenty, any person is able to join a school of their choosing to pursue a career as a Sorce, Artí, or Fencer. Before then, you spend the first eighteen years in Fundamental Academics. For two years Laurie and some of her friends studied the basics of their respective castes. My closest two friends did the same.

I, on the other hand, picked up a book or two but spent most of my time enjoying a two-year long break, and my girlfriend Laurie. We went on several vacations and adventures over those two years, I fell in love with her tenacity, willingness to fight whoever or whatever, the way she was unapologetically herself.

That's how she was on the outside, but I knew a softer, kinder, more self-conscious side of her. I loved her, more than I think I let her know at the time. Maybe she couldn't see that, or maybe I didn't show it, I don't know I'll ever find out now.

Up until now my identity was wrapped around Laurie. Everything she did, her dreams, her aspirations. I didn't realize I hadn't even thought of my own, I was just tagging along for the ride. Maybe that's why she left, maybe I'd grown too complacent with my own life. Not that it matters now. She's gone.

———

EERAH EERAH EERAH! My alarm is blaring at me. Normally I'd be irritated, but I just don't care. I feel an endless void forming in my soul that's trying to drag me down and consume me within it. I stare at the alarm for a moment: 8:30A.M. An hour before my first class. I smack the alarm to turn it off then drag myself from under the covers, then head over to the bathroom. Using the toilet, brushing my teeth, combing my hair, all these mundane tasks feel pointless. I'm definitely in a slump and I have no tangible desire to get out of it.

I put on my relatively new tunic; the one Laurie bought me a few months ago. I normally wear a regular shirt, jeans, and custom-made shoes, but now I'm an Apprentice, a first class Sorce. Which means I have to dress the part. The tunic was a long-sleeved white and black one, with layers of fabric that kept you cool in the day and warm at night. I paired this with black pants and white shoes. It's custom for you to wear symbolic or themed clothing for your first three years, after that, you can practically wear whatever you want. Though, mostly everyone wears some form of tunic, jacket, suit, skirt, dress, padding, or they have specific tastes or a cultural influence.

The day she bought it for me I was shocked, these things weren't cheap since they were made from a special sorce material, as strong as the toughest metals, but softer than most silks. I love this tunic, but now it's just a painful reminder.

I head out to the cafeteria to get something to eat. Not that I'm hungry, I just know that if I don't eat something, I'm not going to be able to focus. I leave my dorm room; the automatic lock makes a beep sound. I notice a couple of other students already down the hall and some leaving their dorms at the same time as me. Is the Master of my first class going to be uptight? It's Sorce Manipulation 103, so they're probably not going to be too harsh.

I did some training over my last summer, getting down the basics of sorce manipulation and some basic elemental skills but nothing too advanced. I walk into the cafeteria and there's a line, of course, and Laurie, a few people away, getting her meal, talking to some of the other students. People I've never met before. My psi-phone and watch vibrate in unison.

SORCE MANIPULATION 103: IN 5 MINUTES.

I'm growing more irritated with these reminders and alarms.

A few of the other students are talking as I approach the line. My sneakers make a distinctive squeak across the cafeteria floors. There's been a rock stuck on the bottom of my shoes for months and every time they squeak it's got the undertone of something being carved into stone. Laurie knows that sound and she turns to see me. We make eye-contact and I feel both happy and sad to see her.

She immediately turns her eyes away and jumps back into a conversation with the guy standing in front of her. Now I've definitely lost my appetite. I bypass the line and go for the snack shelf next to the register. I grab an energy bar and a water. A guy with the nametag that says "Rosh" is standing at the end. Rosh has a huge beard, looks like he's in his late twenties, big but in a muscular way.

"Good morning!" Rosh says.

"Good morning," I reply.

I put my items on a scale and the register scans my items.

"I love those bars! Great for energy, even better paired with an Acceler-aid," Rosh says.

I look over at the pyramid of Acceler-aid cans next to the register.

"You get commission?" I say. Rosh laughs.

"No, I almost got sponsored by them when I was your age though. I'm just a fan."

"Alright, I'll bite."

I swap one can for the water.

"Great choice," Rosh says. "Your total will be D4."

I put my watch up to the payment terminal and it blips with a confirmation.

"You're all set bud," Rosh says.

"Thanks Rosh. I'm Charlie, by the way," I say.

"Nice to meet you Charlie, good luck with your first day!" Rosh says.

He's a little enthusiastic for his job, but his personality is welcome with the hell-of-a-day I'm having. I turn my head one last time. I don't know why. I know who's going to be behind me. For anyone else, it would've been a nice pretty girl who wanted to grab a coffee, or a famous athlete with the offer of front row seats to their next game. For me, I knew it was going to be some faces I didn't want to see. Sure enough, it's the guy Laurie was talking to, with the biggest and silliest grin I'd ever seen. I turn back and make a hasty walk away from the cafeteria.

I make it to the classroom about a minute before class starts. The Master is sitting at his desk with his eyes closed, as if fallen into a deep sleep. Four other students are sitting in class, having already taken their seats. I take another glance at the Master; tall, a long coat with a button up shirt and tie, orange hair and a long-pointed beard to match. A bronze-like nametag floats above his desk that reads "Master W. Uphraeus" with a sticky note attached to it. "Touch Nametag", it reads. I touch the floating nametag and watch as my name appears on the black board behind the Master. The name "Charlie" materializes underneath four other names. The classroom has auditorium seating, I don't want to sit up front, don't want to sit too far back. I find a spot in the middle.

A few moments later, Laurie comes in with the guy she was with earlier, now I'm starting to think I know the reason for the breakup. I watch Laurie and this guy along with four other students take seats two rows in front of me. Great, now I get to look at the back of Laurie's head for the rest of class. We're not just in the same class, we're in the same caste. I'm going to have to see her all day, every day, for the rest of the school year. This realization makes me drop my head to the long stretch of table in front of me, making a loud THUD as it hits. I hear a small snicker from a girl to my right. She speaks with a hushed tone.

"First day of classes. I know the feeling, but it can't be that bad. Can it?" A voice says.

My head rolls to the side. A girl with jet black hair, button nose, and two-tone, long-sleeved tunic with jean shorts. I let out a sigh of air through my nose. She puts her books on the table and slides out the chair.

"I'm assuming no one's sitting here?" She says. I shake my head.

"Go for it," I say.

I should probably pull my book out before we begin. Where's my book? I need my backpack. Where's my backpack? My head falls onto the table again. *THUD!* This time the sound is loud enough that I'm sure everyone is looking at me. I hear a few chuckles around the room. Probably at me, maybe not. I don't know. The ability to care is lost on me at the moment. If I knew a teleportation spell, I'd probably use it to fall into a volcano.

"Does he do that all the time?" another voice, male, chimes in from my right again.

I keep my head down and eyes shut.

"Oh yeah, he's a total drama queen. He's been doing this since we met. And his name is…?" The black-haired girl says.

I say nothing.

"Well..I'm Nathan. Nice to meet you," the guy says says.

"I'm Jessie," the girl says says.

"Nice to meet you, Jessie. I love that tunic!"

I hear him taking the seat next to her. Jessie pokes my arm. "And your name is?" Jessie says.

I raise my head with a red mark where it hit the table. I look over at Nathan, tall, brown hair, I'm guessing a little over six feet, wearing a red cardigan. I have a feeling I'm not going to like this guy.

"Charlie," I say.

"Alright class! Glad all of you could show up." Master Uphraeus looks at his tablet. "According to my tablet, you're all present and accounted for. We have 26 seats in this class I see 23 of you are registered…" He taps his tablet a few times and slaps the sides and mumbles, "Damned machines."

He tosses the tablet onto the table and stands to his feet. "Those of you hoping to crash here can come talk to me after today's lesson." Scanning the room he lets the silence settle in. "I am Master Uphraeus. Today we'll be going over the basics of sorce, but first can anyone explain to me what they think a Sorce is? The profession specifically."

Nathan raises his hand; I assume in hopes to show off in front of Jessie.

"You there, Miss?" Master Uphraeus says.

He points to Laurie who also has her hand up.

"Sorces are those who prefer to wield sorce in its most natural and raw form. Sorces can cast directly from their bodies. With the cost of stressing their physical forms, Sorces create more concentrated and powerful spells in exchange. Sorces command sorce in whatever way they choose, should they be powerful enough to do so," Laurie says.

Master Uphraeus looks at the black board, which rearranged the names to reflect where each student is sitting. He walks around his desk to stand in front of the class.

"Ms. Laurie Barian?" Master Uphraeus says.

"Yes, Master Uphraeus."

"Nice to meet you, Ms. Barian. You're wrong."

"Um, I'm sorry Master? The required text for this class says otherwise, and Sorces are describe—"

"Ms. Barian, I am Master Uphraeus. I've been a Sorce since you were in diapers." Master Uphraeus turns his attention back to the class. "Attention class! I know that the school has required you to purchase a text book by an author who knows nothing about sorce, but that won't be necessary." He continues, taking a copy of the book from his desk and tossing it in the trash.

"They made that text a 'requirement' to seem more prestigious. The stars know why." Master Uphraeus raises a fist in the air. "Follow me to the fields. If anyone wishes to use the restroom, now is the time. You will find us specifically at the Crystal Fields. I'll give everyone a moment to catch up. Now, onward!" He marches to the door.

Laurie looks around, at her group of friends, all of them subtly chuckling. She adjusts her ponytail and crosses her legs. I know that move; she's self-conscious and a little embarrassed. I make an internal triumphant cheer that quickly turns into sympathy. I want to console her, let her know she isn't stupid or that she doesn't have any less value because she got the answer wrong according to the Master. My heart breaks all over again.

"Well, how's that? We get to go on a field trip to the crystals. Master Uphraeus seems very excited. This class is gonna be fun, yeah?" Jessie says.

Before I can reply with my own thoughts, Nathan chimes in, clearly trying to grab Jessie's attention.

"I'll say! We should hurry before the good spots are taken. I have a feeling he's going to breakout some demonstrations!"

"Hmm, you might be right. Come on Charlie!" Jessie says.

I look at my half-eaten bar. It tastes like sawdust with a hint of blueberries. Then chug the rest of my Acceler-aid. Jessie's look of shock turns into a smile, followed by a laugh.

"Shall we?" I say.

A huge belch leaves my mouth before I can react. Jessie laughs.

"I like your energy! I'm pumped!" Jessie says.

———

Most of the students have already packed together, making new friends or chatting with old ones it seems. Master Uphraeus is ahead of all of us, moving very casually and taking in the sun. Jessie is walking in-between Nathan and me, and we're behind the rest of the students. The sun is beaming down but the cool breeze makes the temperature somewhat bearable. The school is huge. As big as a city. Built on a giant island that travels above the ocean. Endlessly levitating through the blue landscape. Although, if you're not looking over the edge, peering out of a window of one of the school's tall buildings, or seeing the school from below, you'd forget you're several miles in the air. I believe the school was founded on a mountainside, but was later cast into the ocean after the Cataclysm. That's when the school was founded by its first recorded Head Master, and was named Sirrus after the clouds above.

The group gets to the gate of the Crystal Fields where Master Uphraeus stands in waiting for us all to gather.

"Here we'll wait for those of us that are falling behind. Now is a good time to stretch!" He says.

I like Master Uphraeus already, he seems really passionate about his work, while not being a complete buzzkill.

"So, Jessie. Where are you from?" Nathan asks.

"Maethril, just off the coast," Jessie replies.

"Ah, an island girl! I like it. So, why'd you choose to come to Sirrus?" says Nathan.

Jessie raises a brow to his "island girl" comment.

"Maybe it had something to do with me being relatively poor and Sirrus being the closest sorce institution near the islands?" says Jessie.

"Well, there's always traveling abroad. Like Uni-Clad?" Nathan says.

Jessie rolls her eyes and ignores the question. "So, Charlie. What's your story?"

I'd zoned out thinking about Laurie and the last argument we had. I was piecing it together to see if there was a clue to our breakup. I have a feeling she's been catching glances of me in the crowd of students and I've been doing my best not to seek her out. I hear her laugh and I instinctually dart my eyes over at her. She's holding onto that other guy's arm while she snorts. That. That broke me. A surreal feeling passes through my body; I see her and this other guy, and it's like looking at us in the past, except I'm not there. Someone else is where I should be, the body I'm in doesn't feel real.

"Charlie?" Jessie is staring at me.

"Hey, sorry. Did you say something?"

"You've been staring at that girl since class started. Looks like she's taken bud." Jessie smirks.

"Yeah, looks like it," I say, barely audible.

"You could do way better. She looks like a psycho anyway. You know, the type that'll say she loves you one day and then key your car the next after hooking up with four other dudes," Jessie says.

She laughs and gives me a nudge with her elbow. "Jessie's right!" Nathan says.

He casually puts himself between Jessie and me, putting his arms around the both of us.

"There's plenty of girls to behold. She looks pretty hot though."

I already don't want to be around anyone, let alone this asshole. I know the next words out of his mouth are going to anger me further and I know someone like him won't know when to shut up. I put my hand on his wrist, the one on my shoulder, and heat it up to something close to unbearably hot.

"Ow!" Nathan yelps, "What the hell was that for?!"

"Don't touch me," I say.

I move ahead to the front of the crowd so I can be one of the first people inside. Master Uphraeus stands at the gate to the Crystal Fields. The gate is circular and metal, floating just above the ground. Master Uphraeus is checking his watch. I decide to move to his flank and touch the border between myself and the field. I'm startled as my hand touches the invisible shield that ripples with iridescent light as it flows around the field.

"A sorce field," Master Uphraeus says.

I'm startled by his voice, not realizing that he noticed me and walked over.

"Can it protect anything?" I say.

"It can protect against most things. No need to worry my boy, pretty soon you'll be able to create your own sorce field," he says, slapping his relatively giant hand on my back.

"I didn't practice at all over the last two years. My whole reason for coming here…kind of, isn't the reason anymore."

"Well, that's alright lad. You'll have plenty of time to figure out what it is you want. But, you seem like a naturally curious one. I bet you'll find your talents soon enough."

"To be honest Master Uphraeus, I only signed up because…" I turn to face him, but Master Uphraeus left me talking to myself. Figures. I hear his watch make a chirping noise in the distance.

"Alright everyone, let's head on inside!" Master Uphraeus says. "First things first. Sorce has various uses, one of these being utility. This sorce field is basic, but strong enough to keep out anyone unauthorized to use it. Anyone willing to try shattering it?"

Silence from the crowd.

"Well, good. It wouldn't work and you'd probably get knocked on your bum. As much as watching one of you getting humbled amuses me, I guess we'll skip it this time."

Master Uphraeus picks up a rock and throws it at the field. The sorce field then ripples again in fractal light like before but much larger this time.

"Sorce fields can be broken or crossed with enough force, disabling its maker, or knowing the correct counter-spell. Or, if you have the right key…"

Master Uphraeus touches the cufflink on his right hand. As he rotates the cuff, the gate makes an unlocking click and proceeds to open.

"It can be opened."

Master Uphraeus walks in through the gate and gestures everyone to follow him inside.

"Come on in! We're almost to the best part!" He says with eager excitement. I quickly move through the gate before the horde of others get their first steps in.

The Crystal Fields is a grassy plain with a forest cluster in the back. Four-foot pillars are scattered throughout the grass with cerulean tear-shaped crystals hovering over them. Master Uphraeus stops in the middle of the field and turns towards all the students, I'm at least a few yards ahead of everyone else.

"Well, you seem to be in quite a hurry to get started," Master Uphraeus says, looking directly at me. "I like your enthusiasm!"

The other students gather around me and make a half circle.

Jessie finds her way next to me again. "Hey."

"Hey."

"I'm sorry if I, or Nathan, said anything to upset you."

"It's fi—"

"Alright! Welcome young Sorces, to the Crystal Fields. These crystals are very special, can anyone tell me why?" Master Uphraeus looks around at the students. Only one has her hand raised.

"Yes, Ms. Barian?"

"The Crystal Fields have been a place to practice sorce for generations. Some even say that the school was founded on the field itself," Laurie says.

I recognize her humble-bragging tone and roll my eyes. The kind of tone she might use with me when she knew she was right, but would let me figure that out after she said it.

"Uhm. Well, yes Ms. Barian. But I was looking for something a bit more specific."

Jessie raises her hand.

"Yes, you! Miss?"

He tries searching for her profile on his tablet.

"Jessie Zirdi," she says.

"Ah, yes, Ms. Zirdi. What say you?"

"Is it because of the crystals sir? These sorce crystals are teardrop shaped and found naturally here on Sirrus. Unlike most sorce crystals that are artificially made by sorce users, these crystals have an above average concentration of sorce held within them and are capable of storing it in large quantities."

"Excellent Ms. Zirdi!"

I glance over at Laurie. I know her pride took a hit there. She's 0 and 2 for questions. Sure enough, she's playing with her ponytail.

"To be more clear, Ms. Zirdi; this place is also a sorce field. Much like the one we came through to get here. Except this one has a different use. The crystals can store, channel, and amplify sorce. Making them an effective source for...sorce!" Master Uphraeus continues.

Master Uphraeus has a huge smile on his face. A single student chuckles out loud and without missing a beat, The Master points off in the direction he hears the laugh.

"I always get at least one." He chuckles to himself then walks next to one of the crystals. "Today, you will start by weaving your own sorce into the crystals. As you do, you can bend the light around these crystals as such."

Master Uphraeus places his hand over one of the crystals and it begins to illuminate a brighter blue. As he moves his hand around, the light changes and becomes green, then yellow and red.

"The point of this exercise is to control your sorce output by not overloading the crystal. You'll know when it's overloading when it becomes a deep orange color. You'll want an opposite effect to complete this exercise, the crystal should have a fractal look to it with multiple colors. And be careful. Too little and nothing will happen. Too much…"

The crystal glows just as before cycling through colors, then turns a bright orange and begins vibrating. A small shockwave of orange light explodes from the crystal, making some of us students at the front lose our balance. Master Uphraeus remains firm.

"That will knock you right on your bums!"

Master Uphraeus lets out a boisterous laugh.

"Luckily for you all, these crystals have been programmed to release before any fatal build up happens and we all end up swimming with the whales." He takes off his glasses and wipes them.

"Now. You're welcome to practice by yourself or with a partner, but no more than two people per crystal. Everyone has to pull their weight. Consider this your first assignment. Dismissed!" Master Uphraeus gestures towards the open field all around us.

———

"Ah there you are!" Nathan says.

He spots Jessie and me as everyone is chattering and breaking off by themselves or going off in pairs. I notice Laurie walking off by herself.

"Well, the Master said three to every crystal." Nathan looks at Jessie.

"He said solo or groups of two. Were you not paying attention?" Jessie says.

I see an opportunity to get out of this conversation before I get dragged into it. Maybe I can catch up to Laurie and see if she'll want to partner up. I slip away as the crowd is still shifting. I spot Laurie walking over to a slightly more isolated crystal from the rest of the field. As I make my way over to her, I notice the guy she's been with all day approaching her from the side. I'm not gonna reach her before he does.

"Laurie!" I shout.

She turns around and sees me. Her reaction is confusing. She gives a half smile and politely waves, like she barely knows me. The other guy turns his gaze to me as well, still approaching her. She notices him and he says something to her.

"Charlie please. Now's not a good time," Laurie says.

"Oh..." I reply. "Okay that's...yeah. Maybe we can talk tomorrow?" My voice has a quiver in it that I don't like.

"Charlie..." Laurie says. "I think you need space...to move on."

"I didn't realize we weren't going to be on speaking terms. Is it because of this guy? Did you—" I say.

"Charlie!" Laurie shouts.

I recoil a bit and a few students in the area notice the loud roar. I feel like a stray puppy, begging for scraps below the table, and everyone can see it. Laurie takes a deep breath.

"Listen, I've got too many things on my mind right now. I can't deal with this," Laurie says.

"So, I'm assuming this is your new boyfriend then?" I say.

"Charlie, that's none of your business. Just leave."

I glance over at this guy who probably has a few inches on me, but I'm not intimidated.

"What's your name?"

"Rhody," he says with confidence, his voice is somewhat deep but I can tell it's artificial. He's trying to intimidate me. Now we're having a stare down, except I'm not really staring him down, I'm actually trying to figure out who's standing behind him. It's a shadowy figure that looks about my height. I can't tell if my vision is blurred from the sun.

I feel a hefty weight on my shoulder. I turn my gaze for a moment to look and see Master Uphraeus has placed his hand on my shoulder. I look back and Rhody is standing there, smug as all hell ,and the dark figure is gone.

"I know your minds are eager to learn, but remember I said groups of two at most," Master Uphraeus says.

I'm not sure if he was around for Laurie's outburst, or the stare down me and this Rhody guy, but he was clearly here to break us up.

"Come along Charlie." Master Uphraeus turns me in the opposite direction. "I'll set you up with your own crystal."

I look at Laurie one last time and she almost looks sad. Rhody turns his back, grabs Laurie's hand and walks towards a crystal. Walking alongside Master Uphraeus, I'm lost in thought about the whole situation. How long has she been with this guy? *Rhody.* Is that why she broke up with me? Did he convince her to or force her? Was he in the shadows of our relationship the whole time?

"Charlie?" Master Uphraeus interrupts my thoughts. "Charlie, what's on your mind son?"

I snap out of my focus to realize we've stopped in front of a crystal.

"Huh? I'm sorry Master Uphraeus, I was lost in thought."

Master Uphraeus chuckles. "Yes, my boy, I can see that. Something to do with that altercation I pulled you from?"

"You heard that?" I ask, slightly embarrassed.

"No. I saw the palms of your hands glowing. It looked like I was going to have to break up a fight and suspend someone or worse, expel them."

"Glowing?" I ask, examining both of my hands and don't see them doing anything unusual.

"Yes. You were channeling a large amount of sorce—and

from the look on your face–it might have ended with someone being harmed"

Master Uphraeus positions himself on the other side of crystal, putting it between us.

"Charlie, I want you to try the exercise on this crystal. See if you can manipulate your sorce in and around it."

I'm looking at my hands. Glowing? What was I about to do? Usually, it takes a bit of concentration to use sorce. I don't think I've ever used sorce subconsciously. I look at Master Uphraeus and he gives me a slight nod.

"I'm here. Don't worry," Master Uphraeus says.

I take a deep breath and position my hands on either side of the crystal. Its blue light gets a bit brighter. I try channeling more sorce, manipulating it through the crystal, but it doesn't do much more than alter the brightness of the blue. I look around and see the other students struggling throughout the field. Most seem to have their crystals shifting to green or yellow. Only a few have made their crystals look like prisms. Then I notice a couple of guys trying to put a crystal back onto one of the pillars and failing miserably.

"Um. Master Uphraeus?"

"It's alright Charlie, just relax."

"I am, but should the crystals be able to come off like that?"

I then point toward the dynamic duo fumbling around with one of the crystals.

"Mighty crustaceans!" Master Uphraeus exclaims. "Y-you keep practicing, Charlie. I'll catch up with you later." He then quickly power walks over to the other side of the field. "Gentlemen! Please step away from the crystal! How in the stars did you manage—"

I focus back on the crystal, attempting to make the color change again. I know if Laurie was here, she'd be able to walk me through this. Then I'm reminded of last week, the last week Laurie and I were together. We'd just watched a movie and everything seemed perfectly fine. Or was it?

"Hey." I hear someone from behind me. It's Jessie. "Mind if I join you?"

"I would say no, but I could use a friend right now," I say.

"Oh! So, we're friends now? Cool…" She moves around to the other side of the crystal and faces me with a big goofy grin, I can't help but laugh.

"Yeah, yeah, I guess we're friends now." I smile.

"It's a pleasure," Jessie says, brightening up even more.

"Where's Nathan?" I say.

"Probably looking around for me. Is it just me or is he *super* clingy?" Jessie says.

I look at Jessie, then turn my head to try and locate Laurie and Rhody. I see the two of them using their crystal. It's changing all sorts of colors with a prismatic aura. They're both laughing and having a great time and I notice Laurie seems relaxed now. Rhody is flailing his arms around acting like an idiot. Does he know all the fun conversations we used to have?

"Charlie."

The arguments? The embarrassing things I've said and done? Did she complain to him about me?

"Charlie."

Was she cheating on me? Has she slept with him?!

"CHARLIE!" Jessie shouts.

I turn my head just in time to see the crystal's bright orange light and low hum. My hands are glowing with the same intensity. A brief second of realization comes to me, then—

BOOM!

II

My head hurts. My hands hurt. My whole body aches.

The sun beams down at me through my eyelids, and the only thing I can hear is a high-pitched whine. The sound slowly fades in, and I can hear a deep muffled voice talking right over me. I open my eyes and see a very concerned Master Uphraeus looking at me, checking my head and the rest of my body.

"Charlie? Charlie can you hear me?" Master Uphraeus says.

"Y-yeah. I hear you," I say.

"My God boy, what happened?!"

I sit up and shake my head, then look around. A few other students are standing around, gawking and murmuring to themselves. I don't see Jessie.

"Jessie?" I squeak.

A group of students are gathered on the other side of me and the crystal.

"Can you stand son?" Master Uphraeus says.

"Yeah. Yeah, I'm fine, where's Jessie?"

Other students are huddled together. I see who else might've witnessed what just happened. The answer is everyone, even Laurie and Rhody. Rhody laughs and Laurie promptly punches him in the arm. I see him grab her arm with more force than I'm comfortable with, and I rise to my feet.

"Take it easy there, Charlie. Explain to me what happened," Master Uphraeus says.

Jessie walks from behind a group of students. I sigh. She looks okay, albeit a bit dirty from the fall. She notices me and gives me a very shocked look. Nathan is standing next to her, an expression of fear on his face.

"Charlie…I need you to answer me," Master Uphraeus says.

He speaks with a coldness that—up until now—I didn't think he had in him. It sends a chill down my spine. I realize that Jessie's okay, and that I'm probably in a lot of trouble. I swallow my words and turn to the Master.

"I…I don't know. I was trying to complete the assignment."

Master Uphraeus looks at me with curiosity. Then like the flip of a coin, his demeanor changes. All the students were gathered around, whispering, watching. I suddenly feel a sense of alienation, or worse…condemnation.

Master Uphraeus lets out a hefty laugh. "No one is hurt. Like I said these crystals have safeguards in place. Albeit this burst of sorce was quite impactful, I think we can say everyone did excellent work! I think we'll end the class here and I'll see you all at our next meeting. I suggest everyone think of a small demonstration of sorce to bring to our next class!"

His booming cheerful tone seems to give everyone else a sense of ease. Except me. I can recognize when someone is putting on a face just to calm the situation down. I don't think our conversation is over.

"Class dismissed!" Master Uphraeus says. "Except you Charlie," he whispers, "I want you to stick around."

Everyone begins gathering their things and departing. Jessie sheepishly approaches me.

"Ms. Zirdi, I'd like you to stay as well," Master Uphraeus says.

"Yes, sir," Jessie says.

Master Uphraeus begins checking on the rest of the students, some of them with questions. I look over at Jessie, I didn't even realize Nathan was standing next to her.

"What was that?" Nathan says.

An irritated tone seeps through his lips.

"Jessie are you alright?" I say.

"Yeah, I'm good, don't worry so much," Jessie says. She gives me a reassuring smile.

"Someone could've gotten hurt! *You* could've gotten hurt!" Nathan says.

"Master Uphraeus said there were safeguards. No one needs to worry about me, especially you," Jessie says.

"I hate to say it, but Nathaniel's right," I say.

"It's *Nathan*," he says.

"You looked like you'd just killed someone. Stop being a drama queen!" Jessie laughs.

"I put up a small sorce shield just before the burst. I got knocked over but I'm fine. Really."

Her eyes are ocean green. The expression she just gave me put me at absolute ease. I can't tell if I'm happier that she's okay, or that she's not mad at me.

"Good, I'm glad," I say.

A smile creeps across my face. I'm really tempted to give her a hug, but Master Uphraeus steps towards me and Nathan.

"Excuse me...Mister?" Master Uphraeus asks, looking at Nathan.

"Toner," Nathan says.

"Mr. Toner. Class is dismissed and I'd like to have a chat with these two."

"Of course, Master Uphraeus."

Nathan gives a proper bow, but doesn't break eye contact.

"I'll see you around, Jessie," Nathan says, staring at me with rage in his eyes as he walks away.

I had a feeling I wasn't going to like Nathan. Now I *know* I don't like Nathan. Him, and his stupid red cardigan, his glasses, brown hair, and overly lumpy shaped frame.

<First Rhody. Then Nathan.>

"What?" I ask.

I look to Jessie and Master Uphraeus.

"What?" Jessie responds.

"Nothing."

I could've sworn I heard a voice say something. I shift my focus to Master Uphraeus, who's currently looking at the crystal I was using. It hasn't moved, and it looks like I haven't even touched it. I shoot a puzzled look at Jessie; she shrugs with her hands in the air.

"I'm sorry Master Uphraeus. I didn't mean to—"

"Nonsense, my boy." Master Uphraeus cuts me off. He waves a hand in my direction, giving me the idea to stop talking. "Tell me, what were you doing just before the burst?"

"I was…"

Trailing off, I remember looking at Laurie, and the thoughts that were running through my head.

"I wasn't paying attention sir. I was lost in thought," I say, regretfully.

"Ms. Zirdi, were you interacting with the crystal at the same time?" Master Uphraeus says.

"I was for a moment Master. Then I stopped when I noticed Charlie had somewhat taken control," Jessie says.

My eyes go wide and I look at her with open palms. Way to throw me under the bus, Jessie. I mean, you don't owe me anything, but still. Jessie returns the gesture but mouths a *what did you want me to say?* to punctuate her pose.

"All my time here and I've never seen a burst like that. To be quite honest, I didn't think that was possible with safeguards. I felt the burst from where I was across the way," Master Uphraeus says.

He's concentrating on the crystal, but I can tell there's something else going through his mind.

"Unless..." Master Uphraeus ponders for a moment. "You told me you weren't sure if you even wanted to be a Sorce. Is that right?" He inquires.

"Yes, sir. I only signed up because...because I was following the wrong path," I say.

I'm a little embarrassed for admitting that.

Master Uphraeus roars a mighty laugh, then puts a hand on my shoulder and speaks in a soft tone. "Sometimes love will turn you blind, my boy. It happens to the best of us."

He turns away from the crystal, wiping the sweat off his brow. Though, I notice it's not that hot out.

"I'm willing to bet that right about now you're feeling like your whole world has just been turned upside down. But I can assure you that doesn't always mean you're lost. You just need a new perspective."

His words are calming and reassuring.

"I think whatever has you feeling lost, will show you the path you were meant to be on." He gives a warm smile to Jessie.

"I want you and Ms. Zirdi to head to the nurse's office, just in case. If Mrs. Poulla is there, just tell her Master Uphraeus sent you. Dismissed."

Master Uphraeus pulls out a notepad from his front coat pocket then walks back over to the crystal. Jessie and I begin walking towards the exit of the Crystal Fields. There's an awkward silence between us. I'm still letting the Master's words sink in. He seems both intrigued and fascinated with what happened. If I show any more potential, I might end up being a star student, or worse...his pupil.

"So, what exactly was going through your mind?" Jessie says.

"I was just thinking about a crappy situation I've been going through," I say.

"Well, it seemed more than just 'crappy'."

She stops walking and stares at me. I turn my head and stop walking as well.

"It's nothing," I say.

"You know just before the burst, after I called your name. You looked at me with tears in your eyes," Jessie says.

Tears in my eyes? Seriously?

"I'm assuming that girl you've been staring at all day is your ex?" Jessie asks.

I nod.

"How recent was it?" Jessie says.

"Yesterday," I say.

"Damn…"

I nod again.

"Well look, I'm not going to pry anymore if you don't want to talk about it right now, but I would like a deeper explanation later—you know—since you almost killed me?" Jessie says. She smiles with a devilish grin.

"You said you were fine!" My shoulders relax a little and I laugh alongside her.

As Jessie and I arrive at the nurse's office together, I take a moment to look at the architecture. The nurse's office is more of a full medical wing of a hospital. At the top of the building is a pink cross with two reptilian creatures carved out of stone on either side. Their bodies move in a wave-like motion. The building is made of a white and coral stone, standing on four floors. The size makes sense considering the amount of people that are stuck on this floating rock. We walk inside and see mostly staff walking around, and we're greeted by the concierge.

"Hello, welcome! How can I help you today?" The woman's nametag reads Mrs. S. Poulla.

"Hi, Mrs. Poulla. We were told to come to the nurse's office by our Master," I say.

"Specifically, Master Uphraeus," Jessie says.

"Yes, Master Uphraeus sent us," I say.

Mrs. Poulla looks exhausted. "Ah, lovely. The semester just started this morning and Uphraeus is already at it. Please put your information into the data pads to your right and I'll be sure the nurse sees you in a moment."

"Thank you," I say.

"Yes, thank you Mrs. Poulla," Jessie says.

We both walk over to the small data pads on the right, which are connected to 40-inch screens that take down all your vitals, and previous medical records for expedited waiting rooms. Jessie is making crude faces at the screen as it scans her.

"I'm assuming you're not a fan?" I say.

"Not really. I hate hospitals. My mom used to practically live in them," Jessie says.

"Oh. I'm sorry," I say.

"It's alright. I'm mostly over it. I got to say goodbye at least." She seems unfazed by the subject, which I'm not sure is a good sign, but she looks alright. "So, how're you feeling?" Jessie asks.

"I'm alright. I thought I might've twisted a joint when I fell, but the doctor said I'm fine," I say.

"I meant there," Jessie says.

She pokes me in the heart.

"Excuse me? The nurse is ready for you, Ms. Zirdi," Mrs. Poulla says.

"Oh?" Jessie says.

"You'll be seen in room 104," Mrs. Poulla says. "And Charlie?"

"Yes?" I say.

"You'll be in room 107. Follow me."

Jessie and I follow the nurse to the offices. We stop at Jessie's room first. Before she enters, she squeezes my hand, takes a deep breath, nods in assurance, then walks inside.

Mrs. Poulla escorts me to my room. The smell of bleach and plastic creep through my nose. I walk inside and sit on the patient's chair, and it has a film on top of it that feels like a soapy bubble. I've been to the hospital before for minor things;

last time I was in one was for a booster shot. I've never had to have anything serious done.

The nurse's office started as a broom closet from what I know. Now it's fully staffed with doctors and nurses, though it's still called the nurse's office. Doctor Shall is the one who comes to examine me and he does a full checkup and doesn't find anything strange. I tell him I'm not in pain, but Master Uphraeus told me to come here just in case. I explain the crystal burst situation.

"Well, those crystals shouldn't have any side effects. If they did, we'd know about it by now," Dr. Shall says looking at me quizzically, "Strange that you were able to cause a surge powerful enough to warrant Uphraeus sending you to the nurse's office. So, you're training to be a Sorce? There are a lot of occupational hazards that come with being a Sorce you know?"

"Yeah."

"Far be it from me to try and convince you otherwise. You just don't look like you're sure why you're here."

"Master Uphraeus told me to come here."

"I meant here at the school," Dr. Shall says. "You're free to go Charlie. If you need anything or any strange symptoms pop up, feel free to call me."

"Okay, thank you, Dr. Shall."

I leave the room and start thinking about what it is I want. I only started this whole thing because I wanted to be with Laurie, but now, here I am without her and everyone tells me I look lost. Probably because I am. I'm lost without her. So, I guess what I have to do is find a way to get her back. Maybe if I become a better Sorce...

"You get lost in thought a lot, don't you?" Jessie says. I didn't notice Jessie at first standing in the doorway.

"Huh?" I say. "I guess?"

"So, what on earth was buzzing around that head of yours

this time? Obviously, it wasn't the same thing that brought you to tears and caused that burst," Jessie says.

"I think I just figured out what I want."

My stomach is rumbling, and now the feeling of soreness and stomach cramps are following. All I had for breakfast this morning was a bar and an energy drink.

"And what exactly do you want?" Jessie asks.

"Food. Wanna grab lunch?" I say.

Jessie laughs out loud and shakes her head. "Sure bud, let's get out of this hellhole."

We leave the nurse's office and head to the dining hall. As we're on our way there, I notice Jessie is staring at the sky deep in thought. Her black hair is softly moving with the wind, and the color of her eyes pop even more.

I suddenly realize my best friends Mat and Zach are probably out of their classes too! I haven't spoken to them in months. The thought of seeing my two closest friends puts a giant smile on my face. Jessie looks over at me as I'm snorting, remembering the time when the three of us were preteens and we went into an abandoned zoo.

We were all scared, but none us of would actually admit it. Mat and Zach were putting on their brave faces as we went down into the lion's den. We laughed and freaked each other out with scary stories and "what if" scenarios of horrendous monsters or ghosts that had taken residence of the place. That is, until we heard something growl. And not just a normal growl, a deep, thunderous growl. We all could've sworn it said something and it wasn't just trying to make loud noises. We never actually found out what it was. To me it sounded like the growl had said "Found you..." Mat and Zach had their own interpretations. Either way we chalked it up to it being the wind because the thought of it being something alive or part of the thereafter was not something we wanted to, or could, mentally handle at the time.

"What're you laughing at weirdo?" Jessie says, interrupting my thoughts.

I explain the story to her in as much vivid detail as I can. "Whoa, that's wicked…Do you think it was a wraith or something?" Jessie says.

"I have no idea, and I'm never planning on finding out. For all I know, the zoo has been torn down and a strip mall has taken its place."

"Well, I hope not! That poor thing could've been scared," Jessie adds.

We continue on to the dining hall and during our little trip, I explain why I was excited to get there. Mat and Zach have been by my side for as long as I can remember, and to see them again —especially with everything that's going on—would be a welcomed break.

Jessie and I arrive at the dining hall, a huge three-story complex with all kinds of eateries, restaurants, lounges, and common eating areas. No matter your diet, allergies, preferences, or choices, the dining hall has it covered. You could eat inside or outside on the 2nd floor patio, which has two options of shaded umbrella tables or grassy turf for a picnic. This place is amazing. The only problem is having too many options. I pull out my psi-phone and send a group text to Mat and Zach.

> Charlie: At the dining hall. Where're you fat losers at? (12:17 PM)

Jessie takes in a deep breath from the surrounding area.

"I could really go for a burger right now!" Jessie says.

I point at her, signaling that she makes a very good point.

My psi-phone buzzes with a new message.

> Z: Ho shit! Charlie's in the house! (12:19 PM)

Mat: Well look what the tiger-cat dragged in! (12:20 PM)

Charlie: You guys eat already? Let's grab food! (12:20 PM)

Mat: Nah. (12:21 PM)

Mat: Zach and I are looking for a spot right now. Burgers? (12:21 PM)

Z: I need a slab of meat in my mouth. STAT! (12:21 PM)

Charlie: LMFAO (12:23 PM)

Charlie: How about Slyder's? They look juicy (12:24 PM)

Z: Never (12:25 PM)

Mat: On our way (12:25 PM)

"Are you done flirting with your friends?" Jessie says. Her tone is utterly sarcastic.

"Yeah, they want burgers too. I told them to meet us at Slyder's," I say.

"Oh, are they aware of me?" Jessie says.

To be honest the thought hadn't really crossed my mind. "They won't mind, but I think we should get you some food before you kill me," I say.

Jessie and I begin walking to Slyder's. On our way we pass by a lot of different students. Some are mixed together; others have decided to stick to their own. There's a table of students looking at complex manuals with metal tools on the table next to their food, obviously those are Artís. Artís can usually be found always tinkering with something mechanical or otherwise, trying to create the next great artifact. At another table students sit watching videos of weapon demonstrations. Clearly, those are the Fencers, the ones that focus on hand-to-hand maneuvers and weapons. Artís usually isolate themselves, Fencers are usually excited about nothing, and Sorces are stuck up. They all have their flaws, and their strengths.

The tables that are the loudest are usually the ones with mixed company, showing off what they've learned or what they're excited most about learning later.

Jessie and I continue to the second floor where Slyder's is located and as we approach, I spot two guys standing outside, one is a bit shorter than I am and the other matches me in height perfectly. It's definitely Zach and Mat. Zach, the taller one, spots me first and throws his arms in the air in celebration. Mat turns to see Zach, and then sees me and starts punching the air in front of him. I quicken my pace ahead of Jessie and clasp hands with Zach in an audible clap. He and I give welcoming hugs.

"Good to see you."

"I see how it is, fuck me I guess, eh?" Mat says.

"Oh, I'm sorry, did you wanna cuddle with me afterwards?" I smirk.

"Maybe…" Mat says.

The three of us explode in laughter as Mat and I give each bear hugs.

"It's been way too long," I say.

"Tell me about it! Wait…that isn't Laurie, is it?" Zach says.

He keeps a hushed tone as Jessie approaches and watches our interactions.

"It's been…a long day and semester…" I say.

"Say no more," Mat says.

Jessie walks up and waves. "Hello."

"Jessie; this is Mat and Zach. Mat and Zach; this is my friend Jessie," I say.

"Nice to meet you," Mat and Zach say.

"Likewise. But let's do pleasantries later, I'm hungry as hell!" Jessie says.

She promptly walks right into Slyder's. Zach and Mat look at me in shock, but nod their heads in approval already. I just laugh and follow Jessie inside. Mat and Zach sit across from Jessie and me at the table. The next half hour is a combination of us remembering the good ole days mixed in with how Jessie and I met and the crystal burst that ended class early.

"Haha! No shit! first day and you're already blowing stuff up? Mad man, I knew you had it in you!" Zach says.

"Well, obviously Charlie isn't *that* skilled, so I'm willing to bet it was a mistake for sure," Mat says.

"I think you're right. Maybe I'll just stay at home next semester and use one of your 'swords' as a butter knife. If it can cut through that," I say.

Zach chokes on his water and Jessie gives a mocking shocked face as if to say "did he just say that?"

Mat uses his middle finger as a rebuttal.

"Sorces think they're hot, but when you come in contact with a sorce blade made by a Fencer who knows what they're doing, then you're crying to a Fencer like me for help," Mat says.

"Oh please, Fencers are glorified, brooding, blacksmiths. Artís are the ones you all need when the shit hits the fan. Who's optimizing Fencer forges? Who's giving Sorces their fancy equipment? The Artís. Why? Cause we run this bitch!" Zach says.

"And yet, without materials, you both would be stuck in the dark ages. Just remember who can break anything either of you two build with raw power and a well-placed sorce burst. Sorce may be pretentious, but there's a reason boys...," Jessie says.

There's a moment of silence between Mat and Zach. They look at me, I look at them. Then we laugh.

"That was disrespectful. I don't know how I feel about it," Zach says.

"She can stick around...For now," Mat says.

Zach nods in agreement. "Yeah, you're cool."

"Cheers! To a new semester with old friends!" I say, raising my glass of soda above the table in the middle of us. "And obviously new ones." I say, looking at Jessie. She smiles and laughs in agreement.

III

CHRING.

My psi-phone pings, notifying me of my next class starting in five minutes. Mat and Zach have their classes in different buildings. Jessie and I have slightly staggered classes together, so we won't be in the same class this time. As I'm walking to my next class, I think about the future and what I want. I know what I have to do to get Laurie back. I have to prove I have my own goals; I can be a Sorce and a good one at that.

Which means I'll have to be practicing and learning a lot more.

I walk into the building known as the Cathedral, the same building my first class was in, the main building of Sorce students and Masters. I head straight for my next class which I'm already a minute late to, hopefully the master doesn't mind. I walk in through the door of the classroom.

"…and although Sorces do not typically use artifacts very often, it is essential that you know the practicality behind them, should you encounter them or be forced to use one." A woman Master is in mid-lecture.

Uh oh. Not even a minute in and I've missed the beginning.

Most of the seats are filled too. I quickly move across the threshold of the doorway, trying not to make too much noise.

As I pass the Master's desk, suddenly, I'm frozen in place. Though I'm not moving I can still see and hear. I look at my hands and notice a silver mist gliding across my skin. The woman who was speaking as I entered, obviously the Master, has promptly gone silent. I see her out of the corner of my eye. She turns her attention away from the other students to look at me and folds her arms. She then smiles and grabs her tablet from her desk.

"Charlie, I presume?" The Master says.

I would nod my head but I'm currently frozen. I also can't talk. I should be in full panic mode, adrenaline pumping, heart beating through my chest, but I'm not. Whatever has me trapped in this stasis is also keeping me extremely calm.

"I'll assume you are since you're late and the tablet has marked you as such," the Master says.

Let me talk.

"Well perfect! You'll be helping me with a demonstration." She sets the tablet down and walks over to me, then past me and over to the door.

"I am Master Sindra. A pleasure to meet you, Charlie. Now class, can anyone explain to Charlie what has just happened?" Master Sindra says.

No one raises their hand.

"I'll give you a hint," Master Sindra says. I hear her knock on the door.

I look around at the other students in the class and see Laurie sitting next to Rhody. Rhody has a smug ass smile on his face, and whispers something to his friend next to him; they both snicker. Laurie cautiously raises her hand, her eyes locked on me and my pitiful looking state.

"Yes, Miss Barian?" Master Sindra says.

"The sigil on the top door?" Laurie says. I've never seen her so unconfident before.

"What about it?" Master Sindra says.

Laurie plays with her ponytail and crosses her legs.

"The sigil, or at least, a piece of the sigil…Is an artifact. With a sorce field attached to it?" Laurie says.

I can't see what Master Sindra is doing behind me, but I'm assuming by Laurie's relaxed body language that Master Sindra has given her some sort of visual praise.

"Very good Miss Barian! Although not quite right about the sorce field, but an easy mistake. This was a tricky one," Master Sindra says.

Laurie smiles in victory. If I could smile, I would. I'm proud of her. She hadn't been so successful in Master Uphraeus' class, so I knew she needed a win.

"Ms. Barian is right. Everyone, jot down notes in your Sorce manuals. Specifically in your artifacts section…The sigil is of little importance, a decorative piece if anything," Master Sindra says.

I hear her tapping on the sigil behind me.

"The center jewel…Is the artifact itself, with a special instruction and timer."

Master Sindra walks to the front of the class while holding the artifact up for everyone to see. Within its crystalline structure, swirls the same silvery mist that's gliding across my skin.

"This one in particular is set to freeze those who pass through my door if they're late."

Master Sindra's gaze fixates on me. The class lets out a unified chuckle. I'd probably laugh at myself, hell I'd probably give the room a bow and shrug it off…but I'm nothing more than a mannequin at the moment.

"Alright then. How about this?" Master Sindra says. She tosses the artifact at Laurie. "Now Miss Barian, since you got the answer correct, I want to know if you can release Charlie from his hold."

She walks over to her desk and leans a hand on it, her other hand on her hip, making sure she can see Laurie and me. Laurie looks around unsure of what to do, Rhody puts his hands in the air as if to say "don't look at me, I can't help you." Then Laurie looks at me, and our eyes lock.

My mind plunges me into a memory of a time when Laurie and I were practicing our sorce on a random weekend. She couldn't understand how to use artifacts, and since neither of us were Artís, the half-baked ones we made out of old items from our garages weren't the best practice. Zach was also practicing on becoming an Artí at the time, so he and I would have long conversations about how frustrating it was for him without the right materials.

Since I understood artifacts a bit more than she did, she'd come to me for help, and I did so because I loved her and would've literally raised an army of the dead for her.

Laurie examines the artifact at her table, but Master Sindra waves a hand to grab her attention to come to the front of class. Laurie gets up and makes her way to me. If I could, I would say "You got this ! You're going to do just fine! Just, please don't split me in half, make me go blind, incinerate my skin, or cause any fatal bodily harm, or horrible disfiguration."

<I'd tell her to kick a bucket full of rocks.> What? No, no, I wouldn't!

Laurie approaches me, takes a deep breath, then gives me a wink. Not just any wink, but the kind of wink she would give me when she knew I was scared or in trouble. That wink she used to give me to make sure I would remain calm and that she had everything covered. For a sweet blissful moment, it feels like everything was going to be alright, because she's here.

Laurie clutches the artifact causing it to make her hand shimmer with the same silver mist. Laurie's hand is now frozen and she's beginning to panic over her mistake. The rest of the class laughs. Master Sindra approaches Laurie with a hand stretched out.

"Okay, Ms. Barian. I can—"

"No!" Laurie says. "I mean…please Master Sindra, I'm okay. I can do this."

Master Sindra nods in approval and takes a step back. Laurie takes her free hand and waves it across the other and the mist follows. She's now freed one hand while containing the mist in the other. Using the hand that's controlling the mist, she pulls the mist from around my body. The silvery clouds move like waves through the air towards Laurie, freeing me from the paralysis. My knees feel like jelly and I almost fall over. Laurie then pools the mist back into the artifact and exhales in relief. Master Sindra and the rest of the class begins to clap, giving applause to Laurie's performance.

"Very well done Ms. Barian! Though, there are many ways to have reversed the effects, and some much more efficient. But, you were phenomenal!" Master Sindra says.

Laurie gives a small bow to Master Sindra and presents the artifact to her.

"You may both have a seat now." Master Sindra takes the artifact from Laurie and waves us off.

"Thanks," I say, looking at Laurie.

Laurie nods, and walks back to her seat next to Rhody.

"Now, let this be lesson to all of you. Including you, Charlie. Next time you show up late to my class you'll be stuck there until its end," Master Sindra says.

"Yes, Master Sindra," I agree, heading up the steps of the stadium seating to find an open chair towards the back.

Back in my room, I think about Master Sindra's lecture. She spoke about the differences in artifacts. Lengthy, but valuable information.

As I had sat there, I wondered about what I would specialize in as a Sorce. They can specialize in specific techniques like necromancy or conjuring. I'm not entirely sure what kind of path I want to take. So, first thing's first:

1. Find out what sorce specialization we want to be.
2. Practice enough to beat Rhody.
3. <*Kill Rhody*> Wait—No, *beat* Rhody…In skills and knowledge. Out demonstrate him.
4. Become a Sorce and make a profit.
5. Win Laurie's admiration and love back by showing I have my own goals and aspirations.

Okay cool, I got this. So, what do I do?…What do I do?

———

I'm lying on my bed unable to sleep. It's 2:31 A.M. A wave of emotions came at me hard, a mixture of unconditional love and undiscriminating hatred, and it feels like I'm being torn apart on a physical level and the epicenter is happening inside my chest.

Flashes of numbness through my body make me wonder what the hell is happening to me. I can't seem to grab hold of a single feeling, everything is coming and going a thousand miles a minute. It feels like I'm dying. Like something inside of me reaching out and consuming my mind, body, and thoughts.

At this point my body feels so mentally and physically exhausted I just want to pass out, but I can't do that choking on my own tears.

<*It hurts. But I'll make this okay. We won't hurt forever.*>

IV

I remember laying on top of my bed last night, not sure exactly how I ended up here; upside down and diagonally across my bed. Must've been a nightmare I was having.

Wom-Ping!

New message? Who in the world is texting me this early?

> Jessie: Rise and shine Mr. Explosion! (7:45 AM)

> Jessie: Wanna grab breakfast before Master Uphraeus' class? (7:45 AM)

Even though I still feel bad, Jessie still makes me laugh out loud when joking about me blowing the both us halfway across the Crystal Fields. Her good spirits make me feel like I just got a second wind.

I respond to Jessie's text.

> Charlie: Can lumibears glow in the dark? (7:48 AM)

I look at myself in the mirror. Yikes. I look like I was just recently rescued from an internment camp. That would explain the funky smell that's been coming in whiffs every two minutes. I walk to the bathroom and begin running the shower and brush my teeth.

Wom-Ping!

> Jessie: Hahaha! Okay cool, meet in the cafeteria at 8:25-30? Then maybe we can talk about what we're demonstrating for Master Uphraeus's class? :) (7:58 AM)

Ha…of course! While wallowing in my own filth last night I completely forgot about Master Uphraeus' assignment. Brilliant! Someone, please help me, I'm co-piloting a plane that's got two engines running on smoke and no captain.

> Charlie: That sounds great! I'll see you there! (8:05 AM)

———

After taking a shower, I jump, skip, and hop my way into some clothes and then head on out to the cafeteria to meet Jessie, grabbing my backpack as I leave.

I get to the cafeteria and check my psi-phone. It's 8:26 A.M. Looking through the area, I see scattered students throughout the building. I check my psi-phone to see Jessie already typing out a message.

> Jessie: He waited…(8:27 AM)

> Jessie: all alone…(8:27 AM)

> Jessie: until…(8:28 AM)

"BOOM!" Jessie shouts.

She got the sneak on me and made me jump, she laughs.

Her laughing starts out normal then turns into a squeal. The transition is cute and the laughter is contagious.

"So, what are you in the mood for?" Jessie asks.

"Hmm, I'm not sure. Maybe a—"

"Breakfast burrito?" Jessie and I say at the same time. We both laugh then nod our heads in agreement.

Jessie and I find a booth to sit in at the center of the eating area. We exchange small talk about Master Sindra's class since she had the class after me and I gave her the rundown of my experience. Jessie laughs so hard she holds her stomach and wipes tears from her eyes as I describe the whole thing, me being stuck in a silvery mist and having to be rescued by Laurie.

"Wow! And then you're saved by that girl from our first class? Laura? Lauren?" Jessie says.

"Laurie," I say.

"*Right*, Laurie. What's the story between you two?"

"Ex-girlfriend. Broke up with me the night before our class."

"Ah, I sort of assumed that it was an ex-girlfriend situation. Didn't know about the whole 'getting dumped the night before classes' but that confirms my other suspicions."

"Yeah, and I can only assume she picked up a new boyfriend that same night."

"Ouch. I'm sorry. Really, do you want me to pull her teeth out? Burn her hair off?"

Jessie conjures a small flame on her fingertips. As nonchalant as she said that, I can't tell if she's serious or not.

"So, what're you going to do for your presentation today?" I change the subject.

"Oh! So, I was fiddling around with two ideas..." She pulls out a small felt pouch from her pocket. "I found this rotator ring under my seat and had it turned into an artifact by one of the Artís who's graduating to Versed this semester. I plan on making it into a semi-sorce crystal. Like the ones in the fields? When you rotate it, it should be able to absorb or expel sorce."

This rotator ring was made of some black metal on the inside with the same crystalline material found in the Crystal Fields on the outside. A rotator ring has two rings; the base ring, and the outer ring. The outer ring spins around the base ring, sometimes creating a neat visual. Though, this ring has an intricate design that feels elaborate and unique.

"And you found this ring? Someone must be pretty upset, maybe you should turn it in to the lost and found?" I ask.

Jessie gives me a blank stare and slowly blinks.

"But I also learned how to do this." Jessie cracks her knuckles and extends her hands out in front of her before slowly closing them together. As the palms of her hands get closer together a small orb of white light begins forming in between them. Crackling and pulsing with sorce, and the size of a peach. She holds the orb steady as it floats just above her left palm.

"Catch!" Jessie says. She tosses the ball in my direction unexpectedly.

After juggling it between my hands, I manage to get a hold of it. I get the hang of it and start throwing the ball around, catching it behind my back and making it do small twirls. Jessie laughs at my tricks, then puts out her left hand and snaps her fingers. The orb descends into my palm and covers my hand and wrist with a shimmering turquoise light.

"A basic sorce field that should protect you from projectiles and physical harm," Jessie says, confidently.

"Wow, that's amazing…Wait 'should?'" I say.

"Yeah! Wanna test it out?"

Jessie makes three darts on her fingertips. I think she might've actually been serious about setting Laurie on fire. She giggles and dispells the darts, and we both end up laughing. I retreat my hand, just in case she's not joking. Jessie immediately asks me what the time is. I check my watch: 9:19 AM.

"Oh! We better head out, I don't want to be late," I say.

Wait…I still don't have anything for my demonstration. Maybe Jessie will let me borrow that ring?

"Shit! Uh, Jessie, can I have your ring for the demonstration today?" I ask.

"You're joking," Jessie says.

"I'm sorry, totally forgot to come up with something. It's a huge ask and I owe you a huge favor."

"Well, I haven't programmed anything into it yet…"

"I'll think of something on the way to class."

Jessie ponders a minute, touching her finger to her chin. "Fine, but you owe me one."

"I owe you three."

Jessie takes the felt pouch out of her pocket and pulls out the ring. She holds it in the air to show it off before she slides it across the table towards me. She then downs the rest of her coffee and wipes her mouth. We both exit the booth and start walking towards the exit.

As we leave, I happen to see Laurie and Rhody, walking towards a snack bar on the other side of the cafeteria. Before Jessie and I exit, I take one last look at Laurie who's now standing in line trying to grab a quick snack from the pre-packaged food. She looks over at me, our eyes meet, a look of resentment crosses her face. Maybe it's sadness? Either way, I'm okay with it.

I look forward at Jessie who's gotten a few steps ahead of me. Jessie hasn't noticed I've fallen behind, and I can hear her talking about theories as she walks with a skip in her step, that puts a smile on my face. Although I've been going through a lot, Jessie has been someone I've needed without even realizing it.

———

Jessie and I get to class about five minutes before anyone else, including Master Uphraeus. We grab two seats in the middle, where we sat yesterday.

"Any idea what you're going to do?" Jessie says.

"Well, I—"

"Hey! Jessie! What's up?" Nathan comes marching through the door.

Obnoxious. Smiling. Getting on my nerves already. Nathan walks up and grabs the seat on the other side of Jessie.

"Hi, Nathan," Jessie says.

"Sorry, I missed you after class yesterday. I had a few extra questions for Master Sindra," Nathan says.

"All good. I wasn't really waiting for you," Jessie says.

"Ouch" I smirk.

"Oh! *Hey*, Charlie, didn't see you there. Blow anyone else up lately?" Nathan asks.

"Want to meet me in the Crystal Fields later?" I say.

I pull out the rotator ring that Jessie gave me and put it on my left ring finger. Since I'm right-handed, I figure if I put it on my off-hand I'll be able to utilize my right at the same time. I start channeling sorce into the ring causing the outer ring to move slightly with a faint blue glow. As I'm fiddling with the ring, more students start pouring into the classroom, Laurie and Rhody enter with their group of friends and take their seats up front.

Usually, an overwhelming amount of dread and pain flow through my chest when I see her, but right now my focus is on getting my demonstration ready. Especially if I want to surpass Rhody and win her back. I still have a goal and I'm going straight for it.

BOOM!

The door flies open. I wasn't paying attention to the classroom chatter until the sudden entrance of Master Uphraeus silences the room. He stands in the room, scanning everyone with intent. There's something menacing about the way he isn't speaking, or being as humorous as usual.

"Why are you all just staring?" Master Uphraeus says. "IT'S PRESENTATION TIME!"

Master Uphraeus must love being overly dramatic in front of students.

"Where's the excitement?! The vigor! The...*exhilaration*!"

Catching the excitement from Master Uphraeus, I crack a smile and the other students give out a few cheers.

"It's Sorce time!" I say, lifting two fists in the air.

Master Uphraeus pauses and looks at me. "Calm down, Charlie."

I drop my fists into my lap, Jessie lets out a snort while covering her mouth.

"But! Before we begin, I must ask; Does anyone's demonstration put this room at risk of catching fire or exploding?" Master Uphraeus is suddenly serious.

A couple students raise their hands. Master Uphraeus lets a wry smile slip.

"Well, to be honest, it matters not to me. I'm taking you all outside regardless. I just like to have forewarning so I can fake plausible deniability. This is my 'shocked' face when the Administrators ask if I knew."

Master Uphraeus makes a dramatic look of terror with his hands pressed to the sides of his face. The class breaks out in stifled laughter.

"Come along then!" Master Uphraeus says. He waves his hand and opens the classroom door, then takes long and fast strides out of the room.

"How does anyone have this much energy in the morning?" Nathan says.

"The trick is to not be such a bi—" I feel Jessie elbow me in the ribs.

"Maybe try getting a regular sleep schedule, Nathan," Jessie says.

"Or maybe you could sorce me to sleep?" Nathan says. He winks at Jessie.

"I'd be happy to use my sorce to put you to sleep Nathan," I say.

Nathan says, "When I need my room bulldozed, I'll be sure to give you a call."

"Can the two of you give it to rest already?" Jessie says.

"He started it," Nathan shrugs.

I take my backpack and walk away, following the rest of the class with Master Uphraeus out of the classroom. The three of us end up behind most of the crowd of students. As the group follows behind Master Uphraeus, we begin passing the Crystal Fields and a student informs him that we're passing it.

"That's because we're not going to the Crystal Fields today! We're going somewhere more appropriate for demonstrations. The Crystal Fields are kept nice and neat, we wouldn't want anything disrupting the groundskeeper's work. Imagine an explosion happening in there? I'd be in trouble for years," Master Uphraeus says.

Chatter begins among the students as to what's going on today. Jessie shoots me a look of curiosity. As we walk, we take a stone path through the forest that surrounds the back of the Crystal Fields. The path of stone passes through trees and brushes, winding and weaving in a downward motion. As we walk, we can hear the ocean and the sound of crashing waves. We must be approaching the edge of the island. I can hear some students are getting excited, others are in disbelief, and some are getting antsy.

As Jessie, Nathan and I come down the path and past the umbrella of trees we see what everyone's talking about. Further down the winding path, in what looks like a deserted area, is a marble white stage with stone benches in a half circle surrounding it. An old ruin-like amphitheater that looks like a place for acting...or battling. Now that I think about it, Master Uphraeus never said what the demonstrations were going to be used for, or if we'd be doing them by ourselves or with a... "partner."

We make our way down, getting closer to the arena stage. From afar the stage looks small, but as we get closer, everything is much bigger. We march through the stands, which split in half, giving a long stretch of dirt leading to the main stage. We step through stone-tapered walls and out into the arena. Directly in front of us is the arena, a large square made of white marble with four pillars on each corner. Beyond the arena is a cliff. Beyond the cliff, the horizon where the ocean meets the sky below Sirrus. To either side of me are the large stadium bleachers of stone, topped with old and tattered upholstery that looks like it's been out in the sun forever and never maintained.

Master Uphraeus is standing at the edge of the stage watching all of us trickle in, forming a half circle around him. The wind is much stronger here and Master Uphraeus's long coat billows in the air, with an ocean that seems to span forever standing behind him. After a few moments, the Master raises his finger to the crowd and waits for silence.

"Welcome, to Breakoff Point! This is an old arena. One of the very first created when Sirrus was founded. Some say this stage, this arena, was the very first classroom built on Sirrus."

Master Uphraeus pulls out a small crystal ball and places it in the air in front of him. With a snap of his fingers, the crystal ball expands and flattens into a tablet. Pressing his finger onto the screen, the tablet makes an audible beep.

"Now, I've randomly selected the order in which you will present. When I call your name, step onto the center of the stage and demonstrate your sorce manipulation technique to the class. There are a few rules to go over:

There will be silence during each student demonstration. Demonstrations will be performed alone. Keep any hazardous spells and or artifact use within the confines of the stage. If I deem a demonstration too dangerous, or a student shows any signs of aggression, or I damn well please...I will end the demonstration myself.

"Should any of you break these rules, you may be subject to

administrative punishment which may include, but is not limited to suspension or expulsion."

His words sound very rehearsed, a list that has probably been repeated more times than he can count. But that last one… about breaking the rules…he was much more present, and I could've sworn he looked right at me as he said it.

"While people are demonstrating their skills, I want everyone to pay attention while seated in the stands. After each demonstration is complete, that student will be dismissed and the next name called will take their place. Are we ready?"

"Yes, Master Uphraeus!" All the students respond in unison.

"Alrighty then! Loving the enthusiasm! First up, Laurie Barian! Everyone else, please find suitable seating on the stone benches."

I give Jessie a nudge and lean my head towards the seating area. Jessie nods and makes her way to the stadium seats. Nathan follows behind her like a lost puppy.

"I wanna sit in the front. This is going to be interesting," Jessie says.

She promptly moves towards the center of the first row. I follow her and take the seat immediately to her right, Nathan takes the seat to her left—of course. The other students scatter around, some sit stage left on the other side of the divide, others are stage right where we are. Rhody and his crew sit a few seats down from where Jessie and I sit. Master Uphraeus takes a stand in the divide between the two sections, facing the stage where Laurie is standing dead center.

She's very calm and seems confident. Master Uphraeus looks around to see if everyone's seated and paying attention. Once satisfied, Master Uphraeus nods at Laurie. "You may begin Ms. Barian."

Laurie begins, "Thank you Master Uphraeus. For my demonstration I wi—"

"No need for explanation! Less talk! More passion!"

Laurie looks surprised, but nods and takes a deep breath.

She clasps her hands together, the dust on the stage begins to spin around her in isolated circles, like the beginnings of five mini-tornados. Laurie then moves her hands around, guiding the controlled gusts in different directions, positioning them in a five-point circle around her then increasing their speed and size. The dust kicks up and small pieces of rock get caught in the whirlwind. Surrounding her are now five, seven foot, tornados which have very faint outlines from the dust dancing between them. Master Uphraeus lets out a hearty laugh and claps his hands.

If this is the bar, I'm screwed. Then again, small tornados are nice, but not all that impressive in my unbiased opinion.

Suddenly, Laurie's eyes begin to shimmer, she extends her hands out in front and then swipes them to her sides as if she just flung open two wide doors. The tornados fill in their shape with a familiar-looking silvery mist. As the wind around her picks up, she strikes what I would call nothing less than a gorgeous pose. Her auburn hair flows around her face and body gracefully as she stares into the crowd of students. If I didn't know any better, I'd say she was doing it on purpose. She looks perfectly in sync with the silver tornados as they dance and circle around her.

"SPLENDID!" Master Uphraeus says. "Absolutely brilliant I tell you! A fine demonstration indeed Ms. Barian! I also see that you've been taking notes from Master Sindra…that silver mist is a staple of hers! Great use of both sorce utility and elemental design, I imagine this is great for keeping attackers at bay or crowd controlling opponents. Though, I will say, that is a somewhat advanced maneuver you've learned in a short amount of time. You wouldn't be preparing to do something…dangerous? Would you, Ms. Barian?"

Laurie briefly has an expression you'd find in a child who just got caught in a lie.

"No Master Uphraeus. Just something I thought looked cool."

Master Uphraeus nods his head slowly as he strokes the tip of his orange beard. "Well! You did a fantastic job and set the bar!" He says. "Feel free to end your demonstration so the next student can come up."

Laurie nods, snaps both fingers, and the tornados fly off the stage towards the ocean.

"Next up! Miguel Tr'ova!" Master Uphraeus says.

The interaction between Laurie and Master Uphraeus was a little unsettling. Laurie isn't very good at lying, let alone to authority figures. Which means she *is* planning on doing something dangerous. Growing up, she had problems with her parents, her stepdad came to the party late and didn't understand her all that well, but he tried. Her mother always second-guessed Laurie's choices, and they would fight nonstop, but they shared a powerful bond. Laurie always wanted to become a Sorce, but I never really stopped to ask her or myself why.

If this was a combat technique, who was she planning on fighting? Was it going to happen soon? What were the motives? Maybe it was only in defense? Had someone recently hurt her? Rhody? Could he be manipulating her, making her do or think things? I look over at Rhody sitting with his friends, smug looks across all their faces as Laurie walks back to them.

"Charlie," Jessie says.

"Sorry. I was zoning out there," I say.

"Yeah, I noticed. You almost had another episode," Jessie says.

She looks at the rotator ring on my hand and the crystal inside was glowing a pale orange.

"As much as I'd like to see you go berserk, you remember what happened last time? You don't exactly have the best control."

I stare at Jessie in frustration. She doesn't have any right to say that to me.

"You can be mad at me, but think about what happened last time; you and I ended up at the infirmary, without even thinking. Imagine you did start thinking, and you still had no control?" Jessie says.

I nod my head in response. She has a point.

We watch the next couple of students go up and demonstrate. A lot of these students are talented. Dancing rings of light, creating temporary duplicates of small animals, mirrors that show different locations. Amazing, yet terrifying for me.

Eventually Jessie's name is called and without any of the usual dramatic entrance or flair, she immediately begins with a meditative stance. After a few seconds her body starts releasing what looks like pollen made of light. She opens her eyes and all the light particles condense into larger spheres, like the one she showed me at breakfast. The spheres begin swirling and dancing around her, then clashing and bouncing off of each other, each time sparking and getting brighter. Then, as Jessie claps her hands together, the spheres encircle her, then disperse into a shockwave of light.

Everyone claps and some—mostly Nathan—cheer. I'm reeling in my seat thinking of what I'm going to do when I get up there. Nathan follows Jessie and displays his sorce prowess with a demonstration by manipulating water, air, and fire. Basic elemental stuff, nothing impressive.

Master Uphraeus has called on all but two people; Rhody and myself, which means one of us is going last.

"Rhody Smill" Master Uphraeus says.

I feel a hand take mine, it's Jessie's, and she's looking at me like everything is going to be okay. I begin to relax a bit, and I glance at Laurie. She's looking right at us. I immediately let go of Jessie's hand.

"Don't do that," I say. Rubbing my hand.

I see Laurie avert her gaze, playing with her hair. Then in spectacular, dramatic fashion, Rhody makes a thunderous clap that shakes the amphitheater seats. Subtle way to get everyone's attention. Master Uphraeus' stance is a serious one, he seems uneasy as Rhody smiles.

"Now that I have everyone's attention! Welcome to my demonstration!" Rhody says.

He dances around the stage as his body turns into stone, then quickly forms a whip in his hand made of pure lightning. He thrashes the electric whip around the arena, flipping in the air and cracking, making the whip spark, causing stray bolts to dance across the stage. Rhody pauses and looks at Laurie, then at me, then gives a devilish smile and snaps his whip in front of us. I look over at Laurie, her legs are crossed and she's nervously braiding her hair, flinching at every time the whip cracks.

Jessie is holding onto Nathan, and Master Uphraeus is balling his fists. I notice the same dark figure I saw yesterday standing behind Rhody. A pitch-black shadow that looks like it's studying its prey before it pounces. The shape is mostly human, but its movements aren't. It fidgets and blurs at times, like an insect caught inside a web, but nothing appears to be obstructing it. This silhouette looks familiar…like I've seen it every day, but for the first time…I'm not sure why.

It feels like I'm watching all of this happen outside of my own body. The tension around the stadium is getting thicker and everyone feels it as they shift in their seats. Rhody has his gaze locked on me, with a look of arrogance and pride, as if he has some personal problem with me and wants to settle it right now. Well, I'm right here. So, if he wants to do this now, I'm ready.

"ENOUGH!" Master Uphraeus says. His voice elevating through the sounds of bolts and strikes as if saying it from a loudspeaker in a long tunnel.

Rhody takes a moment and then disperses his whip.

"Thank you, Mr. Smill, but that's quite enough. This was a simple demonstration, not an exhibition match," Master Uphraeus says.

"Isn't that the point of this school? To teach us how to fight?" Rhody responds.

Rhody shifts his gaze at Laurie, I do the same. She's shaking her head at him. Master Uphraeus grabs Rhody by the arm and whispers something in his ear. After which, Rhody's stone skin crumbles and he returns to normal. Rhody rips his arm away from Master Uphraeus and walks off stage, stomping back to his seat next to Laurie. After that, Master Uphraeus looks over at me, and I stare at him.

"Last but not least!" Master Uphraeus gives a hearty laugh, as if the very awkward and serious encounter didn't just happen in front of everyone's eyes. "Come on, Charlie."

He nods at me, as if he's been intentionally saving me for last. What kind of sick game is this? I hesitate, but take a deep breath and get up.

"You're going to do great," Jessie says, as she grabs my arm and looks me in the eyes.

I head down to the stage. Master Uphraeus is looking at me - or, more accurately, *through* me. He's thinking about something, lost in deep thought. I make my way down to him and he seems to snap out of it then gestures to the stage. I take small steps up to the stage as my heart begins to pound. I still have no idea what I'm going to do and after watching everyone else, espe- cially Laurie, I can't choke while I'm up here. Not when Rhody is watching. I have to do something that'll at least get me by or show that I'm as good as Rhody, if not better. I get to the center of the stage with my back turned to everyone. I'm looking at this beautiful horizon and I have no idea what I'm going to do. I start flicking the rotator ring out of nervousness when I hear someone heckling.

"It's not a race bud!" Rhody shouts. "Let's go, lover boy!"

I turn around immediately to say something, but Master Uphraeus beats me to it.

"Mr. Smill!" The Master erupts. "I will not have you make a mockery of this demonstration or my classroom. Need I remind you that if you step out of line to my disliking or cause any more attempts to disrupt my class, I will not only have the

Administration take full action but I will have you expelled—No, expunged from this institution. Do I make myself clear?"

I lose my train of thought for a moment as I try to make sense of what just happened, I'm hoping that Master Uphraeus would cancel the demonstration and take his fury out on that sack of starch. My hopes quickly fizzle out as Rhody gets up and leaves. Master Uphraeus glares at his exit, then looks back at me.

"Go ahead, son."

I look at Jessie, and I think back to the Crystal Fields…The Crystal Fields…Yeah.

"Excuse me, Master Uphraeus? I'd like to know if I could get a volunteer?" I ask.

Master Uphraeus ponders for a moment. "I'm not sure that's…Well, as long as you are doing most of the work, then I suppose I could allow it this time."

"Great! Jessie? Would you mind giving me a hand?"

Jessie stands up and heads on down the steps of the amphitheater, meeting me on stage with a giddy smile on her face.

"Reporting for duty," Jessie says. She gives me a salute and smiles. "But, what exactly am I doing?"

"Can you make a sorce sphere the size of a beach ball?" I ask.

"Yeah…but what for? Is that it?" Jessie says.

"Yeah, that'll be all for now. Actually, make it three," I say.

"Okay, just let me know what else you need," Jessie says.

Jessie begins weaving her hands together, developing a sphere of light that sparkles and shimmers. The sphere starts out small, roughly the size of an apple, then expands outward and remains steady in the air in front of her.

"Like this?" asks Jessie.

"Perfect! Now, two more," I say.

Jessie nods and creates two more spheres the same size then steps close to me, leaning in for a whisper.

"Why couldn't *you* do that?" Jessie asks.

"Because then I wouldn't be able to stall for time as long," I whisper back.

"Now what?" Jessie asks.

"Take cover."

Jessie snorts then immediately covers her mouth and walks off the arena.

With the spheres Jessie left behind, I pull them through the air and place them around myself in a triangle. One directly in front of me and two behind me. Giving the rotator ring a flick with my finger, I power the ring up using sorce. It makes a high-pitched tone, and the crystal material begins to glow a dim blue. If my theory is right, I can do the same thing I did in the Crystal Fields, but in a more intentional way. I place my open hands out in front of me toward the sphere ahead, trying to connect the sphere to the ring, hoping to create a flow chain between me and the spheres. If I can balance the sorce inside all three spheres at the same time, using them like the crystals from the Crystal Fields, that should be a decent enough demonstration.

Success! I connect to the sphere in front of me, I feel its sorce and mine syncing together. Now, to introduce the ring, just in case I overload myself and pass out. Overload can happen if you've absorbed too much sorce. Overtax happens when you use too much. Either one can paralyze the body, sometimes worse. If you overload past your body's breaking point, you'll essentially turn to dust...if you're lucky.

The ring should serve as a nice conduit to take some of the pressure from my body. Right again! My ring is now the host for the sphere, meaning the sphere is pulling from the ring, and the ring from me. The only visual cue I have is a blue aura swirling around me and an identical one around the sphere. The effect gets increasingly intense around me and the sphere. The chain begins turning the ring a bright orange, like the crystal in the fields. Okay, not bad, but now we need to push it further. I concentrate more on the sphere, and the sphere doubles in size. It's working.

I have to make sure I'm balancing the amount of power in the sphere and ring to make sure the flow chain is distributed evenly amongst them. Only problem is that I'm assuming that the sphere can take more than the ring can. Using the spheres as batteries, I can charge one to full, then split the energy in half and send it to another one. Once all three are fully charged, my hope is to carefully balance them all so they exchange their sorce at a constant rate without overloading them.

"If everyone remembers, our assignment for the Crystal Fields was to create a flow chain between ourselves and the crystals," I say.

"I think we *all* remember, Charlie," Master Uphraeus coughs.

"Well, now I will create a flow chain between myself and *three* sorce objects!"

No one, not even Master Uphraeus, seems particularly impressed or believes it. Master Uphraeus even takes a small step backwards out of caution. That hurt.

I create a second and third flow chain between the other spheres, making sure to balance the sorce between all three. Easy. Now that I have a hang of the flow chain, I make sure to feed more into the newest sphere in the chain, making them all harmoniously sync in a bright glow. The blue aura around myself and the spheres started as calm strings of light, but now they're acting more chaotic. This isn't enough though; I have to show more control of the situation.

The rotator ring and all three spheres are at the same critical point, I need to juggle them at the brink of their breaking point. I flick the ring again with my thumb and the rotator ring responds with a high-pitched tone and begins to ignite in sparks. I then pour sorce into the sphere directly in front of me and the ring dims while the sphere gets brighter, seemingly exchanging brightness and saturation. The sphere is about to overload, but just before that, I redirect the sorce from that sphere to one of the spheres behind me, then the next one, and back to the front.

Master Uphraeus is watching intently. Eventually I pick up the pace of the chain and the bright glow bounces from one sphere to the next, sometimes jumping briefly back to the rotator ring in between transfers. Now, the spheres and the ring are making harmonious high-pitched rings and I'm starting to feel a little dizzy.

The best way I can describe what happens when you use sorce, is that you feel a connection to the thing you're creating, manipulating, or emitting, like an invisible tether. I feel the tether between all the spheres, and I feel the balance of power shifting from the spheres to me and the ring. This feeling is almost overwhelming and I'm not sure where it's going. I was so focused on getting myself here I had no idea what to do once I did it. But I did it.

Every time the sorce transfers from a sphere to another, or a sphere to the ring, there's a pounding within me that pulses through my body, like an earthquake trying to knock me down. I'm starting to lose control of the situation; the transfer is happening so rapidly; I can see it starting to kick up dust and wind around me. I have to figure out how to stop the flow chain now, before these things overload…or I overtax. If I attempt to redirect all of this back into myself, I'll definitely overload. As the sorce is now pulsing through the spheres, I notice that when it shifts from one place to the next, the glow left behind isn't dim, it's getting brighter. This means that eventually they're all going to overload, and by eventually, I mean in the next few seconds with the speed that the flow chain is shifting.

"CHARLIE!!" Master Uphraeus shouts.

I didn't realize that the high pitch ringing was so loud it was drowning out everything else around me. How long had Master Uphraeus been talking to me? I was so focused I couldn't hear him or see what was happening. Breaking my concentration, I look around and notice a sorce field around me containing myself and the three spheres. Master Uphraeus has trapped me inside with the spheres, the look on his face is anger and concern. Mostly anger though.

"What's going on?!" I say.

"You didn't create a flow chain! You created a…"

Master Uphraeus' voice is drowned out by the increasing ringing of the spheres and the gusts of wind inside the sorce field.

"What?!" I yell.

Master Uphraeus lifts his voice over the noise. "I can't help you without risking the safety of the other students! Can you stop this or not?!"

"This isn't helping!" I'm starting to panic. "I have no way out now!"

Shit. Wait, there's a horizon right behind me. I can just throw them off the cliff. Right?

"Wait! Master Uphraeus, I can stop this! Just drop the sorce field!"

Master Uphraeus shakes his head in response. "I can't do that, Charlie!" He yells. "I need you to stop it from the inside!"

I look confidently at Master Uphraeus. "I'm going to *redirect* it. But I can't do that if you're *blocking* me!"

Master Uphraeus hesitates and reluctantly drops the sorce field, then creates a new one around himself and all the students seated behind him. Without hesitation, I send the spheres straight up above my head and off the cliffside as fast as I can.

The spheres fly up as they sparkle and crack. I use what sorce energy is left in the ring and send it towards the spheres like a dart. As the sorce dart reaches the spheres, it causes an explosion that is both beautiful and terrifying. A mixture of blue and orange light fills the sky and air above. I look to see everyone else staring up at the explosion from their hiding places, and Master Uphraeus in awe of the situation. That's when I notice that the stage under my feet had been cracking from the force of the flow chain.

The sorce field drops, and Master Uphraeus runs over to me. "Are you alright son?"

"Yeah, I'm okay. I'm sorry abou—"

Master Uphraeus cuts me off. "You can apologize later."

We see the class coming out of their hiding spots. Jessie emerges clapping, and no one really knows if now is a good time, but Jessie's enthusiasm eventually catches on and there's applause from everyone. Master Uphraeus is also at a loss, wiping sweat from his brow using his tie, but the energy of the students almost immediately gets to him, so he begins clapping as well.

"Everyone did a phenomenal job, and that was a great way to finish up our day of demonstrations! Class is dismissed," Master Uphraeus says.

He then looks at me with curiosity, "Charlie, I'd like to talk to you during my office hours."

"Um…Okay? I-I mean yes Master Uphraeus!" I say.

"Come to my classroom after your next class. We have much to discuss."

I walk to Jessie and she gives me a big hug.

"That was insane! You're insane! And probably going to get expelled! But insane!" Jessie says.

"Yeah, I'm still a little shaken by it—Wait, *expelled*?!"

Nathan isn't far behind Jessie and looks at me with a scowl. "That was reckless and someone could've gotten hurt."

"I know, that wasn't my intention," I say.

"Intentions or not, this is definitely getting recorded by the Administration."

"Are you *trying* to get me suspended?"

"Among other things…"

"What the hell is your problem with me?"

Nathan narrows his eyes. "You're arrogant, reckless, and lack discipline."

"Alright, that's enough!" Jessie says, moving in between Nathan and me. "Charlie's demonstration may have been a bit unorthodox, but it was last minute and he wasn't trying to hurt anyone."

"Thank you, Jessie," I say.

"But he does have a point. You could've hurt yourself out there," Jessie says.

"You can't protect him; he's obviously going to get someone killed and if that someone is you there'll be hell to pay for it," Nathan says.

"Nathan, were you born an asshole or did something happen to you?" Jessie says. She pauses, "Don't answer that, I don't care. Just leave."

Nathan's fists ball up so tight they turn red. He gives me a murderous look before he listens to Jessie and leaves.

"Why do you still hang around with him?" I ask her.

"He hangs around me, and he buys me food. I'll take free food, even if it means dealing with a *puk'lur* like him," Jessie says.

"Puck-ler? What the what?" I try to hold back a laugh.

"It's a word from my hometown. It means fat-ass, or loser, or awkwardly shaped thing."

"Maethril, right? That's a very versatile word, or language?" I say.

"Yup! Where the sands are a fantasy, and the waves are mystical. Our language is pretty weird if you don't grow up knowing it."

"Where can I get a 'puckler' to buy me food?" I chuckle.

"Trust me, you don't want one. Look for a *la'fa* to buy *you* food."

"Lafa?"

"Geez, you're not even trying to accent it. It means fiery spirit, or warrior companion, or partner. Things like that."

"*La'fa*. Yeah. I think I used to have a *la'fa*..."

LAURIE

PART I

I walk to the door and stop for a moment and think to myself. *This is the end, maybe someday it can start again. I've come to terms with this, it needs to end.* I turn back and see Charlie staring at me. I can tell he's not in a good mental state and his eyes are getting red. It breaks my heart to see him that way, to know that I'm the one doing it to him but I need to let this relationship go. I feel a little guilty doing this right before classes begin and that I have Rhody to feel comfortable with, but from here on out I have to be focused on the mission. Have to find the cornerstone, or a way to retrieve it.

—————

I'm jolted awake in the middle of the night, by a dream. My psi-phone says it's 2:31 A.M. Rhody must've left the bed while I was asleep. I assume he's gone home since his shoes aren't by the door. Well, there's no going back to sleep now. I throw on a shirt and underwear and start studying what I can while trying to reinforce what I know.

The Master for our first class could be very relaxed or seriously intimidating. Either way I should be prepared for the worst. Shit, it's already 8:15 A.M. I'm going to be late. I text Rhody and ask him if he's up to grab some food before then.

Laurie: You up? (8:23 A.M.)

Rhody: Yeah (8:24 A.M.)

Laurie: What time did you leave last night? (8:24 A.M.)

Rhody: Shortly after. Why, you miss me? ;) (8:26 A.M.)

Laurie: Look, let's not make this a big deal. Where are you now?

Rhody: Grabbing some food before class with the others. (8:30 A.M.)

Laurie: Cool if I join you? (8:31 A.M.)

Rhody: Sure thing babe, come through (8:38 A.M.)

Laurie: Cool omw (9:00 A.M.)

Ugh, "babe." I hope he really doesn't think I'm taking our fling last night seriously. Whatever, he's company I can keep around and a friend to have right now. I catch up with Rhody and our friends at the cafeteria, just in time before they reach the front of the line.

I don't know why my heart sinks into my chest after I hear a very familiar squeaking scratch across the floor. It's the same screech that I'd hear when Charlie came over to my house and walked across the kitchen floor. I look over and there he is, wearing the tunic I bought him, and immediately I'm filled with regret. Not just for us, but for what happened last night. Staring at him I feel an awful lump in my throat and want to focus on something else.

Rhody and the others are going to make me late by waiting for them to finish their food. I should've just done what Charlie did and went for the snack bar. They finally finish and we head to class and get there a couple minutes late, but luckily, we weren't the only ones. I see Charlie sitting in the middle, I grab a seat down front so I don't have to have him in my line of sight throughout class. Now I feel trapped, I can't face him, not after yesterday and last night. I'm a nervous wreck right now. I need to get my head back in the game. I tried answering a question by Master Uphraeus and was told I was immediately wrong… great start.

Master Uphraeus has us all walk to the Crystal Fields, thankfully that means we don't have to be confined to a room. Even better that we're told to break off by ourselves, I need time to myself right now. As Master Uphraeus dismisses us, I promptly take off before being asked to be someone's partner. Then I hear Charlie call my name and my heart stops for a moment. I turn to look at him, but Rhody is also approaching me. Charlie can't know, Charlie won't be able to handle it. I also can't have him hate me for the rest of his life, it would kill me. I also can't have him distracting me right now.

Things start getting heated between Charlie and Rhody, so I tell Charlie to leave. Then Master Uphraeus shows up and now I'm concerned that we're all about to get reported to the Administration, the exact opposite of what we need right now. Master Uphraeus takes Charlie away and I realize that Charlie's probably already pieced things together. As he walks away, I notice his hands glowing orange. I don't think he noticed, at least I hope he wasn't intentionally about to fight Rhody.

———

It's over. I'm over it. I think to myself. I wasn't going to be able to rise to my true potential with him. I don't know which one hurts more; the fact that I let Charlie go to pursue something that isn't even promised or the fact that he seems to have moved on. No, he hasn't moved on, I won't make assumptions.

But that girl with the black hair…Jasmine? Jackie? Whatever the hell her name is she's not worth losing sleep over. Charlie is…Charlie *was* a huge part of my life, and I'm going to miss that. I'm going to miss the days we would laugh together and talk about our future, but if life has taught me anything, it's that you have to take opportunities even if it means leaving some behind. Hopefully one day Charlie can forgive me.

Like my father did…at least that's what my mother tells me whenever the conversation about him leaving us comes up. He was evil and selfish. I found out the truth a few years ago. I never told her, and I won't, not unless she tells me herself. Dad left us for another family he had, then died while out on a sorce-for-hire mission. I like to think he died the way he lived; surrounded by regret.

I guess karma works in mysterious ways, because now Rhody wants me all to himself and I want arms that aren't his. His ambition is what pulled me in about a year ago. Charlie was too busy to come with me to this meetup that was happening for "aspiring Sorces who want to change the world." So, I went by myself. Next thing I know I'm in a room with Rhody and a handful of other people talking about Sirrus, the world around us, and how most of us don't do anything about it. It started with the one meeting, then more meetings and more meetings, each one getting more secretive than the last. It felt like I was part of a new movement that would actually be advocating for change.

At least, that's what I have to believe now.

I was initiated a week before I started at Sirrus. Our leader, Master Krain, performed the initiation on myself and about thirty others. In that group there were five people who were also going to Sirrus: Abigail, Sanderon, Sia, Oni, and Lias. We were invited to our final meeting as prospects by Rhody and we all followed him through a portal that led us to a candlelit ballroom. The flames were a pale green, and banners draped from the walls with the same symbol, one I didn't recognize.

Master Krain stood at the head of the room with a mask of what looked like a demon-bat with two large antler-like horns and an uneasy engraved smile. I remember him asking the whole room first: *Why are you here?* We all stared at him in confusion. How should we answer? He asked again but not as nice, and that time it was to me directly. My hands were shaking and I had no answer for him. *Useless…*he called me.

Master Krain turned his back on all of us, and I turned to Rhody. He was looking at me with such contempt. That's when I shouted "I want to prove everyone wrong!" and the room went silent. Master Krain turned back to me and the rest of the group. Master Krain looked at Rhody and Rhody smiled back at him and nodded his head. He told us to get on our knees as he spoke these words:

> *My glory shines to the next world*
> *My loyalty in the great beyond*
> *My freedom will be afterlife*
> *My allegiance is hereafter*

Myself and the others repeated these words in echo of Master Krain with our heads bowed. When he ordered us to lift our eyes, we looked to see the room was filled with at least fifty more people, maybe more, all wearing masks similar to Master Krain's. Even Rhody, who I assume is the person standing in the same spot, the only difference being the mask of a vulture.

Master Krain held up a figurine of an animal that was mixed of different animal limbs, tails, heads, paws, and talons. He held this figure in the palm of his left hand, outstretched towards us, then with a wave of his right hand he summoned a mist from the figurine that spread to us who pledged ourselves. The mist made its way into our senses and came back out, covering our faces, forming our own masks. Master Krain told us to stand and embrace our new lives as members of the Queen's Wraiths and repeat his words:

My allegiance is hereafter.

From that night forward, I was part of the Queen's Wraiths. An Alignment that looks to create a new one-world government. As it stands the world is a free one, but with freedom comes a responsibility to ourselves and each other. Everyone forgets the hard times, no one knows the souls that are damned due to the actions of those unchained. Rhody told me that his mother was killed in a fight between two warring Alignments. They'd been fighting over territory and access to resources. Those men, to this day, go unpunished. The Queen's Wraiths are rising to put an end to groups like that and restore an order that was long lost.

V

"I still can't believe she dumps you *hours* before classes start, turns around a few hours after *that* and gets frisky with a 'friend' the same night, then has the audacity to get mad at *me* for simply existing in your presence?! Seriously, Charlie, she's got it out for me," Jessie says.

"When you put it like that, it sounds pretty bad," I say.

"Is there another way those events happened?"

"No. Kinda. It's complicated? What do you mean she's got it out for you?"

"No, it's not complicated. She's messed up, and you need to stop apologizing for her. Yeah, anytime I see her with her group of clowns, she stares at me with a hint of disgust."

Jessie puts a small space between her thumb and finger. "The only reason I haven't done anything about it, is because the rules of engagement are *very* strict. She has to act first, *then* I get to put her…in her place."

"Rules of engagement? Isn't that only in a violent situation? Like, hostile, life-threatening?" I ask.

"Yeah! That's the one!" Jessie snaps her fingers.

Time to change the subject. "…So! I heard about what happened to Nathan in Sindra's class. Explain that to me."

"Oh, hohoho! You're going to love this."

She tells me all about her life growing up on an island and how the tourists and trade systems make everything worse for her family and the other natives. I told her all about what I was up to over the two years prior to Sirrus and what lead up to my life when we met.

It's been about a month since the semester started and I've gathered my friends on campus to have a game night in my dorm room. Jessie showed up a little early so we could discuss Master Sindra's homework. She wants us to enchant our own artifacts that either heal, distract, or contain another sorce user. Jessie and I agreed to work on the assignment together, even though our schedule with Master Sindra didn't line up.

"So, when is everyone else showing up?" Jessie says. "Well, it's only 7:45 P.M. you got here pretty early," I say.

"Geez your honor, it was just a question. I have no further questions for the witness," Jessie says.

"I'm sorry, I didn't mean it like that," I laugh.

"Zach and Mat said they'll be here around 8-ish. Which means anywhere between 7:55 P.M. and 8:15 P.M."

"Ah, well, only lame people show up on time," Jessie says.

"So, what does that say about the people who show up early?"

"Hey! We're doing...Homework and stuff."

"We've gotten through exactly two sentences on how to enchant artifacts, the rest has been shootin' the shit about life."

"Yeah! That's crucial for studying!" We both laugh again. "Okay fine, seriously. You got any ideas?" Jessie says.

"Well, this rotator ring is nice, but Master Sindra has probably recognized it by now so I can't use that. But I was thinking about making an artifact that creates a sorce field programmed to create illusions of its wielder within a small radius."

"That seems pretty advanced; doable, but advanced," Jessie says.

"This wouldn't have anything to do with your recent 'office hours' with Master Uphraeus, would it?"

She was absolutely right. After the demonstration incident, Master Uphraeus asked to see me privately. He and I talked about the nature of what happened.

He asked, "What is giant crustaceans was that in the arena?"

I explained to him what my initial goal was, which was to create a flow chain but something went wrong.

"You created a feedback loop. Not a flow chain," he told me.

A feedback loop is like a flow chain, except with a feedback loop, the sorce builds on itself and compounds until it overloads. When physical forms overload, the sorce inside them escapes...violently. But when sorce itself can't escape, it too can overload, and if sorce overloads, well you get giant explosions that cause irreparable damage.

"Charlie, I believe you might have an...ability. A sort of...mutation among Sorces. Have you ever heard of something called an echo?" Master Uphraeus had said.

I'd heard of the word 'echo' before sure, but then he explained further:

"Echoes are like a sorce...condition, that manifest within Sorces, Fencers, and Artís. It takes the host's sorce as its own, and expands upon it, copies it, outright corrupts it, making its host's abilities more intense or concentrated. Echoes can cause...problems if not handled correctly."

I had no idea what he was talking about. He said he'd like to keep meeting to test this theory. For my safety and everyone else's. Before I left his office, Master Uphraeus turned and asked me. "Charlie, have you had any...unsettling things happening to you?"

I wasn't sure how to answer that considering the semester I'd been having.

My girlfriend breaking up with me? Her new lover? I'd dream of something unsettling or abnormal to take me away right now. I said nothing about my personal life and kept my answer simple and said I'd been under a lot of stress but nothing more.

"Alright, well then! I think that concludes our meeting. I want you to see me every day after your classes so we can get a hold of this."

He was masking his concern with a mock of his usual enthusiasm; it was very unsettling.

So, for the past two weeks I've been seeing Master Uphraeus after my classes and he's been teaching more in-depth techniques. He let me know that he wasn't going to teach me how to pass my classes, but if it happens that these lessons have a beneficial outcome, then so be it.

"Hey, about that, I don't think I'm supposed to tell anyone about that so keep it between me and you?" I say.

"You know, this whole 'mysterious boy' thing loses its charm when you turn out to *actually* be mysterious. Then it's just weird." Jessie rolls her eyes.

"Please, Jessie?"

Clasping both my hands around hers, I give her the puppy dog eyes. She pouts while trying to avoid eye contact, but the ghost of a smirk travels her face and she folds.

"Ugh, fine! You're lucky I like weird too. But you owe me two now." Jessie mocks turning her nose up in disgust.

"Two?" I gasp.

Jessie starts counting off her fingers.

"Overloading at The Crystal Fields. Borrowing my ring for your disastrous demonstration at Breakoff Point."

"Oh yeah…" I say.

"Need I go on?"

"No…"

"Well, just so you know, Master Uphraeus hasn't been teaching me anything out of the ordinary. It's mostly testing my capabilities. Checking my limits so I don't overtax or load myself. Turns out my limits are above average for someone my age and especially an Apprentice."

"Hm, well that doesn't sound like too much cheating," Jessie says.

"Cheating? Hey, I didn't ask for any special treatment," I say.

"Yeah, but even if you were Versed, you'd have to have a good argument or a special case that makes you eligible for private tutoring from a Master; otherwise, you both would be accused of favoritism. So, since you're definitely an Apprentice, what's your special case?"

"I have no idea. Apparently, I've stumbled upon a new technique called echoing?"

"*Echoing*? Like, e-c-h-o, echo?"

"Yeah, but not like when you scream into a big cave or something. Master Uphraeus says I'm showing signs of it but he's taking me under his wing to find out if it's the real deal. You've heard of it?"

"Yeah, most information about it is speculation. Either because there's little information or because it's something so powerful that if people knew about it they'd be able to take over...the world."

"Wait, seriously?!"

She just blinks at me.

"No, you dork. I've never heard of anything like that," Jessie says.

We both laugh. There's a little awkward silence between us. Her smile makes me smile, and my smiling is making her smile even more.

Slam!

Zach and Mat come through the door. Zach didn't even knock before barging in with a bag of chips and Mat followed behind him carrying chips and soda.

"Play time is over!" Zach says.

"The CHAMPIONS...have arrived!" Mat says.

Zach is wearing a pair of fingerless gloves and Artís' goggles. The black smudges on his fingers are likely from a project he's been forging. The aroma of grease and oil is still faintly on him as we clap hands and give each other hugs. Mat has on a pair of all white athletic shoes, the kind that emphasize the arc in your foot, a pair the Fencers usually wear for active training. We exchange the same hand shake and hug.

"So, what? You guys just get out of class? I thought you were done an hour ago?" I say.

"Well, I was but I had an idea for an artifact I'm working on so I stayed a half hour later than usual," Zach says.

"I don't know about Mat, he's always ugly," Zach continues. Jessie giggles.

"Really? I'm pretty sure your last girlfriend had a very different opinion," Mat says.

Zach makes his way to the small table in the room. "You wanna die tonight?" Zach jokes.

"Ready when you are babe," Mat says.

"Anyway! One of the duels ran a bit over-time, and I didn't have time to shower so I changed out of my fencer fatigues and headed over. Luckily, I wasn't dueling today so I'm not all sweaty as usual," Mat continues.

"Still smell like a dog though," Zach says. Jessie laughs aloud again.

"We haven't addressed the lady in the room! How're you doing Jessie?" Zach says.

Zach flashes his charming and flirtatious smile.

"What's up Jess?" Mat says. "I can call you Jess right?"

"Hi Zach, hi Mat. Hmm, 'Jess' is weird, but I'll allow it. I've been great! Well, as great as being stuck with this nerd can get. Has he always been like this?" Jessie says.

"Oh, you have no idea, this guy won't shut up once he gets going," Mat says.

"He went on for days about oysters when he found out that's where pearls came from," Zach says.

"Oh wow, you guys have known each other a long time— like really long," Jessie says.

"Well yeah, but the pearl thing was about a week ago," Says Zach.

Zach, Mat, and Jessie burst into laughter together. Though, as hard as I try not to, the laughter is too contagious for me not to laugh with them.

"You are—all of you—beneath me!" I say.

"It's been almost two decades since Charlie roped us into being his friends. Sixteen years of misery and torture. You still have time Jessie…Run," Mat says.

Jessie laughs then gets off the bean bag chair she'd been sitting in and up on her feet.

"I'm going to the bathroom; I vote we play something with teams," Jessie says.

Jessie walks into the small hallway leading to the bathroom. Zach and Mat look at me with wide eyes and raised eyebrows.

"So, you two were alone before we got here?" Mat says. "Didn't mean to crash the party, I should've knocked," Zach says.

"Ha. Ha. Funny. No, we weren't doing anything, and no, there's nothing happening," I say.

"Really? That's a shame. So, she's single?" Zach says.

"I guess? Can we not talk about this when she's right here?"

"Oh, so there *is* something to talk about?" Mat says.

"We're not having this conversation," I say.

I hear the door to the bathroom open and Jessie walks out adjusting her short sleeve cardigan, revealing more of her tank top. Her blue washed jeans weren't baggy whatsoever. Jessie's black wavy hair rests just below her chest, in stark contrast with the rest of her outfit. The way her hair falls reminds me of the way lakes ripple after a rock is thrown into them. I feel an overwhelming amount of guilt and pain as memories of Laurie flood me.

"So, what're we playing?" Jessie says.

"Well, I heard someone say teams, so let's start with a game of Zolar," Zach says.

"Zolar? Wow I haven't played that game in years," Jessie says.

"I got Mat on my team," I say.

Mat and Zach shoot a look at each other with curiosity.

"Huh, okay," Mat says.

"Don't worry Zach, we got this!" Jessie says. "I will gladly take Charlie down."

"I hope so, because this is Zolar: Gunwater Edition," Zach says.

Zolar is a card game that can be played with up to six people. The three of us used to play it all the time in high school. Every few years they come out with a special edition that tweaks the rules or adds new ones altogether, but keeps the base rules of the game the same. Since I am already feeling like crap and have Laurie on my brain, I know I don't want to be on the same team as Jessie. The game requires, at minimum, constant communication with your partner, and I know if I don't select Mat as my teammate that the "Chessie Committee" will end up getting me closer to her. "Chessie" being a mixture of "Charlie" and "Jessie" which I'm sure is what Zach and Mat will call us, as it is both over-the-top and cheesy.

———

After about an hour into game night I start relaxing and having a great time. Consistent trash talk is had by everyone, even between partners during Zolar. Zach would make a snarky remark about his next move and Jessie would return with a comment about her having to carry him there. Mat and I would banter back and forth about who had the best hand. Zach would make a joke about my play-style; I'd return with a question about his or the lack thereof.

We end up sitting on the bean bag chairs and pillows that are around, talking about the events that happened with everyone over the past week. I get the feeling that Jessie is waiting for Zach and Mat to leave, but they are waiting for her to leave.

"Welp! I think it's time for me to get out of here," Zach says.

"Yeah, I'm calling it too. I have some artifacts to build, and I mean the heavy-duty stuff," Mat says.

"Alright fellas, it was good seeing you. Same time next week?" I say.

"You know it," Zach says.

"Obviously," Mat adds.

Mat walks out of the door first, followed by Zach who turns to me and gestures to his psi-phone as if to say "I expect a call later." I smile and shake my head.

"Goodnight, guys!" I say.

Now I'm standing in my dorm, alone, with Jessie. Except this time there's far more tension in the air, at least for me there is. Jessie is still sitting on a pillow looking at the game cards. She peeks up to look at me and smiles.

"Well, that was fun! Your friends are pretty cool," Jessie says.

"Y-yeah no, they're the best. I could tell they like you too."

"I wouldn't mind trading you in for them as far as friends go," Jessie says.

"Oh really? The empty feeling of my absence would only be filled with the fact that you. Aren't. Me."

"Well, I think I'm going to go too. It's pretty late," Jessie says.

"Yeah, I'll uh…See you tomorrow?" I say.

"What's tomorrow?"

I forgot it was the weekend

"Right! I mean I'll see you in class," I say.

"Well, *if* you want to see me tomorrow…" Jessie says.

"I actually, have a thing I have to do."

"Oh…Like a 'if I tell you I have to kill you' thing?"

She gives me a half smile, trying to cover her disappointment.

"Haha, yeah something like that."

"Well, whatever it is, it sucks. Taking my only friend!"

Jessie speaks with an overdramatic tone and flips her hair in mockingly angry fashion.

"Only friend?" I laugh.

"No of course not, I'm not socially awkward like you." We both chuckle.

We spend the next fifteen minutes standing at the door saying goodbye, then telling another joke, then saying goodbye, then making a witty comeback. Finally, she walks down the hallway and I watch until she turns the corner. I go back inside my dorm and realize that the tension I'd felt was replaced with mesmeric conversation. I feel at ease. I clean up what little mess there is after the party and head to bed.

———

The next day I wake up without an alarm, allowing myself to sleep off all the stress without being disturbed. I get showered up and ready to head out. I check my watch: 11:13A.M. I don't have to meet Master Uphraeus today, but I'm not taking the day off. I'll go practice what he's been teaching me and see if I can get any more ideas as to what this "echo" situation is. I walk to the cafeteria to get some food in me before I head out for the day. I get a pre-made sandwich, a bottle of water, and a bottle of Acceler-aid. As I walk up to pay for my stuff, I see Rosh tending the register.

"Yo, what's up Charlie?" Rosh says.

Rosh and I have a personal handshake.

"Sup Rosh? How's the life?"

"Ah you know. Same old same old. You know that girl I was telling you about?"

"Nope, no idea what you're talking about. Certainly not someone you work with."

"Exactly! Things are going well, we uhh…had a little desert."

"Last night?"

"An hour ago."

Rosh grabs my items and scans them in the register.

"So, what about you? Got your ex-girlfriend situation sorted out yet?" Rosh says.

"Not even slightly. The main plan is still on, but I'm gonna have to take this whole Sorce thing seriously if I want it to work," I say.

"Well, what about that other girl you've been talking to? Jasmine?"

"Jessie."

"Jessie! Yeah, what about her? She's pretty cute."

"I'm not sure you can say that out loud as faculty," Rosh points to his black uniform.

"I'm not exactly making tenure here." Rosh says, and I laugh.

"I guess not."

"Just want to make sure you're gonna be alright."

"I will, thanks Rosh."

Rosh and I clap and slide hands together as I head off. I look around the area and there's no sight of Laurie or Rhody. I stuff my food in my backpack and take off towards the Arena.

———

As I approach the arena, I stand next to one of the four pillars on each corner. I prop my backpack on the ground and pull out the rotator ring and walk to the center of the arena. The ring seems to be fine; it has a few scratches from wear and tear but the crystalline material on the outside is still a nice deep blue. I place the ring on my left ring finger and give it a flick with my thumb. The outer ring begins to spin. As the sorce inside me begins to fill the ring, the outer ring starts to illuminate.

Next, I create a dynamic iris sorce crystal, or *DISC*. DISCs are like the sorce crystals from the fields, except they're fabricated with the user's sorce energy instead of coming naturally from the crystal itself and has a trillion shapes it can form aside from the usual tear shape. Maybe not exactly a trillion, but it's a lot. I set-up three more DISCs around me in a diamond formation, with me at the center. With the rotator ring ready and spinning, I launch a small dart into the DISC in front of me. Because DISCs are dynamic, they can be programmed for different functions. I've set these DISCs up to create small pulses, and exhaust their sorce just before they overload, to avoid causing another explosion.

Master Uphraeus has taught me a few advanced techniques, including the DISCs, but told me not to use them during class so no one gets suspicious. I mean, I'm not cheating or doing anything illegal...I don't think. But like Jessie said, getting lessons directly from a Master outside of a class setting is a pretty big deal. We've been testing my abilities to confirm whether or not I have this "echo" thing he was talking about. Apparently, if I'm capable or have the capacity or the ability or whatever, these exercises should prove it. The idea is to see how long I can sustain a smaller feedback loop like before. Master Uphraeus said I need to try and hold the loop for over thirty minutes. I'm not sure what the effects of having an echo are and Master Uphraeus hasn't been very forthcoming with any information and instructed me not to go digging for any more information about it. Holding a feedback loop for that long means my capacity is much larger than an average Apprentice, potentially rivaling a Versed or greater.

The beginner level, also known as an Apprentice, have the potential to manipulate sorce on a small scale. Influence basic elements, like water, fire, air, etc. Creating simple shapes, or sorce fields the size of a door. An intermediate level, or Protégé, can take things further into illusions, hallucinations, levitation of objects or themselves.

The advanced level or "Tertiary" sorce users can do everything an Apprentice or Protégé can do but on a much larger scale or affect multiple people at a time. To put it simply; an Apprentice uses sand, a Protégé uses a pebble, and a Tertiary uses a rock. Then you have the most advanced students of sorce; the Versed. Versed can move boulders. They're the ones who graduate from schools with the potential to become Masters in their lifetime.

Apprentice, to Protégé, to Tertiary, to Versed. All of these titles are assessed and given by institutions like Sirrus. Institutions are primarily run by Masters. The title of Master is not earned through school. The title of Master is granted only by another Master. Most often, and the most boring way, is a Versed finds a Master to work under; until hopefully they demonstrate enough skill and knowledge to be recognized. What rarely happens, but is the coolest way, is to be recognized in the heat of a moment or after a crisis. In those moments you're pushed to your limits, and without realizing it you earned the title in a trial by fire. I honestly find it hard to believe that there's anything noteworthy of myself, that a Master has decided to take me on. Whereas Versed can move boulders, Masters can move mountains.

There are three castes: Sorces, Fencers, and Artís. Sorces apply their knowledge of sorce directly to sorce itself, this takes time to practice, learn, and also train the sorce within yourself to withstand the taxing abilities they perform. Fencers apply their knowledge to hand-to-hand combat, more often than not in the form of weapons like swords, shields, hammers, projectile launchers, etc. Whatever they can literally get their hands on becomes a deadly weapon. Rather than drain themselves or waste time trying to think, Artís use their abilities to craft accessories, charms, articles, tools, and whatever they can think of to turn into artifacts. Artifacts can be programmed with specific sorce instructions to activate abilities, give passive ones, or help enhance the power of its wielder.

Master Uphraeus told me that the ring is a crutch, an Artís' tool, and I shouldn't rely on it for sorce manipulation. I need to learn how to do that on my own like a Sorce; I haven't made much progress in that area. Well, there's no time like the present! I pull the rest of the sorce from the ring and form it into a tennis ball sized orb, then stuff the ring in my pocket. I focus on the DISC in front of me, still glowing, and close my eyes. first, I get a sense of the sorce in my hand, feeling the power. I take a deep breath and focus on the slight rhythm humming from within. Reaching out with my free hand, I try to feel the same rhythm coming from the DISC in front of me; I feel nothing.

Unless concealed, or too far away, a Sorce should be able to feel the presence of sorce around themselves. Since I slacked off over the last two years, I never really honed that skill. Though, if I have an echo...do I *have* an echo or *can* I echo? It's still confusing. If I understand correctly, an echo is the ability or trait that can feedback sorce onto itself using your own without overtaxing or overloading yourself. Echoes are reverberations of sounds normally, so what does that mean for sorce? Can I bounce sorce back and forth? How would that even work?

Wait...I open my eyes for a second to refresh the scene in front of me then close them again. I tap into the rhythm of the sorce in my hand again; 1.. 2...1.. 2...1.. 2...I can feel it! Okay, now, if this works, I'm going to lose my shit. The orb in my hand has a pulse, I'm going to try and extend the range of that pulse to meet the DISC in front of me, without increasing the size of the orb.

I extend the pulse by a few feet, and it gives me goose bumps; it feels like I've just tapped into a secret I shouldn't know right now. I try it again and this time I feel the pulse ripple throughout my body and out in a circle. Not quite there, but the next one I'm cranking up to 10!

I wait to get ahold of the rhythm again, and on the next pulse I let loose. The pulse ripples through my body again, it feels like I just chugged a bottle of adrenaline. The pulse travels across the arena and I can feel how fast the pulse is moving outward all around me. Then BAM! It hit something. It hit a lot of things. Though my eyes are closed, the invisible pulse acts as an extension of myself, like a giant stick I can use to poke around the dark and figure out my surroundings. The pulse reached out far enough to hit each DISC in the formation around me. Now, time to try and create a feedback loop. I pull out a small hourglass from my pocket and set it up to move around my head for 30 minutes, that's all I need. I send another pulse and the DISCs send it right back to me, causing me to lose my footing a bit.

As I open my eyes, I see that the DISCs I created are now flickering, but they're flickering between bright and *brighter.* So, the sorce in them remains but gets sent back tenfold? Or just the same amount exponentially? Let's try that again, this time starting from fresh. I transform the orb into a rod and throw it at the DISC to my right. The DISC throws the rod right back at me. I anticipate its movements as it leaves a trail through the air. Immediately catching the rod, I throw it at the DISC to my left, it bounces back. I catch it, throw it, it bounces. Catch, throw, bounce, catch.

Can't stop now, gotta keep going. This is where I start the feedback loop. After a minute of catching and throwing the rod, I get rid of it entirely. Now I'm directly exchanging sorce from the DISCs to myself. The energy is chaotic and untamed, every passing pulse through my body to the next DISC causes my muscles to tense up. This is why I used the ring for the flow chain I tried to create. Without the ring, my body is simultaneously overloading and getting overtaxed at the same time. Sorce is leaving as fast as it's being taken. It hurts. After a few moments I start getting used to the feedback. There's so much sorce, I can feel and see it moving around my body and the DISCs in a dance of streams and sparks of light. Before I know it, the hourglass passes my eyes for the last time and stops.

"Holy shit," I say. "I've got it!"

Whatever the hell *it* is; I have an Echo! I *can* Echo? *The* Echo? I don't know, whatever, the point is, I have it and the implications here are badass! If I can sorce to echo itself, or echo other things…wait do they have to be tethered? I assume so. Maybe once I get better, I can make tethers to anything? Are they even called tethers? I'm learning as I go. I take a moment to hold the feedback loop a bit longer and practice getting a sense of this new feeling.

As I'm looking at all four DISCs I feel another pulse, but it's not in line with the others. This one feels off, not just rhythm wise. It feels stronger, and it came from outside my practice area. Caught up in all my excitement there are two things I didn't realize until just now:

It's nighttime. And Rhody is here, sitting in the stands a few rows up.

How long has he been here? Was he here the whole time? Did he just get here? If not, why am I just now noticing his pulse? Too many questions, not a lot of time to even get a cohesive thought. Rhody grins and slowly claps his hands. He gets up from his seat and walks down the coliseum steps, that stupid grin still on. He doesn't say a word, just pulls out a piece of paper and leaves it on the first row of seats as he leaves.

I dispell the DISCs around me and they shrink out of existence. Hopefully he has no idea what I'm doing here. Though, Master Uphraeus is not going to be happy that someone saw me. He's been trying to keep this a secret. On that note he's been doing a great job because I don't even know what's going on right now. I walk over to the first row of seats and open the folded paper:

MMCV Sorce Games
!!!HEADLINER: SORCE FIELD SPARRING BRACKET!!!
~TOMORROW – 9PM~ D-DRINKS-D

LOCATION: STAR FIELD (KNOCK ON THE DOOR –
PASSWORD: BLUE GROTTO)

It's a flyer? What in the world are the "Sorce Games?" Wait, "sparring bracket?" Is this a challenge? Is Rhody calling me out? Okay pal, if it's a fight you want, it's a fight you're going to get. You have no idea what's coming to you, especially with this echo thing. I stuff the flyer in my pocket and continue practicing so I can use my newly trained ability. Or, that I'm still training it. Whatever.

VI

I'm exhausted and it's 7:29 PM. I call it a night for practice and start packing my stuff. I'm wondering if Zach and Mat have any idea what the Sorce Games are, so I decide to give them a call.

"Yo what up Charlie?" Mat says.

"Are we on a three way?" Zach says.

"Yeah. Have you—" I say.

"Ew, is that Zach? Tell him I said no one likes him," Mat says.

"You know I can hear you right?" Zach says.

"Charlie? Can you tell him?" Mat says.

I'm trying my hardest not to laugh.

"Zach, Mat can hear you. Seriously, I have a question for you two," I say.

"Shoot."

"Have you guys heard of the Sorce Games?" I say.

"Hell yeah! Everyone's been talking about it for a couple weeks now. Lots of food, drinks, activities, dancing. Some demonstrations and games with prizes. And a big ol' fight arena thing. It's like an underground student carnival with a cage fight," Mat says.

"Underground? Cage fight? I'm sorry, what?" I say.

"Yeah, none of the faculty are going to be there. Well…they shouldn't be there. If they show up the party is over. Especially since the bracket isn't monitored by Masters. I hear less than 100 students have ever died at one. Seems pretty chill," Zach says.

"*Died?!* Wait, roll it back. Underground? Cage fight? No *Masters?* How is this my first time hearing about this? No one told me!" I say.

"Probably because you're lame," Mat says.

"Yeah, you do kinda suck," Zach says.

"I'm going to kill you both," I say.

"Well, anyone can come. But it is a low-key invite only. That's how they keep the Masters out of it. Rumors spread about different days and different locations to keep them off the scent," Zach says.

"No wonder Rhody gave me a flyer. He's probably planning on breaking my legs in the tournament."

"Flyer? There are no fliers. Someone made a flyer?" Asks Zach.

"Rhody? You're joking. That lunch meat is signing up?" Mat says.

"Yeah, I'm looking at it right no—"

I look down at the flyer Rhody left me, and it slowly fades away, like an eraser on lead.

"I guess it was an illusion."

"Isn't Rhody that the guy Laurie is seeing right now?" Zach says.

"Yeah…for now," I say.

"What do you mean 'for now'?" asks Zach.

"You're not thinking of getting her back, are you?" Mat says.

"And what if I am? It's my choice, isn't it?"

"I mean…" Zach shrugs.

"Yeah, if you're dumb enough to not see the other path in front of you," Mat says.

"Other path?" I say.

"Regardless of that, Matty boy, Laurie is done. I never liked her anyway," Zach says.

"You never told me that."

"Well, it's not that I didn't like her, but if she's so quick to toss you to the side like that, then she was rotten to begin with," Zach says.

"Hey, I get it, you're looking out for me, but honestly I think she's valid in her choices."

"You know what you sound like right now?" Zach says.

Mat jumps in, "Don't even try to justify it. Right, wrong, whatever it is, you need to get your head on straight. Can we get back to the serious question though?"

"What serious question?" I ask.

"The bracket?" Zach says.

"Exactly. If this Rhody guy wants to brawl we can do it before the tournament. I have a project I've been working on and I'd love to start testing it on actual people and Rhody sounds like he's been wanting to see the other end of it," Mat says.

"Give me two seconds and I'll make it look like an accident," Zach says.

"As much as I would love to see whatever it is you guys have cooked up, I want to beat this guy on my own."

There's a moment of silence. Uncomfortable silence.

"What? You guys don't think I can beat him?" I say.

"It's not that, Charlie. It's just…" Mat says.

"Wow…" I can't believe these guys.

"You only joined the Sorce caste because of Laurie. You've never really had an affinity for this stuff," Zach says.

"WOW!" I say.

"Are we wrong?" The two speak in unison.

"I didn't join just because of Laurie…And I've just found out that I have a…a new technique that I'm pretty sure can lay him out. I just need to practice a bit."

"New technique? What is it?" Zach is curious.

"I'm not entirely sure myself."

"That doesn't sound very convincing. And from what's been said it sounds like this guy is loose in the head with power," Mat says.

"Guys, just trust me, worst case scenario: You guys jump in and break it up."

"You forgot the part where I said you can die," Zach says.

"Wait, I thought that was people getting drunk and doing stupid stuff. Do students die during the *brackets?!*" I say.

"Well, no, not that we know of," Mat says.

"Or that's been reported. But then again, there's a reason the Sorce Games are underground," Zach adds...

Eventually, the conversation ends. I hang up my psi-phone and head back to my room. I'm not usually jumpy at night, but those two got into my head and now I'm realizing how eerily quiet it is. I'm starting to wonder if Rhody has plans to come after me before the fight, maybe he showed me the flyer as an unofficial challenge beforehand? It's a long walk back to my dorm and it feels longer the more I think about it. I hear footsteps behind me and check to see who it is.

Halfway back to my dorm I hear another set of footprints behind me, I'm really hoping it's a groundskeeper again, but these steps suddenly picked up the pace and were getting closer until they sounded like a full-on sprint towards my direction. I turn around to see my assailant, but it's too late.

"GOTCHA!"

My heart sinks into my chest as I hear the words before I realize who it is. Jessie jumps me and gives me a hug but my body remains rigid and shaken.

"What's up kid? You look like someone just hit you with a quartz arrow. Did I scare you that bad?" Jessie says.

I nod my head slowly.

"Yeah, sorry. I'm just on edge right now. Rhody showed up during my practice today and unofficially invited me to the Sorce Games tomorrow night."

"Really? I thought you knew about the Sorce Games already?" Jessie says.

"Well, you thought wrong. I'm headed back to my dorm, what are you doing out here?"

"I like walking around at night?"

"I can't confirm whether you're lying or not but that does sound like something you actually like."

"Well, have I lied to you before?"

"Not that I know of," I say.

"And how sure are you that you know what I like?" Jessie says.

"I guess I'm not."

"You're a dork, and also being very paranoid," Jessie says.

"I'm sorry, I'm just nervous about this tournament thing."

"The bracket? You're not participating in that are you?" Jessie says.

"Well yeah, Rhody basically said he wanted me to fight him and I'm more than okay with getting a few hits in on him myself."

"Charlie, no. The Sorce Games are fun and there's plenty to do other than the bracket," Jessie says.

"What? You don't think I can take him? You don't think I'm strong enough? You sound like Mat and Zach. Do you guys really think I'm that squishy?" I say.

"Did you see his demonstration? Regardless of what you already don't know and your lack of control, Rhody isn't right in the head. He's got psychopathic tendencies. This is suicide. You needed my help for your own demonstration. You weren't even sure about becoming a sorce when you got here and people like Rhody look like they've been waiting their whole lives to get here," Jessie says.

"Suicide? That's a little dramatic don't you think? I'm pretty sure as angry as Rhody is he isn't going to risk getting expelled or locked up because of me," I say.

"Charlie..." Jessie looks at me. "Rhody doesn't have to kill you but he sure as hell can make you wish you were dead."

"I want to win, Jessie. I want to let them know they were wrong about me."

"Fine. When I'm visiting you in the hospital bed, I'll make sure you tell me how 'right' you were." Jessie starts to walk away.

As much as I want to ask her to stay, I don't. I keep my eyes forward, and walk back to my dorm.

———

In my room I drop my backpack on the floor and barely make it to my bed before I collapse onto my bed.

I'm terrified to take on Rhody, I don't know if I can beat him. Maybe everyone is right, but how am I supposed to prove myself to Laurie if I can't beat him? How am I supposed to prove that I'm not a waste of space? How do I prove to myself that I'm better than that? That I haven't come this far just to back down? I'm not going to just sit around and wither away, I'm not going to be silent, I'm not going to sit here and do nothing about it.

———

I wake up on my floor the day of the Sorce Games.

As I go about my day, I notice everyone I see has a slight grin on their face. Some students are huddled into small groups organizing things on boards and tables. Others are practicing dance moves or songs, spells and fighting stances. As Masters walk by, they wave and dismiss any speculation about their activity. Students are secretly out of control with excitement, and everyone knows. I even hear someone talking to his friends; they're trying to convince him that the ring he bought is probably fake and the idea proposing to his girlfriend tonight is a terrible idea.

During lunch time I sneak off to meet Master Uphraeus to tell him what happened yesterday. I knock on his door twice, then three times rapidly, to let him know it's me. He came up with the secret knock. A little dramatic in my opinion, he could just enchant the door and let him know who's knocking, but he said that would be even more suspicious.

"Ah, Charlie! Come in my boy!" His muffled words coming from the other side of the door.

The door swings open, and I see Master Uphraeus studying multiple things on his table. Two crystals hover just above the desktop with a small distance between them. Master Uphraeus taps one of the crystals and it lights up. At the same time, the crystal on the opposite end lights up as well. Both crystals shimmer in a pink-blue type color. Master Uphraeus gestures me to come in as he concentrates on the crystals. I quietly shut the door behind me and move closer to him and the table. He then taps the crystal he did before. The crystal rings and begins to turn counterclockwise. A second later the other crystal does the same.

"That's pretty cool. Is this some sort of copy technique?"

"No. I'm creating an experiment to better understand your abilities," Master Uphraeus says.

"Oh! Speaking of which—"

"I know. I've been following your studies and I have to say you've done quite well. The only problem is that you haven't been very discrete about your practices."

"You've been watching me?"

"Yes, and I saw Mr. Smill invite you to the Sorce Games."

I lie. "Sorce Games? I'm not familiar."

I'm not sure why I lied. I guess it was just instinctive not to be the one person who ruins it for everyone, or maybe it's because I didn't want to ruin my chance to fight Rhody.

"I keep my ear low to the ground, I know what goes on

around here even if the other faculty members don't. If lying isn't your strong suit, I'd recommend being silent," Master Uphraeus quips.

"So, you're not going to try to shut it down?" I say.

"No. I was an Apprentice once, I had my fair share of the reckless fun."

Master Uphraeus opens a small drawer in his desk and pulls out a small trophy. A very old version of a Sorce's hat; wide brimmed, with a long top that curves slightly at the end. The inscription on it reads:

WILLIAM J. UPHRAEUS
1ST PLACE SORCE GAMES
BRACKET MMLXXV

"I was a Tertiary at the time," Master Uphraeus says, leaning back in his chair with a very self-satisfied grin.

"Whoa…"

"Since I became a Master and started teaching at Sirrus, I've always kept an eye on the games. Students need an outlet and a time to unwind, who am I to deny them that?"

I place the small trophy on the desk. "Did anyone ever die when you were at the games?"

"No one has died at the games for over a thousand years."

"Oh thank the stars. Wait, so you *can* die at the games?"

Master Uphraeus stares at me blankly. "Charlie, focus. Have you spoken to anyone about what we're working on?"

"Jessie knows that I've been taking private lessons with you…Rhody saw me at Breakpoint…Other than that, I don't think anyone else knows."

That, technically, wasn't a lie. I just omitted the part where I told Jessie about echo.

"I thought I made it clear that I didn't want this getting out to anyone else?"

"I know, I'm sorry. Though, I couldn't lie to Jessie, she's been a great help to me and she's very smart. She would've investigated further if I hadn't told her about echo."

"You *told her* about echo?!"

Shit.

Master Uphraeus rubs his temples, inhaling and exhaling deeply.

"It's not entirely your fault. Ms. Zirdi isn't as much a problem as Mr. Smill. He wasn't just watching you; he was tailing me."

"What?"

"He's been tracking my movements since the semester started. I'm not sure if it has anything to do with our collective encounter at the Crystal Fields. He hasn't broken any strict rules, he's very careful, so I haven't been able to report him to Administration."

"So, Rhody only found me because he found you?"

"Watch your words and make no mistake; you have compromised yourself and may be putting others at risk."

"Master Uphraeus, I feel there's something you're not telling me, and if I don't have all the information, how am I supposed to know the seriousness of the situation? I held the feedback loop for thirty minutes. So, what does that mean?"

"It means my theory was correct. You have an echo. This means that your ability to handle sorce is…unique. Also, very volatile."

"Volatile, how? That doesn't sound normal. Is it curable? Will I grow out of it?" I ask.

"No, it's not something you grow out of, it stays with you until you die. Charlie, let me see your ring."

He takes the ring and places it in between the two crystals he was observing earlier. He spins the outer part of the ring as it floats in between both crystals. As Master Uphraeus taps the crystal on his right, it changes color and shines a bit brighter. After a second, the ring spins vertically, and the crystal on the left mimics the actions of the one on the right; changing color and increasing its shine. Master Uphraeus picks up one of the books on his desk, an ornate, brown, leathered, old book. He flips through a few pages till he finds the one he's looking for. Nodding and murmuring to himself, he whispers words while reading intently from the book. He gestures with his finger at the ring, making it spin horizontally. He taps the crystal again, making it change shape and color, but this time the other crystal doesn't copy the result as it did before.

"This won't be able to stop you from using echo, but in theory it should help dampen its effects until we can find a more permanent solution," Master Uphraeus says.

Master Uphraeus moves his fingers through the air, like using small invisible tools to carve out the outer ring, and replace it with pieces from the two crystals. He pulls the floating ring from between the crystals and hands it to me.

"What do you mean 'dampen' echo? I thought the whole reason for me to figure out if I had it was so that I could start using it? So, I could get better at it?" I ask.

Master Uphraeus removes his glasses and rubs his forehead as he lets out a long sigh.

"Charlie, I know what I'm doing. I'm sorry for keeping you on a need-to-know basis, but that's all I can do right now. I need to talk to a few people before things move forward. You can be a danger unto yourself. Please, just put the ring on and don't take it off until I say so. I need you to trust me," Master Uphraeus says.

"I didn't sign up for this, I don't even know what I've signed up for! How can I trust you when you're clearly not being up front with what's going on with me. And I don't think you understand what's at stake for me here. I need to use this," I say.

"You've had more than one occasion of endangering me, yourself, and others, yet I have been lax and patient with you. This isn't up for debate. And how do you suppose that it works, hmm? Go ahead, if you can tell me what an echo is, what it does, and how it…affects you. I won't force you to wear that ring" Master Uphraeus says.

He's right, I have no counter for that. If it hadn't been for him, I probably would've blown up half of Sirrus at this point. I have no clue what's going on, or what echo is or isn't. My silence is compliance.

"Put on the ring, son," Master Uphraeus says.

I snatch the ring from his hand in frustration. I stare at the ring for a moment and have half a mind to throw it across his office and storm out. I take a deep breath and slide the ring onto my left ring finger.

"There. Hap—?"

A sharp pain rips through my hand causing it to ball into a fist. I scream out in pain and panic as the feeling stretches its way through the rest of my body. It's a feeling that I've never felt before, but it feels familiar at the same time, like experiencing a memory and remembering it at the same time. I've dropped to the floor and I'm shaking.

<Take it off.>

"What?" I say.

Master Uphraeus rushes to me.

"Charlie, are you okay?" Master Uphraeus asks.

<I said take it off! It hurts!>

"Okay! I'll take it off!" I say.

"No, don't!" Master Uphraeus says.

"He…just…told me to…take it off!" I manage to get a few words out through the pain.

Master Uphraeus looks around the room. "He, who? Who, Charlie?"

"Whoever was standing behind you."

"It's just me here Charlie, don't take off the ring. Stand up son."

I pull myself up, leaning on his desk for support as the pain slowly dulls and fades away. As I look around the room, I realize there's no one else here except me and Master Uphraeus.

"Charlie?"

"What was that? Why does it hurt now?" I say, inspecting the ring.

The ring now has a brighter sheen than usual, and the outer ring has a new color along with a more intricate chain-like design.

"Your reaction to the ring tells me it's far worse than I thought."

"Worse?! What do you mean, *worse?!*"

"You said something was telling you to take off the ring?"

"Yeah, a voice. I could've sworn it was coming from inside the room, but it must've just been in my head. What do you mean worse?"

Master Uphraeus quickly moves to his bookshelf on the opposite side of the room. He frantically searches until he pulls out a small, dark blue, old looking book. "Don't panic."

"Too late for that! Also, telling someone not to panic in an unclear situation, doesn't help them not to panic!"

"Your mental state is very important here. You don't have to agree with me, you don't have to even like me, but if you want help, which you're going to need, then you have to trust me. I will explain what I can, when I can, but for now I need you to remain calm and let me think. And whatever happens, do not take off that ring. Do you understand?" Master Uphraeus says.

I can't tell if the look on his face is concern or fear or both. My question is: is that fear for me, him, or the rest of the school? It feels like I can't breathe, but I'm also hyperventilating.

"Charlie? I'm losing you…"

"Yeah? No shit."

"Language."

"What? I'm sorry, I'm not exactly having the best time right now."

"Then sleep."

Before I can protest, Master Uphraeus makes a Z shape on my forehead with his thumb, and everything fades to black…

———

I wake up in my room, feeling dazed and my head feels filled with rocks. I see a note on my nightstand that reads:

Charlie,
I suggest you stay away from the Sorce Games tonight and
wait until I can find a better solution for you and give you
more answers. Do not take off your ring in the meantime, at
this point it's keeping you from getting worse but I don't know
for how long.
~M.U.~

I've already put the ring on, I'm not missing the games. I check my clock: 9:17 PM, I'm already late. I look at the rotator ring on my hand and remember the searing pain I felt after I put it on. I still feel like my skin is warm on the inside, trying to escape. I put on a fresh pair of clothes and head out to the Sorce Games.

———

The Star Field is only half the size of the Crystal Fields, and on the opposite side of Sirrus in the North West section. A glassy black dome covers the field, covered in tiny lights that sparkle and shine like stars. The entrance is protected by two sorce fields shaped like doors. I walk up to them and give the door a knock with my knuckle, but unlike the usual iridescent shimmer, these sorce fields were dark with constellation formations that were connected with lines. I check to see if anyone is nearby, then knock three times on the door. Each knock made the constellations move and shift in different formations. After a few seconds the doors show me a constellation in the shape of a question mark. I've passed by the Star Field before, maybe once or twice, but I don't think I've ever seen this happen. Is it asking me for the password?

"Grotto."

The question mark fades away and the doors return to normal, highlighting different constellations. In frustration I knock on the door three times again and the question mark returns.

"Blue Grotto."

The question mark fades away again and the doors shift in color to a dull gray. Then a small orb of light appears in the middle. I attempt to open the door but it bends forward, shrugs me off, and the orb shines a bit brighter. Great, another riddle? I touch the crystal and it turns pink. Then the doors open revealing a dark hallway. Only the light from outside is making the first few feet visible. This isn't the Star Field. The doors must've become a portal to wherever this hallway is. I can hear the faint bumping of music, so I take a few steps inside when I notice two guys standing in the hallway, waiting in the shadows. Shit. I wait for a moment running possible scenarios. For all I know this could be a trap. I never actually confirmed the location of the games with anyone, I just assumed Rhody was telling the truth. Mistake number one.

"Well?" One of the guys says.

"Hurry up, before someone sees you, dumbass," the other guy says.

I walk forward a few steps, not entirely confident, when the doors slam shut behind me. Now, it's pitch black. I can feel my heartbeat starting to pick up. I position myself and get ready for a fight in the dark when two dim lights appear. The two strangers in the hallway are each holding a small bird in one of their hands. The birds are made of light that gives off a soft glow to illuminate the immediate area.

"Sorce Games?" I ask.

One guy tilts his head towards the long hallway ahead, a bit peeved at my question. I nod and continue walking down the hall where the faint music is coming from. It's so dark I can barely see what's right in front of me. Suddenly, as I walk through an invisible wall, the hallway lights up. Huh, an illusion barrier, fancy. Changing the doors to the Star Field, setting a portal to activate after you give the right keyword, and setting an illusion barrier just in case? Changing any aspect of the campus grounds, without express permission, is strictly forbidden and hard to do. There's no doubt it took a handful of Versed to put all of this together. At the end of the hallway is a wide opening, where I see silhouettes of people and flashing lights. As I approach, I can feel the bass of the music pulsing through the floor. A bit of adrenaline rushes through me before I walk inside to see everything; Laughing, shouting, dancing, and loud music. It's complete and utter chaos. I love it.

VII

Charlie: Please tell me I'm not early and
someone else is here (9:39PM)

Mat is typing…(9:39PM)

Z: Zen tables (9:40PM)

Charlie: There's a Zen table?! (9:40PM)

Z: Yup (9:40PM)

Mat: At the buffet table. You sign up for the
bracket yet? (9:40PM)

Charlie: It took you that long to type? (9:41PM)

Z: LOL (9:41PM)

Mat: You two type too fast (9:41PM)

Charlie: Where's the sign up? (9:41PM)

Mat is typing…(9:41PM)

Z: He's been sipping (9:42PM)

Charlie: How many? (9:42PM)

Mat: Sign up is at the booth in front of the arena and yes, sipping smooth baby! (9:42PM)

Z: Two? Idk it's my turn at the at the table (9:42PM)

Charlie is typing…(9:43PM)

Mat: One and a half. I'm also trying to talk to this Fencer girl (9:43PM)

Z: She cute? (9:43PM)

Mat: No (9:43PM)

Mat: Go away (9:43PM)

Z: So, she's not cute? (9:44PM)

Charlie: Alright, I'll head over and register for the bracket then hit the buffet table and help Mat strikeout quick so we can meet you at the Zen tables. (9:44PM)

Charlie: LOL (9:44PM)

The music is obnoxiously loud but creates a mood that keeps up the energy, while lights literally dance around the room. Crystals, fireballs, and glass orbs move through the air, setting the atmosphere with the light that shines through them. I make my way towards the arena on the other side of where Mat and Zach are. This whole complex is huge, the ceiling alone has to be at least seventy feet. Hovering above the archway to the arena is a giant plastic banner that reads:

SORCE GAMES MMCV
2,105 SORCE GAMES

I frequently forget how long schools like this have been around. Though the school is older than that, pretty sure the games didn't start in year one. At least, none that were *recorded*. Right in front of the opening to the arena is a black stone archway, underneath the arch is a banner and table with signup sheets. A boy and girl sit at the table helping people sign in, I walk up and see their name tags: Braeson and Talker. Braeson has a sleeveless grey tunic with black roses embroidered on it, putting his muscles on display, his hair is straight and dark brown, wrapped in a long ponytail. Talker is wearing a green shawl over her vest and skirt, three tones of light and dark green, blonde hair braided down one side.

"Name?" Braeson asks.

"Charlie," I say.

"Last name?"

"Omitted."

"Fine."

"Year?" Talker asks.

"Apprentice," I say.

Braeson rolls his eyes looking at Talker. Talker giggles in response.

"It's always the fresh meat," Braeson says.

"Alright Charlie, here's your number." Talker hands me a die with the number 12 on it. "Bracket starts at 10:30, wait for your number to get called, if you're late you forfeit your match," he says.

"Um, is there an Apprentice named Rhody Smill on the roster?" I ask.

Talker takes a minute to look over the names.

"R-h-o-d-y?" Talker asks.

"Yeah, I'm pretty sure."

"Yeah, he's number six."

"Thanks."

"No problem."

I look around and see a few other people with dice, some

wearing them as bracelets or necklaces. I look back down at the table and see a pile of strings and chains, so I grab one and link it to my die, putting it around my neck like some of the others. I walk to the buffet table where Mat should be, and sure enough, I see him, drink in hand, talking to a girl with short hair, wearing a hooded tunic around her waist. She has small scars on her forearms, a telling sign of a young Fencer who hasn't mastered the art of not cutting themselves on their weapons. She's cute, and doesn't look completely disinterested in Mat. This'll be fun.

I approach Mat and the girl; Mat almost instantly glares at me to go away but I tap my imaginary watch back at him. I stay and chat for a moment, Mat surprisingly doesn't blow it and starts exchanging numbers with the girl. After Mat secures the girl's digits, he and I head over to the Zen table to meet up with Zach. Zen is a game where two to four players stand opposite each other, around a large round table with sand and rocks. Each game, the rocks are randomly moved around, creating space where they cannot play. At the start of each round, players choose a style; marbles or sticks. Sticks are used to create paths; marbles are used to travel those paths. The objective is to create a design given at random to each player, while stopping other players from completing theirs.

Zach has always had a knack for Zen, and never backs down from a game. At one point during his childhood, he was thought to be a prodigy. I was the only one of his friends that knew how he really felt about the game. One day when we were nine or ten, he said "I just play for fun", and that's when I knew he was going to be one of my best friends. He didn't care about going pro, or getting popular; he simply enjoyed the art of the game.

Just as I would expect, Zach has defeated the other two, leaving one guy to beat. The other guy is sweating his eyebrows off and doesn't look like he's caught a break since they started. Zach studies the sand on the board and he's as calm as ever. I can tell he's a little…giggly, as he rubs his chin. The other guy makes his move and Zach yawns. Out of what I can only assume to be boredom and impatience, Zach switches to his marbles and places them gently onto the sand path. With the motions of his hand, Zach moves the marbles gracefully through the design he previously made using sticks. The marbles dance, splitting off on different paths, eventually merging back together on top of the other guy's design, moving his marbles off their paths.

"Zen," Zach declares, then bows.

Everyone around the table cheers and Zach collects a few coins from each of the players.

"Did you really have to do that?" I ask.

"Do what? Win?" Zach says.

"That wasn't just a win, that was a poetic beatdown. I don't think it's really fair that most people don't know how good you were as a kid."

Zach looks around and puts his hands around Mat and my shoulders as he walks us out of the room.

"Say it a little louder, will you?" Zach says.

"See? That's what I'm saying," I say.

"Hey, I didn't say I was bad at the game, everyone stepped up to the plate assuming they would win. Not my fault they didn't do their research," Zach says.

Mat and I laugh.

"Besides, are you saying I should stop? You sound like a keeper," Zach says.

"No, not at all actually. I'm not saying anything, I'm just saying," I say.

"It's a dick move, but a respectable one," Mat says.

"Exactly!" I add.

"Don't you have a fight to get to?" Zach asks.

"Oh shit!" I exclaim.

I check one of the clocks on the wall and it's 10:29PM. I break free from Zach and rush to the arena gates. No one is sitting at the sign-in table, so I rush in to hear if my name's being called. I hear the announcer, a girl in a luxurious purple gown, calling out the names and numbers of matches. Past the arena gates are eight rings arranged in a circle, each ring is closed off by a sorce field in the shape of a dome, and each one looks around 50ft in diameter. Not exactly what I pictured. I was expecting some grand square stage made of exotic stone and pillars. This feels more like an underground cage match… oh. That's what Zach and Mat meant.

"3rd ring! #6 Sorce Apprentice, Rhody versus #11 Fencer Tertiary, Fae," the announcer says.

"Crap, I hope I didn't miss my name," I say.

"No, they haven't called you yet," a familiar voice says.

I turn to see Jessie, and I almost fall over since I wasn't expecting her to be there.

"Don't look so shocked to see me," Jessie says.

"4th ring! #8 Fencer Protégé, Sable versus #9 Artí Protégé, Percy," the announcer says.

"I don't. I-I mean, I'm not. I just thought you didn't want to see me again," I say.

"Over a small thing like that? Come on, Charlie," Jessie says.

"5th ring! #12 Sorce Apprentice, Charlie versus #5 Sorce Apprentice Niko," the announcer says.

"That's you. Try not to get your ass kicked too hard," Jessie says.

"Thanks."

Zach and Mat follow up behind Jessie, just in time. "You got this man," Mat says.

"We'll be watching!" Zach says.

The three of them walk off to find seats on the wooden bleachers surrounding the fighting rings. Each ring has a number sign just outside its sorce field. I walk around each of the rings looking for my number, the announcer is calling the rest of the names and numbers, I see the other fighters and try to smile and wave at a few. One or two people return the gesture but everyone else looks like they're about to go to war. I take a small jog to ring 5, getting there before my opponent. I can see ring 3, and Rhody is already inside his ring with his back to his opponent staring at me. He puts both of his thumbs up and mouths the words "good luck" to me, with the sleaziest grin on his face.

My head starts to get dizzy; my heart starts racing out of my chest. I touch the ring to see if it's still on; it is, but outer ring is slowly turning. I take three deep breaths and try to calm down. I shift my focus on the crowd of students getting to their seats. Mat, Zach, and Jessie have spots on the 8th row of the bleachers where they can get a good look at the fight. It must be obvious something's wrong, Jessie has a concerned look on her face. I give her a thumbs up and smile just as my opponent steps into the ring. He's short with dirty blonde hair, and a tunic that looks like a hand-me-down. He almost looks too young to be here, at least by a year.

"Charlie, is it?" Niko asks.

"Yeah. Niko?" I ask.

"Yup. Figures, they put me against another Apprentice," Niko smirks.

"Lucky for us, yeah? I was worried I might go up against a Versed in the first round. Hell, I'm still worried I might later."

Niko narrows his eyes. "Only thing you need to be worried about is me."

"I can tell you're a *really* fun person to be around. Good luck, Niko."

Niko just scoffs at me. The announcer walks into the center of the eight fighting rings, and materializes a megaphone in her hand. She taps the back of the megaphone, amplifying the sound throughout the arena. She snaps her fingers, making a metal screech come out of the megaphone to get everyone's attention, for dramatic effect.

"Alright everyone listen up! Welcome to 2,105[th] Sorce Games! As is tradition for the games, you can thank your

Versed classmates, superiors, or peers for putting on this well known secret event!"

The announcer pauses for applause.

"We, the Versed class, would like to thank everyone for coming out and partaking in a tradition that lives strong here at Sirrus! We have a *great* set of fighters here tonight, so let's get this show on the road!"

She takes another pause for people to cheer.

"But, before we begin, fighters! Here are the rules:

1. Each fighters is only allowed to use their <u>own</u> artifacts or weapons to incapacitate their opponent, force them to surrender. This means they can only use whatever they bring into the ring, no outside help.
2. Use of fatal spells, potions, weapons, or using lethal force of any kind is strictly prohibited. If you're caught by the refs, you're disqualified and more than likely reported to the Administration. Lethal force in this case is causing permanent damage to organs, or dismemberment. Cuts, bruises, broken bones, or anything else that can be fixed with a potion or healer is free game. You don't have to go easy on your opponent, but don't make us shut you and this whole tournament down.
3. You are allowed to surrender or you can leave the ring through the red highlighted opening in your sorce field. Please note that exiting through the red opening for any reason means you've lost the match. No bathroom breaks.
4. You are allowed to call a draw if both of you agree to surrender at the same time. To do this, both of you must grab your left or right wrist and raise it above your head. If you both agree to a surrender, you cannot take a cheap shot afterwards. If you do, you're DQ'd.

Now, all that said! Let the games…BEGIN!"

The announcer throws her megaphone into the air, then in a burst of light, the megaphone shatters into spiraling fireworks.

Cheers, screams, and whistles. The crowd goes insane as music ramps up. Each ring has a referee, and mine is…

"Nathan?!" I gasp.

"Sup, Charlie? Just here to make sure you don't blow anyone up. But, if you do, I'll disqualify you quick. No need to thank me," Nathan says.

Out of all the people in the world, it had to be this guy. Is he ever going to get off my back about the Crystal Fields situation?

"Alright, I'm Nathan and I'll be overseeing your match today. No funny business, alright Charlie?" Nathan says with a smirk.

Niko looks at me sideways and then back at Nathan. "You know the ref?" Niko asks.

"Sadly. I don't like him very much," I say.

"Yeah, I don't think I do either," Niko says.

"Fighters ready?!" Nathan says.

Niko and I walk to opposite sides of the ring and face one another. Niko gets into a fighting stance with his legs spread apart and both hands clasped together. At this moment I realize that I haven't actually trained in Sorce Combat whatsoever, that's a Protégé class, and Niko looks like he knows a few stances. Oh shit, this is why Rhody wanted me to come. He knew I wouldn't refuse the chance to fight him and I'd rush into this and get worked around by all the other students. As this sudden realization happens, Nathan steps out of the ring and puts a sorce field around it, trapping Niko and me inside.

"Begin!" Nathan declares.

I plant my back foot and ready myself for a full offensive attack. Niko drops to the ground and sweeps his leg out, suddenly I'm knocked onto my ass. How in the…? We're standing 50ft apart, how did he…? Before I can stand, a portal opens just a few inches above my head, but I manage to roll out of the way. Niko's foot comes through the portal a half second later and I see him standing across the ring with another portal cutting off his shin. Being able to use mini-portals is something an Apprentice shouldn't know, let alone be this good at, not by a long shot. I jump to my feet and Niko creates another portal to the left of me and hits me right in the face with his fist.

As I recover, I notice Niko is already slightly out of breath and holding himself up on his knees. He's overtaxing himself too soon, he doesn't have a lot of control yet, which means he has to use quick-long-range attacks. If I can get closer to him it'll break his rhythm and strategy.

Niko opens another portal behind me and spins me around, then a portal behind me again to kick me in the back. Cheap shot. Another portal opens in front of me. Niko throws a punch through the portal, I weave and grab his arm. Now, he can't close the portal. Niko expands and steps through the portal, throwing a punch right at my gut, causing me to lose my grip and stumble backwards.

"Nice reflexes. Will you be fighting back soon? What's your thing? Levitation? Familiars? Mind games?" Niko asks.

"A bad day," I say.

I put my foot forward to throw a punch at him, but Niko opens a portal right in front of me. That'll work. I clap my hands together as I move through his portal, this causes a small shockwave that collapses the portal behind me. Now, I'm positioned on the opposite side of the ring again.

He opens two small portals this time, continuing his long-range assault. He feints a low sweep with the first one, throws a punch through the second one. I hop over the sweep, but I take the hook from the second. I turn to grab Niko's arm through the portal, but something has changed. The portal looks as if it's on fire. A numbing sensation passes through me, and I subconsciously release Niko's arm.

Something is happening to me. My ring starts glowing and the sharp pain I felt when I was in Master Uphraeus' office shoots through my body again. It's the echo. Niko notices that I'm compromised and tries to attack me again with a portal kick from the side. I catch his leg against my torso, then focus on the portal itself. Let's see if I can make the portal collapse with a feedback loop.

"What the?!" Niko says.

Niko kicks his leg away from my grip and pushes himself back to close the portal. He sees the portal starting to whirl in an unstable mess.

"What are you doing?" Niko asks.

I pull the portal open with my hands and step through it. Niko opens another portal to run, but not before I start making it feedback again and step through behind him. He goes through a portal. I follow. This happens for a short time before I can tell Niko is getting tired. I stop my charges and taunt him.

"What's wrong Niko? Portals can't keep up?" I say.

Niko gets frustrated and starts throwing punches out of thin air through his portals. I put my arms up and block every strike. Then Niko throws his punch through another portal, then pulls away but the portal doesn't close. It's operating on its own now. I didn't realize, or even know, the feedback loop I created on one portal would affect them all. The portal expands and turns violently before freezing in place. I see a silhouette of a man through the portal. The figure holds up his hand, wearing my rotator ring. I look down and see the ring is still on my hand. I look up at the image, that now almost looks like a mirror.

"Echo?"

The figure slowly nods.

The portal collapses, and causes a shockwave. The detonation knocks Niko and me back. I stand to my feet and brush myself off. I walk over to Niko and he looks pretty hurt. I feel bad. I look around and notice Nathan watching with shock, as if he doesn't believe what just happened. I look back down at Niko who's trying to get back up, but he falls back to the ground. I rush over and kneel down to help him up.

"Niko, you okay?" I ask.

"Fighter! Are you continuing the fight?" Nathan asks.

"Does he look like he still wants to fight?" I retort.

"That's not your call," Nathan says.

His eyes are glued onto Niko. Niko grabs his left wrist and raises it above his head.

"No. I surrender."

Niko starts to cough in between his laughs.

"That was a nice trick. What was that?" Niko asks.

"Trade secret, I'm afraid," I say.

"Ha!…Asshole," Niko says.

Nathan drops the sorce field around the ring for Niko to step out. Nathan watches Niko leave, then glares back at me and rolls his eyes. He fires a sorce dart into the air that creates a white light over the ring.

"Winner! #12 Apprentice, Charlie!" announces Nathan.

I hear the cheers and screams of the people watching. I see Mat, Zach, and Jessie whistling and clapping. I look around and see a few other white lights, Rhody's included. I'm not sure when they finished their fights, but it was long enough for Rhody to look like he's been watching me the whole time. Once all the fighters finish, we're allowed to leave our rings for our next match.

"Next round is in five minutes!" the announcer says.

Jeez, five minutes? This isn't a tournament; this is a gauntlet! "Charlie!"

I hear Jessie call out my name and turn just in time to see a water bottle coming straight for my head. I grab for it, and the bottle tumbles in my hands for a second, then I give Jessie a smile and a wave. She returns the gesture while Mat and Zach make greasy smiles at me. Rolling my eyes, I turn away to hear who my next opponent will be. With a twirl of her finger, the announcer summons a giant board with specific names scratched out, as it reveals the next round of fights.

"Fighters! Check the board and find your rings! The second round fights are about to begin!" the announcer says.

Looks like my next opponent is an Artí named Noira. A Protégé level too. I'm still pretty sore from my fight with Niko.

Not bad for my first fight, but this is going to take a lot more thought. The refs from the other fights break the sorce fields and other rings to make room for the new rings. Eight rings in total are now four. Each one with a new number and I'm in ring three.

"Fighters! Take your positions!" the announcer instructs.

As I walk towards my ring, I lock eyes with Noira, standing off to the side with her arms folded. Deep red hair, with light freckles moving from the inside of her cheeks and across her nose, wearing a long braided a ponytail. Unlike me, Noira looks like she just got back from a meditation class; calm, cool, collected, and no sign of fatigue from her fight.

Suddenly, Rhody walks straight into my shoulder and almost throws me off balance. I instinctively turn to confront and attack, but not before my ring starts glowing and the sharp pain shoots through my arm. This is barely enough to stop me until Nathan shouts, "Charlie!"

I see Nathan watching from the sidelines.

"Don't get disqualified before you get your ass kicked," Nathan admonishes.

I glance back over at Rhody and he blows me a mocking kiss before looking at Nathan and giving him a wink. Nathan subtly nods his head. Are these assholes working together now? That's when it all dawned on me; Rhody, Nathan, Laurie, all of them. This was a plan to take me down from the get-go. I walked right into a trap. This is the lion's den, but I can't forfeit, even if I'm backed into a corner.

I get into the ring with Noira and Nathan puts a new sorce field around us. Artís are good at using gems, charms, necklaces, rings, or whatever else they can enchant using sorce. Unlike

Sorces, however, they're better at sorce deflection and containment rather than manipulation and utilization. An Artí is more likely to trap you in a cage, poison you with mist, paralyze you with a cane, or summon some sort of golem to fight for them using whatever artifact they have at hand. Their spells and enchants are more potent and concentrated, but are restricted to the number of things they have and they can't change them in the moment.

Upside: Significantly less odds of overtaxing.

Downside: Very limited strategies.

I take a deep breath in—

"Begin!" Nathan says.

Not "Fighters, ready?" Not: "3.. 2.. 1!" Nathan starts the fight immediately, knowing I'm not ready. I take a moment to glare at Nathan, on the cusp of asking him what the hell he thinks he's doing. That's when I hear Noira's footsteps coming up fast. I turn just in time to see a bracelet flying towards me, but I'm quick enough to catch it. As it turns out, that's exactly what she wanted me to do. The bracelet turns a bright ruby color and wraps itself around my wrists, tying my hands together in a beaded knot. Noira strikes the back of my knee quickly, knocking me to the ground. I notice she's wearing a necklace, which she takes off and clasps it around my neck.

"Ficium!"

I have no idea what she just said, but I can only assume it's a trigger phrase. When Artís are dealing with artifacts that are programmed to do something tricky or dangerous, they take precaution and give it a trigger phrase. This stops the artifact from accidentally activating, potentially causing unwanted damage or harm to themselves and or others. Noira uses her trigger phrase, jumps back and activates the necklace. Within seconds, a large transparent purple box materializes around me. I'm trapped. I rise to my feet and try to break free from the bonds, but every time I try, they seem to get tighter. I slam my bonds against the box, and break out. At least, that's how it plays out in my head. Instead, the restraints bounce back and knock me in the head.

"Yer bonds won't break. Nor the box, lad," Noira says.

Her dialect is foreign, it has musical intonations and has a flow that sounds like she's from Piquer. I look down at the floor where the box meets the ground and it looks like the box has shrunk.

"You're from Piquer?" I ask

"The box'll only shrink if ya try ta break it. Ya've lost, surrend'r now, so I can rest a bit 'fore me next fight."

"I've never been to Piquer," I continue, "but I hear it's a beautiful place."

"A gorgeous place 'tis. Perhaps one day yu'll see her."

I test to see if I can use a feedback loop to break the prison, but the cuffs drain me before I can muster the power.

<We can break this.>

I know, I can figure a way out of this. I can break this.

<*Take off the ring.*>

What is this voice in my head? Is someone psychically messing with me? The stress of this situation is really taking a toll. Master Uphraeus said I can't take off the ring so that's not an option. Maybe there's something I'm not seeing, some flaw here I can exploit. Assuming nothing can get out, Noira is most likely locked out as well. I close my eyes and try to concentrate and focus on the sorce around me.

In my mind I can see the restraints around my wrists as a glowing red knot. The box is like purple glass, and there's a blue line connected between them and Noira. If I can't break the chains or the box, maybe I can break the connection between her and the artifacts? No, that's not how artifacts work. Master Sindra told us that artifacts are as dangerous as they are versatile, there aren't many ways to counter them unless you know enough about them to know how they or the user work.

What else is inside the ring that I can use? The ring. The sorce field around us! I can see it, and it's connected to Nathan.

Okay, that doesn't help much. Unless...the box isn't perfect! This box only has five sides; no floor. Okay, I think I can do this, but the binds around my wrists are going to absorb any large spell I try to cast. So, it has to be something small.

"Taking a nap?! You surrender yet, Charlie?!" Nathan says, gleefully.

He shouts at me from the other side of the sorce field. I can sense him and Noira; both are in my mind, appearing as faceless glowing white bodies. I notice Noira moving one of her hands in a clockwise motion, at the same time the box is starting to get smaller. She's going to keep closing this box in and force a surrender out of me. I don't have a lot of time; I have to get this right on the first try. I get down on my knees and create a small sorce dart between my index fingers, making it slightly bigger over time until the binds absorb it. Now, I have a feel for the limit I can use before the restraints negate whatever I use.

"C'mon, Charlie. No way out fer ya, ya've lost," Noira says.

I create another dart, just before the limit the restraints will activate, and shoot it into the floor. This'll act as my conduit. These binds trigger if I pass a threshold, hopefully they're not sophisticated enough to stop something *else* from reaching that threshold. As for the box, it's still closing, but I can tell Noira is focusing more on closing the box, than what I'm doing. Perfect. I push the dart further into the ground till my finger is touching the floor. I can feel my body starting to tremble, I'm overtaxing myself. I don't have it in me to reach Noira, but I can definitely extend this dart to the edge of the box, I just have to concentrate a little longer. With the dart in the ground, I can control it hands-free to draw a line to the side of the box that's closest to the sorce field.

As soon as I draw the line to the edge of the box, I extend it further, making sure I don't trigger the effect of the bracelet. I'm manipulating the dart just underneath the surface of the ground, which makes it easier to conceal what I'm doing. The line travels underneath the box towards the sorce field, resurfacing just enough to connect to Nathan's sorce field around the ring. Now, I have a direct link to the sorce field.

"What do you think you're doing?" Noira asks.

"He's lost it!" Nathan laughs.

I send a pulse through the line, just like the DISCs at Breakpoint. The sorce field bounces the pulse back to me. I open my eyes to see with my own eyes. What was once an iridescent dome covering the fighting ring, appears to be vibrating and flickering. Nathan falls silent, as does Noira.

"Noira you might want to end this," Nathan says.

"Aren'cha s'posed to be impartial?" Noira asks him.

Keep talking, Nathan. You might be an idiot, but you're a great distrac—Uh oh, the pulse I sent out is coming back to me and it's stronger. I have to keep it on the line or the binds might destroy my connection. I stop the charge just in time, sending it back to the sorce field, just as the box starts closing faster. Noira's attention is back on me. Dammit! Another pulse through the line; the sorce field gets brighter and flickers more violently. Box is closing faster. I send another pulse and the sorce field starts shrinking. Got it!

"How'er yew doin' that? What're ya doin?!"

Nathan quickly realizes his sorce field is now shrinking—Well, it's *our* sorce field now. I just hijacked the field, and now he's trying to regain control of it. A sharp pain goes through my arms as I notice that Nathan and I are sharing a tether. I rub my eyes to make sure I'm not hallucinating. I can only see tethers in my head when I'm concentrating. I'm not sure what's happening, but I have to hurry before Nathan regains control. I send three more pulses through the line I made with the dart, and I can sense that it's now traveling towards Nathan instead of the sorce field directly. Nathan flinches, he must be able to feel it, but since he doesn't know what's happening, he keeps a stronghold on his tether to the barrier; making Nathan another conduit.

The pulses pass through Nathan, but not as strong. There's a new outline around Nathan that wasn't there before. With every pulse he endures, the outline gets smaller. My echo can affect other people too? As Nathan and I fight for control over the sorce field, it flickers and flashes while making distorted sounds. It's going to overload while Nathan is struggling to regain control. Noira's trap is closing in on me. I only have about two feet in any direction before it completely collapses on me.

"It's getting a little c-cramped in here, but I'm willing to negotiate your terms of surrender at any time!" I say.

Noira takes a moment to think, but the box isn't stopping so I send another pulse, a big one, through the tether and Nathan. His outline almost completely fades away, he was trapped in my feedback loop and now he's overtaxed. Nathan drops to his knees, giving me direct control over the sorce field again. I take it without hesitation. One more pulse and this ring goes boom, but this time there are no safeguards like in the Crystal Fields. I'm risking a lot here, if she calls my bluff, I lose; if I don't end this in time, a lot of people are probably going to get hurt. I definitely should've thought this through.

Noira stands with her own outline. I can't tell if the expression on her face is one of confidence, or disdain. Probably both. Her trap is now inches away from crushing me into submission. Just as the words of surrender are about to leave my mouth, I hear Noira:

"I yield!" Noira announces.

With a snap of her fingers, the restraints fall apart and slide off my wrists, and the box shatters into harmless shards. Though, the sorce field around us is still flickering at an increased rate. I attempt to dispel the sorce field through the dart in the ground, but the pulses coming from the feedback loop knock me on my ass. This isn't going to be fun...Here's to hoping I don't overload myself.

When I place my hands on the sorce field, the sharp pain returns, as it was when I first put the ring on. I muster all that I can, pulling from the sorce field itself. I feel the sorce field collapse all at once as it gets absorbed straight into me. The force of it all sends me straight into the ground on my back. I was expecting to feel more pain than I did. Instead, I feel charged. I feel as if nothing can stop me, like I'm invincible! I jump to my feet and almost attack Noira, till I see the look on her face and the eeriness of the quiet stadium. I look around and notice Mat, Zach, and Jessie. Everyone in the arena looks like they just witnessed a crisis. I look at my hands and body and notice the crackling light radiating from all over.

"You...you cheated. There's no...no way you...did that on your own," Nathan says, exhausted. He is bent over his knees.

"I didn't cheat! Everything I did was in the rules!" I say.

"Ay, the lad 'as an intrestin' way...but he ain't a chea'er. I lost fair and square," Noira says.

"Bullshit. He's disqua—" Nathan is cut off by a hand on his shoulder.

"Looks like Charlie won fair and square to me," Rhody says. Nathan snarls at Rhody, but he quickly gets quiet. Rhody bends down to whisper something in Nathan's ear. Nathan responds with something inaudible, then stands to his feet.

"Apprentice Charlie...Wins!" declares Nathan.

Thunderous applause immediately breaks the silence. Noira claps along with them. I look over at my three friends in the stands and Zach is losing his mind with his hands clapping furiously. Jessie looks like she's doing all she can not to run down and give me a hug, as if I just won the whole tournament.

VIII

A Tertiary Fencer named Ducane Sanderon is my next opponent in the semi-finals. Sanderon stands at about 6'3", a solid four inches taller than me with dirty blonde hair, beady little eyes, an awkward nose, and peach fuzz on his chin. If it wasn't for his height, he'd look like a scrawny little half-gremlin.

"The semi-finals begin in 5 minutes!" the announcer says.

Zach, Mat, and Jessie come down to the arena and run straight towards me, stopping just a few feet away.

"Hey, guys!" I say.

Jessie gestures at me with concern. My body is still pulsing with sorce, I almost look like a human sorce crystal.

"Oh! Uhh…let's see."

I look at the rotator ring and notice that it's cracked in the middle. That's probably not good, if taking it off is out, then I'd imagine it breaking isn't good either. As I try to exhaust the sorce flowing through me, I feel an internal tug, like something is stopping the sorce from leaving.

<I want more.>

What?

<We need to keep this for the next fight and the ones to come after.>

Who are you? What are you? Are you in the arena?

<*The ring is broken. Take it off. I don't need it. We don't need it. Master Uphraeus is wrong.*>

How do you know about Master Uphra— …Get out of my head, whoever *you are!*

The tugging gets stronger with every word the voice speaks. Something isn't letting me get rid of the sorce built up inside me. I concentrate harder and force the excess sorce inside of me out. As soon as I stop glowing, Zach picks me up and bear hugs me.

"I won't lie I thought you were gonna lose!" Zach says. Zach puts me down to let Mat get his turn.

"Man, that was insane! Where did you learn how to do that? Wait, what did you do?" Mat says.

"Were you controlling the sorce field from inside the trap?" Jessie asks me.

Jessie walks up to me and there's a second where I'm not sure if I want to hug her or shake her hand, and neither of us move. We awkwardly stand in front of each other smiling until I can't take it and say something.

"Uhh…I'm not sure? I just kind of learned through practice," I answer.

I'm hesitant to talk about my echo, knowing that I might become an even bigger target in this tournament, and other students as a whole at this school.

"I've never seen or heard of anything like that," Mat says.

"Must be really absorbing the class materials, huh?" Jessie says.

Jessie knows I've been meeting with Master Uphraeus, and gives me a sly grin.

"Yeah, I guess so! I've had a goal set in mind," I say.

My eyes search the room for Rhody, he's with Laurie, Sanderon, and a few others. The only one I meet eyes with is Laurie, she looks scared.

"Hey, buddy. You alright?" Zach says.

I turn my attention back to the group. "Yeah, yeah I'm fine," I say.

"Whatever happens you made it to the semi-finals your first year. It's dumb luck, but you should be proud!" Mat says.

He slaps my shoulder and gives it a squeeze and I laugh. "Thanks Mat, really appreciate the positive reinforcement," I say.

"No problem," Mat says, grinning.

"Semi-finals are in one minute! fighters, find your rings!" the announcer says.

"Alright, I'm up. I'll see you guys after the fight."

"Give'em hell man," Zach says.

"I bet on the other guy, but I really do hope you win," Mat says.

"Good luck, Charlie," Jessie says.

Jessie gives me a hug before she leaves and I feel a connection between us. I hadn't realized it with Zach or Mat, but my echo sensed something different about her. There's the feeling of a faint tether between us, though I'm not entirely sure why. Jessie turns away to catch up with Mat and Zach.

I walk over to my ring; Sanderon is there waiting for me. I can see his weapon sheathed at his side; a sorce powered zapier, which is a long-thinned blade with a round hand guard. His stance is elegant and smug, he looks like he's moving with grace even though he's standing still. I hate it. A new referee walks into the ring.

"What happened to Nathan?" I ask.

"Apparently, he was overtaxed after your fight. So, we made him take a break. No one saw you cheat, but I promise if you are cheating, I'll know," the ref says.

"Thanks for the pep talk," I say.

"No problem," he says.

The ref opens a small hole in the sorce field to let me pass through. I walk inside and he shuts it behind me. Sanderon is still standing there, watching me with his sword still sheathed. He looks like he's already begun the fight in his head.

"Fighters! Ready!" the announcer says.

I immediately take a fighting stance and flick my rotator ring with my thumb. The crack in the ring must be allowing me to use more of my echo and I have a feeling I'm going to need it for this fight. Sanderon switches his posture to face me, his feet sideways and his shoulders squared.

He's extremely calm, not even in a cold sweat from his last fight. A knot the size of a golf ball turns in my stomach. There's something off about all of this. The timing, the rounds, who I faced. I'm an Apprentice in the semi-finals of a popular tournament. I shouldn't be here; I shouldn't even be at this schoo—

"BEGIN!!" the announcer shouts.

Again?! Okay, maybe I missed the ready-check this time, I wasn't really paying attention. I take a half step back preparing for Sanderon's first move, my hands are shaking and my heart is racing. Sanderon lets out a small laugh.

"I'm not going to let you surrender," Sanderon declares. He slowly draws his zapier from its sheath. "Not that you plan to. I like that about you."

He walks sideways towards my flank as he points his zapier at me.

"You have a lot of courage, and seem like a fine gentleman. That said, I'm going to break you now."

CLICK.

I hear Sanderon flipping a switch on his zapier. The zapier then creates green and white sparks that dance around the blade's length. He walks slowly and deliberately towards me. I walk away from him with each step he takes forward; keeping my distance. Sanderon and I walk slowly in circles around the ring, periodically making quick steps to close or further the gap between us. He must be stalling or trying to wear me out before the fight starts, or maybe I'm too scared to fight a Tertiary.

I'm getting tired of his smug face and posture but there isn't a lot I can do without provoking an attack, and since I don't know what he's trying to do I don't want to make the first move. I don't care. I didn't come this far to lose and if he's not going to strike first then I am. Flicking my rotator ring, I charge it up and create a DISC, walking away from it to draw him away. Sanderon takes a few steps towards it and slices the DISC in two; making it disappear.

"I'm not letting you setup any tricks," Sanderon says.

I create two more DISCS on either side of me and stop walking away from him. This makes him hesitate his approach.

"How does it feel?" Sanderon says. "Knowing that the love of your life is with another? That you weren't good enough? That you're following her around like an abandoned puppy? She is quite beautiful. Tell me, do you think after Rhody's done; I'll have a chance?"

Something switches inside me. I know he's just trying to provoke me. I know this is a trap. I know he's trying to throw me off my game so I'll react irrationally…and…It. Is. Working.

<This. Ends. Now.>

The voice in my head returns. Sanderon takes a step forward and extends his sword in my direction arcing a lightning bolt at me. I take the hit head on, the electricity dancing around the surface of my skin; a burning, searing, numbing pain flows through my body.

<Big mistake.>

Something about the voice is off, I hadn't noticed it before but the voice sounds like me. Although I know it's *not* me, it *sounds* like me. Sanderon looks a little more cautious now. I can only guess that he assumes I should've gone down from that strike, but as I stare him down with unfiltered rage, I now see a tether between myself and his blade. Another visible tether. Usually, I have the intent of creating a tether but this one mani-fested itself on its own. I wave my hand through it, but nothing happens. Sanderon doesn't seem to notice it either. Otherwise, I'd imagine he would attempt to get rid of it.

"You're more durable than you look," Sanderon says.

Sanderon lunges towards me, charging his blade for another attack. I look down at the ground, watching his foot movements. It feels like I'm almost a passenger in my own body now. Sanderon swings his blade towards my head. Instinctively, I send a pulse through the tether, throwing his zapier off balance, sending his strike veering left. This leaves Sanderon wide open for an attack and I jump at the opportunity.

I lead with a quick right hook; he dodges. He's still off balance; I go for a leg sweep. He moves his leg straight up, then falls back on it, regaining his posture. I examine my body to see if there's a noticeable change, but I can't see any. That's when I look back at the tether and Sanderon.

"Ah, so you see it too then?" Sanderon says, gesturing at the tether between myself and his sword.

"You can see it?" I ask, stunned.

"Of course. Is this technique of yours supposed to be invisible to the naked eye? Is that how you've been winning your previous fights, with this trickery?"

"It's not a trick. Well, not really."

"What is it then? What do you call it?"

"My ec—"

I cut myself short. My hands are still shaking and my voice quivered. I almost told him about my echo. I think he already suspects as much; he just needs me to confirm it.

<Let go, Charlie. Let's take back our strength.>

"No!" I shout aloud.

Hearing me suddenly shout, Sanderon raises an eyebrow. "No? You're not going to tell me?" Sanderon says.

<Master Uphraeus was wrong. We need this ring gone or we'll never get stronger. We'll lose.>

"I'm not talking to you!" I say.

"Then who are you talking to?" Sanderon says, looking around the ring.

"Not you, moron."

Sanderon frowns in disgust.

<Give in to the call. Listen to the pulse of his sorce; it echoes throughout the field.>

The voice in my head is getting louder now, like an entirely separate consciousness. Am I going insane? I've snapped. There's sweat beginning to bead around my brow. My ring is flashing, how long has this been happening?

"Enough of this. I'm ending this now!" Sanderon says.

He isn't speaking to me directly; he's projecting his voice out in general, as if to get approval from someone else. I'm in the middle of arguing with my own mind when Sanderon alters his stance and approaches me while swinging his blade, arcing more bolts at random in my direction. I would be scared of him if it weren't for this feeling, this feeling of something trying to move me out of the way, out of my own body.

<He's coming. Move now!>

No, I don't want to, I'm not letting you in.

<I'm already here. Let me out.>

No, you're not in control, I am.

<We're in control. We need to win. Rhody has to lose. If we lose, he wins.>

I don't want to fight anymore; I don't want to be here. We're forfeiting.

Sanderon draws his sword back, going for a piercing strike. Surely the ref isn't going to let him kill me...right? Everything has slowed down. I see the blade moving every inch through the air, straight at my head. Everything begins to fade to black. Is this what death is?

<Yes. DEATH!>

Echo

As Sanderon's zapier lunges at Charlie, in the flash of a second, the light in Charlie's eyes blinks out. Sanderon lets out a victorious roar as the blade pierces Charlie's shoulder, but there's no cry of pain. Instead, Charlie's eyes lock with Sanderon's, and Sanderon sees the cold blackness of someone, or some*thing* out for blood. Sanderon notices that Charlie's eyes are colored differently now; gold and silver, mixing and pushing against each other like rivers that are fighting for the same territory.

Charlie's bare hands grab the blade of the zapier, pulling Sanderon closer. Out of complete fear Sanderon clicks the switch on the handle of his blade, causing a surge of lightning to crackle and spark around the blade. Charlie is unphased by the amount of electric sorce energy that now courses through his body, and thrusts a fist into Sanderon's chest. The lightning surges from the blade, to Charlie's fist, and back into Sanderon, creating an explosion of light that sends Sanderon flying across the ring still clutching his sword, pulling the blade from Charlie's shoulder and breaking the visible tether.

Sanderon barely lands on his feet, using his sword as a way to balance himself. Charlie stands practically unaffected by the force that distanced them, aside from the bleeding wound in his shoulder.

"What in the world?" Sanderon asks quizzically.

Charlie's expression is one of joy, like a child who was just told they could purchase any toy they want. The devilish grin sends an ice-cold chill down Sanderon's spine. Moving with unprecedented speed, Charlie rushes towards Sanderon still grinning with two hands, open palmed, flickering and sparking with the same electricity that Sanderon's blade uses. Sanderon poses for a counter move and charges his blade with sorce again. Charlie anticipates the move and launches a dart at the zapier, creating another tether between his hand and Sanderon's sword. Using the tether, Charlie pulls the sorce from the sword.

Once again, Charlie within range of Sanderon's blade and dodges left, barely missing Sanderon's counterattack. In the same motion, Charlie reaches out and grabs Sanderon, discharging the sorce into Sanderon. Sanderon cries out in pain but quickly regains his senses and uses his zapier to slice Charlie's forearm. Charlie jerks backwards and winces from the attack. Sanderon goes for another strike but Charlie catches the blade in both hands again.

<"You-u. Die.">

His words coming out broken and raspy, like someone talking again for the first time after having their mouth sewn shut. Sanderon's blade turns from metallic silver to a glowing gold that shines like a dim flashlight. Charlie immediately backs away from him, holding up his left hand, then slowly closes all of his fingers except the first.

"W-what is this?" Sanderon quivers.

<"I-I'll s-show you.">

Charlie points his index finger at the sword; the sword rings, pulses, and sends a dart along the tether to Charlie's finger. The dart bounces back and forth, causing the sword to dim and glow with each bounce. Charlie utters something that Sanderon can't understand, as he flails his sword and attempts to dispel the tether.

"What is this?!" Sanderon says.

<"H-hope that steel is durable!">

Sanderon admires the glow of his blade.

"So, you're using sorce to amplify the blade past its limits? Impressive, but not enough to stop me. And what's happened to your voice, Charlie? It sounds...augmented and broken," Sanderon says.

Charlie frowns, and shakes his head, like a bug just landed on it.

<"I'm. Not. Charlie.">

"Interesting...So, all I need to do is make sure I'm expelling more energy than you're putting out. And it seems you're not putting out as much as you think you are."

Charlie's eyes glare at Sanderon then the tether; turning his gaze to the rotator ring on his finger.

<"No.">

Sanderon smiles and rushes Charlie with his zapier, fully extended towards him, casting a single massive bolt of lightning in his direction. Charlie evades Sanderon's attack; trying to pull the ring from around his finger, but his fingers stop around the ring. Sanderon charges at him again, Charlie dodges. With his back against the sorce field, Charlie slams his fist into it, worsening the crack in the ring.

<"Take it off! I don't have time for these games!">

Sanderon chases Charlie's movements with his sword, leaving scorch marks everywhere. Charlie tries pulling off the ring again, but he's met with much resistance. As Charlie argues with himself, Sanderon notices his strange behavior. For a moment, Sanderon remains still to watch Charlie.

<"You had your chance! But you wouldn't listen to me, so now we're doing it my way!">

"Who in Tredius' name are you talking to?" Sanderon says.

<"A dead man.">

Sanderon looks out at the crowd that now surrounds the ring. This is the last fight before the finals, and a crowd has formed around the dome. He looks specifically to Rhody who's been watching for some time. Rhody shrugs at Sanderon. As Sanderon turns back to face Charlie, he's met with the blast of sorce energy straight from Charlie's hand that cuts the right side of his face. Sanderon feels the flesh wound on his cheek and sees the blood on his fingers.

<"You incestual parasite. Lurch over here, so I can put you down like the pestilent rodent you are.">

Sanderon ignites his zapier once again and dashes towards Charlie with a flurry of strikes. Charlie maneuvers around his blade but for every slash he evades, Sanderon uses his off-hand to send a bolt of electricity straight at him. Charlie moves left, a bolt into his right abdomen. Sanderon slices downward, Charlie backs away, a bolt to his knee. Charlie attempts to counterattack with blasts of sorce of his own, but Sanderon uses his blade to deflect or take the force of each attack to his tunic.

Sanderon stomps his foot on the ground, causing a flare of sparks to blind Charlie. Gripping the handle of his blade with both hands, he swings it in a horizontal arc that sends a concussive wave of lightning forward, knocking Charlie out onto the ground. Charlie's body lies there, motionless…

Give me back my body!

<"No! You've had your time. We would've lost if I hadn't come to the rescue.">

So now it's back to "we"? I'm not arguing with you. The fight is over, I want my body back.

<"I'll give it back when we win.">

We're slumped over on the floor. It's over.

<"It's only over because you keep fighting me. I'm only going to tell you this once; you and I need to work together.">

Sanderon slowly approaches Charlie, who still lies on the

ground, but seems as though he's talking to someone. As Sanderon gets closer he readies his blade for any surprise attacks. As he hovers over Charlie, he ignites his zapier once again with lightning that flows through his sword and up his arm until it completely envelopes his whole body. Charlie turns over to see his opponent hovered over him with the blade held above his brow; preparing to pierce Charlie where he lies.

<"Do it.">

Charlie's head turns to look Sanderon in his eyes. Sanderon braces to thrust his sword; he stops in thought and peers up to see Rhody on the other side of the sorce field, standing behind where Charlie is on the ground. Rhody doesn't look pleased; they both exchange glares, and Rhody slowly shakes his head.

"You can't be serious," Sanderon sighs.

"It's not your place," Rhody says.

"Why do *you* get special treatment?"

"Where is your allegiance?"

Sanderon frowns and takes a deep breath.

"My allegiance is hereafter," Sanderon says through gritted teeth.

Sanderon sheaths his blade and snaps his fingers; dispelling the shroud of electricity.

"I forfeit!" Sanderon claims.

<"What?!">

Sanderon walks away from Charlie towards the referee.

"You forfeit?" The referee says.

"Yes. I concede victory to, Char— ...to whoever that is," Sanderon says.

The referee looks confused, but reluctantly drops the sorce field around the fighting ring and allows Sanderon to leave. Charlie's body moves to get up, but can barely get onto his knees.

We won.

<*We didn't win. He humiliated us.*>

You won. Deals a deal; give me back control.

<You've always been in control. I didn't force you out; you let me in.>

What? No. No, that's not true.

<You stopped me from taking off the ring. You could've taken control at any time. You simply refused to do so.>

IX

The moment I dropped to my knees in that fight with Sanderon, I wanted to be anywhere but there. That's when something took over. *It* took over. The rest of the fight was like being in a dream state where I couldn't tell if what I was seeing through my eyes was actually happening. Coming back into full control of myself feels like waking up from a dream that you never had. I can still feel it in there, inside my head, lurking, echoing. Wait…Is that?…Is that what echo is?

Is that what you are?!

<Yes.>

You're the echo?! You're not just an ability, you're like an entity?!

<I am sentient. Yes.>

I don't know if I should be terrified or amazed. How does this work? How did you get here? Why me? Are you trying to kill me?

<I don't know. But I want to live, so I've been trying to help you.>

Help me? You've been trying to get me to take off this ring, and you almost got us killed in that fight with Sanderon. You must be joking.

<I helped you get out of a sticky situation, and yes, I am trying to get you to take off the ring. Because it hurts me, and whatever happens to one of us, echoes to the other.>

"Charlie!" Jessie roars. I flinch. "Are you okay?"

Jessie kneels down and examines my wounds. Jessie uses the sleeve of her tunic to wipe the blood from my nose and other spots on my face, staining the sky-blue fabric. I didn't even know I was bleeding.

"What the hell happened? You looked like you blacked out for a second and then you started going crazy!" Jessie says.

"I mean you look like you just got hit by a truck, but you won, right?" Mat says.

Mat and Zach walk around to the opposite side of Jessie. "Yeah...he 'won' alright," Zach starts.

"But he surrendered when he had you on the ropes. I don't like that."

"You noticed that too huh?" I say.

As Jessie is looking over my wounds, I notice Laurie looking at me from afar; She looks sad and scared. Laurie averts her gaze when she notices I've caught her looking. Seems she was actually looking at Jessie, not me.

"Hey, Jessie, thanks but I think I got it from here," I say.

I try pulling my arm away from Jessie but she pulls my arm back with force and I wince.

"Sit your ass down. You are in no position to get up, let alone fight right now. Zach, can you get me a bottle of water and a rag please?" Jessie says.

"I gotcha. Mat, come help me find either of those things," Zach says.

Mat says, "It doesn't take two peo—"

"Come on!" Zach says, cutting him off.

Zach pulls Mat up by his shoulder and they leave the ring. Sounds of chatter around the tournament room fill the air, I can see some people acting out the fight I just had with Sanderon. A slight pain from my arm pulls me back to Jessie.

"Ow!" I say.

"Sorry," Jessie says.

"I think you might have nerve damage, or fracture, I'm not sure."

"You're a medic now?" I say.

"As of right now I am. Please, tell me you're not going to fight in the finals."

"Of course, I am. I can't stop now, I'm so close!"

"Close to death, Charlie! You can't be serious. You're going up against Rhody in the final match. You saw what he was capable of at the demonstration; he hasn't lost a fight or broken a sweat since the tournament started."

"That's not possible. He's gotta be as beat up as I am."

"He won every fight in less than a minute, either through force or surrender. You don't have to prove anything here Charlie. You made it this far, take the win and leave it."

"I'm sorry Jessie. I have to."

"For what? For Laurie? Charlie, you have to let that go."

"I think we're done here, Jessie."

Zach and Mat arrive with a water bottle and cloth. Jessie stares at me, I can tell she's about to start tearing up out of frustration.

"Get him cleaned up. He's your problem now," Jessie says. Jessie drops my arm, stands up, and walks away.

"Whoa, what happened?" Mat says.

"Jessie?" Zach calls.

Jessie keeps walking.

"She mad, cause you're not fighting again?" Mat says.

"Quite the opposite," I say.

"I was really hoping you weren't gonna say that," Zach says. Zach hands me the bottle and the cloth.

"Thanks," I say.

"Seriously, Charlie, don't go in there. Something isn't right about all of this. It feels like a…" Zach trails off.

"Like a trap?" I ask.

"Exactly," Mat says.

"Look, even if it is a trap, I can't stop here. I'm so close to fighting Rhody."

"Fighting him isn't going to get you Laurie back. You're smart enough to know that right?" Zach says.

"Maybe it's not about Laurie, okay?!" I say.

Zach and Mat are a bit taken aback by my exclamation. "Maybe I want to fight him for myself. Maybe, maybe, I want to prove to myself that I'm someone worth fighting for, that I can fight if I had to. Being a Sorce can be dangerous, right? If I can't hack it here, then the real world is going to eat me alive."

Zach and Mat nod at me.

"Fine, but if this next round gets too hairy, you have to promise you'll get out of there," Zach says.

"Okay," I say.

"Seriously, Charlie. As soon as you feel like you can't put up any more of a fight, you surrender," Mat says.

"I get it!" I say.

"Yeah, makes sense why Jessie left," Zach says. I scowl at Zach.

"Sheesh. C'mon Zach, you don't have to be so harsh," Mat says.

"You both know what I meant; she doesn't know what you're like, Charlie. It's very off putting when you get stubborn like this," Zach says.

"Yeah, well, I'm not having the best day," I say.

"Doesn't mean you have to be a dick," Zach says.

Mat nods, "He's got a point."

"Who?" Zach and I say.

"Pick one," Mat says.

Mat offers me his hand and I take it to pull myself up to my feet.

"How're you feeling?" Mat says.

"Well, the adrenaline is wearing off, so, like shit?" I say. All three of us share a laugh.

"Final round starts in five minutes!" the announcer says.

"Five minutes? They're crazy! The last fight just barely finished," Zach snaps.

"It's fine Zach. It's a gauntlet. Not meant for the weak," I say.

"Still," Zach says.

"I'll see you guys after the fight?" I say.

"Of course," Zach says.

"You know it. Right after we beat the other guy's ass," Mat says.

The three of us laugh together again before the other two walk-off to the stands again. I take the cloth that Jessie gave me and wipe my face off one more time. Now that we're in the final match, all of the rings have been consolidated into one. Now the circle takes up the entire center of the room, leaving only a few feet of space between the bleachers. Everyone is taking their seats and getting ready for this final showdown.

My body is starting to ache and crack. I can feel the residual sting from Sanderon's blast. I'm surprised I can still move after something like that.

<It's because you gave something a little extra.>

Please, not you again.

<One more fight.>

This shouldn't be as hard as the last one.

<Rhody isn't as strong as Sanderon is; Sanderon was a Tertiary, Rhody is just an Apprentice.>

I can do this no problem, right? Wait. Are you influencing my thoughts?

<No.>

Are you lying?

<Can I lie to you?>

I don't know. Can you? Do you even know?

"Next round begins in one minute! fighters, get ready!" the announcer says.

I take my stance in the ring on the side closest to where Mat and Zach are sitting. I turn around just as the referee puts on the sorce field to see them. I notice Jessie's empty seat and look at Zach, he and Mat shrug. Just before I turn around, I notice Jessie making her way back. She takes her seat next to Mat and glares at me. There's a strong look of concern on her face but she mouths the words "good luck" to me and gives me a half smile. I nod then turn around to face Rhody.

Rhody is standing on the other side of the ring, soaking up the cheers from his section and putting on a preshow for his "fans".

<Take off the ring.>

No. We're not having this conversation. I'm going to beat him, if not, I'm at least going to let out some overdue frustration.

"Let the final fight…BEGIN!" the announcer says.

A huge wave of claps and cheers erupt around the room, some people standing up and waving whatever items they have nearby. I see Laurie past Rhody for a moment, and the way she looks at him; it's the same way she used to look at me. With those eyes, those eyes that let you know everything is going to be okay…

Rhody is still standing there watching the crowd on his side, with his back still turned on me. I can feel the anger in me boiling and that's probably exactly what he wants.

"Hey asshole!" I say.

Rhody doesn't react to my taunt. He does react to the sorce dart I shoot at the back of his head. Not enough to knock him out, but just enough to get his attention. I should've cleaned his clock right then and there, but I don't have the energy in me to last if I miss. The crowd *ooooos* in reaction to my attack. Rhody rubs the back of his head and looks at me with more than enough contempt.

I immediately set up two DISCS on my left and right. I'll use these as my defense against any attacks Rhody might bring my way. Sanderon had lightning, and from the demonstration, Rhody seems to also know how to use the element of chaos. If I use them right, I can use the DISCS as lightning rods and redirect some of the surge coming my way.

Rhody cracks his neck and knuckles. He reaches out with both hands and pulls the ground up from beneath to cover himself in stone. Same trick as his demonstration. Next, he's going to use lightning as whips. Which is what I was assuming, until he uses lightning to make the rocks covering his body into glowing stones; fusing them together to look like shimmering scales across his body.

"You like the new look? Made some improvements," Rhody says.

"Yeah, you look *really* pretty. I think I'll call it…*Glitter*scale!" In a single burst of strength, Rhody jumps straight at me and attempts to use an aerial stomp. I rush forward underneath him to dodge the move but the shockwave from his landing shakes the whole ground, so much that it ripples throughout the sorce field around us. The crowd goes wild again. Rhody turns around swiftly and shoots a lightning bolt at me. I respond with the DISC to my right and it absorbs the whole strike. I return the bolt to its owner, with added sorce of my own.

Rhody side-steps the incoming hit and swings an arm in my direction, causing small shards of the armored scales to fly off at me. Covering my face with my arms, I feel the shards flying past me. A few actually hitting, slicing and digging into my skin. The shards are as small as pebbles but feel like pieces of glass. While I'm still defending myself from the onslaught of shards, Rhody punches me across the ring with what feels like a giant hammer. I roll a few times before I'm lying on my back staring up at the roof.

<Charlie, we really need to take off the ring.>

I don't think that's a good idea.

<We're bleeding, two or more of our ribs are broken, and you don't have the strength alone to do this.>

I'll beat him or die trying.

<Is that what you want? For what, Laurie?>

Yes. No. I mean yes. I want her back. That's why I'm fighting in this stupid tournament. I…think…

<No, you don't. You want to win. That's what we've always wanted. What exactly is it worth? She's already gone, and now you're enduring more pain than necessary and what happens after this fight? You think everything will go back to the way things were? Let's say it does; what then? Is the pain going away? Is the trust coming back? Do you honestly think any of this is going to matter to Laurie or you?>

I guess not.

<Take. Off. The ring. Now.>

But-

<NOW!>

I put both hands across my chest and place my fingers on the ring. I turn my head to the left to look at Rhody. He's gloating and getting riled up by the crowd. I notice Mat, Zach, and Jessie standing at the edge of the sorce field on the other side, beating on it and screaming at the referee. I turn my head to the right and see Laurie. I cling to the ring tighter.

Laurie looks down at her feet and covers her face with one hand to avoid looking at me further.

<Let go Charlie! LET! GO!>

Rhody notices me moving and starts walking towards me with what looks like an intent to murder.

I take one more look at Laurie…then I pull off the ring.

I feel a sudden rush of adrenaline and sorce coursing through my body.

I don't feel any more pain, all I feel is determination.

<Now. Let. Me. Out.>

Take it away, Echo.

My body rises to its feet and I notice that Rhody is outlined in a yellow glow, while everyone else is outlined in purple. I notice my own glow is blue with spots of yellow where Rhody's shards are stuck inside my arms. I feel as if I'm a passenger in my own body again, but this time I'm giving in and not fighting. It almost feels like my instincts have taken over, like I'm at peace and I don't have to worry about this anymore; I'm no longer in control.

Rhody throws a larger scale of his armor at me, straight at my chest, and my hands catch it. Then I trace the shard back to where it came from, visualizing the tether between Rhody and the shard. The tether slowly disappears, letting me know that Rhody isn't controlling the shards after he throws them. I watch as my body transfers his shard's sorce into mine; giving it the same blue glow as myself. My body moves to throw the shard back at Rhody, straight at his head. Rhody barely has any time to react as the shard just barely grazes his cheek, knocking off a chunk of his glitterscale helmet.

Rhody then charges at my body with full rage and force, breaking off larger pieces of his armor to throw at me. My body reacts by moving backwards and catching the scales and turning them into DISCs and throwing them at the ground around the arena. Rhody's attacks are relentless; growling and throwing volley after volley of shards. Each scale is either caught or deflected with a small sorce field my hands have projected. After catching and planting the deflected scales in the ground, my body catches two more and throws one back at Rhody, causing him to pause his attack.

I see the tether between the scales planted in the ground and the one in my hand. Enchanting the scale, I watch as the sorce is shared between the rest of them, creating a minefield of DISCs that shimmer and glow all around the ring, both of us surrounded. By all accounts, I think my body should be over-taxed by now, but I can see the shards pulling from me and me from the shards. Becoming a self-sustaining feedback loop. This is what an Echo must be; an everlasting battery of sorce. I see it now.

Rhody sees the scales in the ground and removes his glitter-scale armor. Changing tactics, he crosses his hands together and locks his fingers. A blue flame ignites from his fingertips and makes its way across his entire body, covering himself in a bright blue flame that burns the ground beneath his feet. The DISCs are now ready to detonate the entire arena, and at the rate they're charging—probably more. My body dashes towards Rhody with speed I didn't even know my body could reach. Being a passenger in my own body is surreal. I can feel the blood rushing through my veins, the scars and bruises, the emotions; all of it. An experience that's happening around me, but not to me. Empathizing with the shell I'm in, yet disconnected altogether. Part of me just doesn't want to lose, the other part of me wants to kill this guy where he stands. I don't know which one is Echo, and which is me.

Just before I make contact with Rhody, he launches a spiraling fireball at me. My arms block with a sorce field; the heat is so intense I can feel it as it makes contact. first lightning, then scales, now fire. It looks like Rhody has been practicing just as much as I have. As the flames surround me, Echo senses the closest shard to Rhody. There's one shard two feet behind him. Echo can only concentrate on one thing at a time; the sorce field stopping us from becoming a piece of coal, or the DISC shard right behind Rhody.

<I can focus on the crystals. You handle the sorce field.>

Echo? Are you sure?

<Trust me.>

Rhody's flames grow more intense with every second. I put all my focus into reinforcing the shield while Echo takes care of the shards. While Rhody is focused on breaking the barrier, I feel Echo moving around my mind, pushing me back into some sliver of control. The flames spread apart as they hit the shield, giving me a slight glimpse at Rhody and standing behind him is the same shadowy figure I'd seen back at the Crystal Fields. That's when it hit me; that figure was Echo the whole time. It was Echo that appeared behind him every time. The sudden realization terrified me, breaking my concentration on the shield, which gives the flames the leverage they needed. Before

Echo can finish the plan, the sorce field breaks, creating a small concussion that blows me back into the main sorce field that surrounded the arena.

Propping myself up on my elbows, I see Rhody walking towards me. One arm is engulfed in blue flame, the other in glitterscale. A sadistic, eerie, and genuine smile stretches across his face. He was enjoying this.

<Get up, Charlie.>

I can't. I'm too tired.

<Overtaxed already?>

Considering I've been crushed, kicked, stabbed, and almost scorched; I'd say I've been doing pretty goo—

Shhtt!

A fiery glitterscale pierces my shoulder, where Sanderon's zapier hit. I release a scream of pain, the searing scale burning my flesh.

"I'm going to enjoy this. Very, *very*, much," Rhody says.

Shhtt!

Another scale in my leg.

Jessie, Zach, and Mat rush to the sorce field, beating on it with their fists.

"Stop it!"

"End the fight!"

"Charlie, get up! Get out of there!"

The referee continues to watch. He looks over at Sanderon, and Sanderon shakes his head.

"The f-fight, will continue unless s-someone surrenders or is rendered u-unconscious!" The ref stammers.

SHHTT! Another scale. *SHHTT!* Another. *SHHTT! SHHT! KRRRRSSSSHHHH!!!!*

Suddenly, the sorce field shatters. Rhody is about to launch his final attack at me, when Master Uphraeus, out of nowhere, appears in between us. He grabs Rhody's hand and dispells his flames and glitterscales. Rhody lets out a groan; Master Uphraeus twists his arm and tosses him backwards.

"ENOUGH!" Master Uphraeus shouts. "The Sorce Games, are over!" His voice booms throughout the entire arena.

Master Uphraeus turns around to look at me, his eyes are glowing a bright green. I've never seen him like this before; angry, disappointed, intense. His gaze moves across the room.

"All of you are dismissed for the rest of the night. Leave now and none of you will be at risk of being expelled," Master Uphraeus says.

There's a brief moment of silence. Everyone too scared to move. A Master has come to the Sorce Games.

"Now!" Master Uphraeus says.

All of the students jump out of their seats and begin scurrying out of the entire complex. Some try cleaning up whatever mess they'd made but are convinced to just leave it behind. Zach, Mat, and Jessie rush over to me instead of leaving.

"Charlie are you okay?" Zach says.

"We told you to get—" Mat is interrupted.

"I understand your concern with Charlie's health, but I need all three of you to leave—immediately," Master Uphraeus says.

Jessie is inspecting my wounds and hands.

"Jessie, I'm fine," I say.

"Shut up," Jessie says.

Her eyes glisten as water builds around them, her voice choking up, but she continues to monitor me with determination.

"Ms. Zirdi, I'm not going to ask you again," Master Uphraeus says.

Jessie looks at Master Uphraeus. Then looks around the room. She releases my hand and walks off with Zach and Mat. The Master stares at a powerless Rhody, who holds his wrist in pain. Rhody isn't afraid, he's annoyed and angry.

"Mr. Smill. I would suggest you take your victory and remove yourself before you get into any more trouble," Master Uphraeus says.

Rhody looks at me, we stare at each other, both of us willing to finish what we started. If I didn't respect and fear Master Uphraeus as much as I do, I would launch an attack. Rhody is sadly smarter than that. He picks himself off the floor and walks away. Now, it's just me and Master Uphraeus in the room, his eyes still glowing with intensity.

"I'm sor—"

"No," Master Uphraeus says. "We are far beyond apologies. You were a fool to come here. Though, I am also sorry. Sorry, that I didn't explain the situation to you sooner. I did ask you to wait…to give me more time."

"My Echo…it told me to take off the ring."

"Dammit Charlie!"

"I'm sorry! I just wanted to win!"

"Where is the ring now?"

"I don't know. Somewhere around here."

"Can you walk?"

"I think so."

Master Uphraeus pulls me up by my arm.

"Ow!"

"Then walk." <says The Master.>

"Where are we going?"

"Silence, my boy."

I follow Master Uphraeus out of the complex. We pass by empty cups, spills, knocked over chairs and tables. It looks like a fight broke out everywhere. Precautions for faculty presence are supposed to be fool proof, but I guess Master Uphraeus knew, so he must've known how to get around all the safe-guards. We get to the exit when Master Uphraeus takes a pause.

"Charlie, is there anyone else here?" He asks.

"I don't know?"

"Can you use your echo?"

His question surprises me. I thought he didn't want me to use my Echo, but I guess the circumstances have changed. I nod and I try to use Echo to sense anyone else around.

Echo? Is there anyone else here?

<I don't like him.>

What?

<He doesn't want me here. He doesn't want us to speak. That's why he gave us the ring.>

You don't know that. I just found out you're alive. He probably has no idea himself.

<There's no one else here. I checked as we were walking.>

Are you sure?

<Trust me. No one else is here.>

"No one else is here," I say.

"You're positive?" Master Uphraeus questions.

"He's positive."

"He? Who is *he*?" Master Uphraeus tilts his head in curiosity.

"Echo. That's it's—er, *his* name. I guess? That's what I'm calling him."

Master Uphraeus gives a look of suspicion, then holds his head up to the exit portal I used to get to the Sorce Games. The portal shifts to a wavy iridescent portal. Master Uphraeus gestures for me to go through first as he looks behind me. I take a look over my shoulder then proceed through the portal.

X

I limp into the portal and arrive in a small living room. A lit fireplace illuminates the room and the smell of pine trees fills the air. In front of me is a set of chairs, and to my right, a sofa. Master Uphraeus steps into the portal after me and closes it.

"Eve, are you here?" Master Uphraeus asks.

I hear the *click* sound of a switch. One of the chairs begins to fracture like glass, revealing Master Sindra who'd been sitting there the whole time.

"I'm right here William," Master Sindra says.

"It's gotten worse. The seal didn't work," Master Uphraeus says.

"Obviously, William. Oh my!" Master Sindra says.

Master Sindra notices my wounds and blood-soaked tunic. "What in the stars?! My poor boy, come sit."

Master Sindra ushers me to sit in the large leather chair she previously occupied.

"Who did this? I want names!" Master Sindra demands.

"Rhody Smill," Master Uphraeus responds. "I saved the boy from the Sorce Games. He took off the ring, he's probably on the brink of overtaxing himself to death."

"That ring wasn't supposed to cure him. You moved too hastily."

Master Sindra inspects my wounds. Moving her hand over them, then pulling a vial of lilac-colored liquid from a small end table next to the chair.

"This will burn, but try to hold still," Master Sindra says, handing me the vial.

I move to pour the liquid on my shoulder wound, when Master Sindra stops me.

"No, my child. Drink it," Master Sindra says.

I take a second look at the vial, and see little white clouds floating in the potion. I take a deep breath, and chug the whole thing. She was wrong, it didn't burn. It felt like it just ignited my throat in flames. I burst into a coughing fit, and Master Sindra hands me a handkerchief.

"Hold it down, Charlie."

Master Sindra turns to look at Master Uphraeus.

"The ring wasn't supposed to be a permanent solution, we weren't positive that the boy was even…affected. Let alone how bad his condition is."

"It's worse than that. I've been keeping an eye on the others, I'm almost positive Krain is behind their…*rapid*, improvements," Master Uphraeus says.

The wounds heal slightly, at least the bleeding has stopped. The scales still need to be pulled out, and I'm still feeling fatigued. Master Uphraeus walks over to a desk on the left side of the room, opposite of Master Sindra. Above the desk is a board with pictures of shadowy figures and creatures that mirror the gestures and poses of the people they're connected to. Old, damaged, and withered books rest on the table on top of a large sheet of paper.

"Krain? William, I know you've had quite the grudge with him but you know the Head Master won't take you seriously unless you have solid proof," Master Sindra says.

"You don't believe me?" Master Uphraeus accuses.

Master Uphraeus waves his hands over the old books, making them float neatly into place one right next to the other. He then takes two fingers and waves them through the air, turning the pages of the books. He glances over his shoulder at me.

"Charlie, whatever you do, do not talk to that…*thing*. If it can be helped," Master Uphraeus says.

"It's not that I don't believe you—"

"Is it a matter of trust?" Master Uphraeus says, cutting off Master Sindra.

"It's not that simple. I trust you with my life William, you know that, but there's nothing we can do without evidence. I've been watching the girl like you asked and she does seem to be very suspicious with her questions in advanced artifacts, but that hardly constitutes an all-out war with someone we can't even find."

Girl? What girl?

<I have a guess.>

"So, we're just supposed to sit around and wait for him to attack?" Master Uphraeus says.

"What other option do we have? Do you even know if he plans to attack, let alone *what* he plans to attack?" Master Sindra says.

"I cannot wait for the worst to happen before I act. We have to act. Now."

"And what if that's exactly what he wants you to do?"

"We'll talk about this at another time. For now, we have to focus on Charlie here."

Master Sindra and Uphraeus both glance over at me, then back at the books on the desk.

"He says he's already hearing it speak, it also may have temporarily taken control of him during this year's Sorce Games," Master Uphraeus says.

"If the myths are accurate, that means he's about to have the fight of his life," Master Sindra says.

Master Uphraeus points a finger at me without looking in my direction. Master Sindra looks at me with a face I can only describe as concerned grief and now I'm getting slightly worried.

"Charlie?" Eve Sindra says, looking over at me with a look of concern on her helpless face.

Uphraeus notices the look of concern. She's scared of me, and probably should be. Uphraeus also turns to look my way.

"Charlie..." William Uphraeus nods toward my hands and then back up at me.

I don't realize that I'm standing up with a charged ring until Master Uphraeus calls my name. How long have I been in this position? One that says "I'm ready to attack". I look at my hands, glowing with sorce, my rotator ring spinning.

"It's okay," Master Sindra says.

"I didn't know I was standing up," I say.

That's when the realization that I wasn't in control of my body hits me. Was I ever in control? Am I in control now? Have I always been in control, but never wanted to admit it? I stare at my hands, tears forming in my eyes.

"What's wrong with me?" I say, concerned.

Master Sindra gestures me forward, I clumsily walk towards her. She embraces me and looks at Uphraeus.

"Nothing, my child. You're going to be fine," Master Sindra comforts me.

Master Uphraeus stares at both of us, as if he's not quite sure what to do. He brings us both into his arms and hugs us tight, then moves us over to the table.

"Charlie, there's something you should see," Master Uphraeus says.

I spend the next few minutes looking over the images, books and papers on Master Uphraeus' desk. He explains that I have a sort of condition that doesn't appear often. So rare that there's barely any research about it, only myths and legends. "Echo" is a part of me, a being that manifests itself through the sorce of the one afflicted. It is both independent and symbiotic with its host.

There is no definitive name for them, other than the ones given by different cultures. The closest translation is "echo." It reflects our emotions and behaviors, while simultaneously reverberating the sorce around us. Throughout time these "echoes" have come and gone without a trace. Which is why most of them don't appear in any written history and not much is known about them. What is known about echoes is that they're bound to their hosts, they come from a "dark place", as folklore would have it. Both the host and echo have a tendency to disappear within their early twenties. I'm turning twenty-one at the end of this year.

The concept of an echo isn't new. According to Master Uphraeus's findings, each story has its own reasoning for the disappearances; Sorces with echoes turn to monsters, are taken away by their echoes, or are called to a higher plane of existence. The main takeaway for me is that I'm going to disappear whether I like it or not.

"I told you this was too much for the boy. We should let him rest," Master Sindra says.

"Sindra, we can't hide this from the boy forever. Too soon isn't the problem, I'm hoping we aren't too late," Master Uphraeus says.

"Charlie, can you explain in any detail how the echo started talking to you?" Master Sindra says.

<She wants to get rid of me. Kill her.>

Kill her? No! You need to calm down, seriously, this isn't helping either of us.

<I've been keeping us alive; I've been helping you.>

Is it "us" or "you"? Because this is starting to get annoying. Can we at least agree to work together? After everything we've just read, do you really think it's a good idea for us to start arguing right now?

<There is no "you" without me.>

Yeah, and by the looks of it, there's no 'you' without me. So, how about we figure this out together before you get us both killed?

<She's not stronger than me.>

Okay, even if that were true, and it's not, do you really think Master Uphraeus is going to let that happen? The fact that you think my body can take one Master is bad enough, but do you really want to gamble with two after we barely beat Rhody?

<…fine.>

So, is it "you and me"? Or "us"?

<…>

I need an answer…

<…>

Now, Echo.

<Us.>

Thank you.

"Charlie?" Master Uphraeus says.

"Sorry, it was taking a while for…us to come to an agreement," I say.

"What do you mean…'us'?" Master Sindra inquires.

"I've been hearing him for a while now. We just made an agreement, he's very arrogant," I answer.

"And stubborn?" Master Uphraeus says.

"Extremely," I say, cracking a slight smile.

"Then I guess that makes two of you," Master Uphraeus says.

"I'm sorry," I concede, my hint of a smile disappearing.

"Well, there's no use in keeping it a secret now. Do you think the boy and the girl know?" Master Sindra asks.

"You mean Rhody and Laurie?" I ask.

Master Uphraeus and Master Sindra exchange looks.

"Yes," Master Uphraeus says.

"I figured," I say.

"I don't know what their plan is, but I have a feeling it has something to do with you, Charlie," Master Uphraeus says.

"But! Until we have proof, there's nothing we can do," Master Sindra says.

"We?" Master Uphraeus questions. Master Sindra nods.

"Yes, we, William. Until we have proof that there's something more to this, we have to be wise in our next moves," Master Sindra says.

Master Uphraeus nods slowly in agreement.

"We have to assume Rhody is aware of your situation, and echo. If that's the case, we have to figure out what he intends to do about it. Charlie, do you have any idea why he's been so keen on you? What's your history?" Master Uphraeus says.

"Laurie's my ex. Rhody is her...I don't know."

Master Uphraeus and Sindra exchange looks again. "Oh."

"Yeah."

Master Sindra places a hand on my shoulder as a means to comfort me.

"Well, at any rate, I don't think it has anything to do with hormones and lovers," Master Uphraeus says.

"William! Be more considerate," Master Sindra scolds.

"I'm serious Eve. Imagine what might happen if Krain gets ahold of Charlie; is he going to kill him? Use him? What if he knows more about this echo than we do? What if he's found a way to weaponize it?" Master Uphraeus says.

Master Sindra lets out a deep breath and taps me on the shoulder. I take the hint and move out of the way. I feel like a child watching his parents' fight.

"All right William, if what you're saying is true, we need to find out what he's up to, and we need proof; actual proof. Then maybe we can take it to the Head Master," Master Sindra says.

"We also have to consider...other options," Master Uphraeus says.

Master Sindra and Uphraeus both look at me, as if they're trying to size me up.

"W-what other option?" I ask.

"We separate you from the echo," Master Uphraeus says.

"And what exactly does that mean?" I say, hesitation in my voice.

"We're not even sure if we can. Can we, William?" Master Sindra says.

"Maybe, maybe not. Either way, we have to make sure Charlie's stunt back there doesn't happen again any time soon and we find a decent reason to cover it up. Just in case anyone else at this institution gets the wrong idea," Master Uphraeus says.

"Perhaps barging in and ending the party on Charlie's behalf wasn't such a smart idea?" Master Sindra inquires.

"It was either that, or wait for him to blow up half the students," Master Uphraeus says.

I turn my head down towards the ground in shame and rub the cracked rotator ring on my finger.

"I think we can find a good explanation for all of this, but it will cost Charlie a bit of his reputation," Master Sindra says.

"Charlie," Master Uphraeus says.

I look up at Master Uphraeus, his look of concern becomes grim and stern.

"I'll fix your ring. Your echo is too powerful now, so the ring won't be of much use, but at least it'll help you concentrate your abilities until Eve—Master Sindra and I can find a better solution," Master Uphraeus says.

"Fix the ring? I don't think it's necessary. Echo and I are… cooperating, now. Though, Jessie might be mad, so maybe fixing it won't be a bad idea."

"It isn't up to you and…'Echo.' Whether you like it or not, your fates are intertwined, and don't trust a thing it says. It only has one goal; to kill its host. So the ring gets fixed and stays on. Eve, be ready."

Master Sindra moves over to me, standing at my side with a hand on my shoulder.

"Masters, I honestly don't think we need to take this much of a precaution."

"Give me the ring, Charlie."

I slowly pull the ring up to my knuckle. I hesitate for a moment, my hands starting to sweat. Okay, here we go. Things are going to be fine. *Right, Echo? ...Echo?* I take a deep breath and pull the ring off.

<Finally.>

The glitterscales in my body flare to life, causing a searing pain. I scream out in horrendous pain.

"Eve, now!"

———

Luckily for me, the Sorce Games were on a three-day weekend, so when I wake up, it isn't to my annoying alarm. I'm not sure when I blacked out, or how I got back to my dorm, but I assume Master Sindra and Uphraeus are responsible. I turn to my nightstand to check the clock but immediately notice a letter. I rub my eyes for a moment then sit up and grab it. I see the rotator ring on my hand again. It looks brand new, but the part that rotates has been split into two rings instead of one. I turn my attention back to the letter, it reads:

Charlie,

Things are going to be a bit complicated from here on out. I'm not sure it's wise for us to keep up with our usual private lessons since we've established you do in fact have an echo and if Rhody is part of Krain's plans we need to get him off your trail.

As of today, you are on academic probation for "stealing a Master's artifact" and "using an advanced artifact for personal gain" which means you can only practice or use sorce in desig- nated areas like the Crystal Fields, with written permission from a Master. That's the cover story we're going with. Hopefully it's enough to clear up any confusion on your end. We do hope you understand my boy.

I've modified and fixed your ring to better help you control Echo without inhibiting your sorce manipulation. The extra ring should act as an exhaust to relieve some of the sorce feedback that happens if Echo becomes more active, making it a bit easier to maintain control or at least not lose it so quickly. Continue with your classes as scheduled, just try to stay out of trouble while your probation is in effect.
If anyone asks, tell them you're not allowed to discuss the situation or your punishment outside of Administrators. I'll speak with you again as soon as I have more information.

Best regards,
W. Uphraeus Master of Sorces
P.S. Vanish this letter after you're done with it.

Great, I'm on probation and Rhody walks away with a clean record. Even though he and his friends were definitely trying to get me killed, or worse. Wait, if the goal was to kill me, they wouldn't have tried to do it in the open like that. They might be morons but they're smarter than that. No, actually they're probably not, but Laurie, Laurie is smarter than that.

I grab my psi-phone to text her, but then I freeze. It never really hit me until now, but Laurie's…gone. I think about last night at the Sorce Games. She just looked away. She didn't cry, she didn't ask someone to help, she just looked away.

———

CHARLIE: Hey, anybody wanna meet up at the crystals? (1:31 PM)

Z: HE LIVES!! (1:32 PM)

JESSIE: Sure, I'm down :) (1:32 PM)

MAT: Someone said you got expelled? But
maybe later I'm out with Clara. (1:33 PM)

Z: Clara? From my history of metals class?
(1:34 PM)

CHARLIE: No I wasn't expelled (1:34 PM)

Z: Yeah what happened after the games?
(1:34 PM)

CHARLIE: Actually, I can't talk about it outside
of the Administration (1:34 PM)

JESSIE: Apparently he stole the ring I gave him
(1:35PM)

MAT: Speaking of giving rings, I'm thinking
about proposing to Clara (1:37 PM)

Z: From my history class?? (1:37 PM)

CHARLIE: I'll be there in 15 Jess (1:38 PM)

MAT: …Maybe (1:38 PM)

JESSIE: See you soon! (1:38 PM)

Z: Kiss my ass Mat, you met her last night
(1:39 PM)

Z: I hate you (1:52 PM)

I'm standing in the middle of six sorce crystals on podiums, organized in a hexagon outline. I give a flick to my rotator ring, and it whistles as it spins with a faint glow. I launch darts towards two different crystals, causing them to ignite in colorful fashion as they usually do. I slow my breathing down, taking a moment to focus. Reaching out with my hands, I pull the sorce from the crystals back to me. A sudden rush of energy fills my body like a shockwave. I dispel the energy back towards two different crystals, they crackle and spark with a vibrant glow, letting me know they're about to reach their limit.

"So, the sorce we take gets amplified. Correct?" I say, speaking to Echo out loud.

<Correct.>

"Is there any way we can…not…do that?"

<The sorce you receive and use is added to my own, whether or not we want to. It's automatic.>

"You're saying you have no control over that?"

<I do not.>

"Well what good are you then?"

<…>

"I'm kidding. Jeez, I didn't realize I was subconsciously a stickler."

<Perhaps the ring can help?>

"Oh yeah! Master Uphraeus said in the letter the ring could help exhaust sorce buildup, to keep that to a minimum. Let's give it a test run."

I concentrate on the ring and halt its spinning. Extending my hands once more, I absorb the sorce from the two crystals back to me; the shock is even more intense than the last one.

"Let's try spinning it in the opposite direction this time."

Spinning the ring to the right this time, I notice the ring changes from a whistling sound, to a low hum. Instead of the usual blue glow, the ring is now a deep yellow or gold. Time for the moment of truth.

A feedback loop is a constant sorce connection between at least two things. Person A and Person B create a feedback loop between each other. Person A sends a spell to Person B. Person B takes the spell, and sends it back to Person A, but the spell is now stronger. Each time the spell is transferred, more strength is added to it. Until eventually, the spell overwhelms one of them. If the spell doesn't overwhelm, then the other outcome is both persons dying from overloading and overtaxing. Two people don't usually create feedback loops together, unless they both have a death wish. Typically feedback loops are created between two sorce conduits and left to destroy something nearby. Feedback loops are popular for miners and sorce users who like to demolish things.

A flow chain is much less dangerous and has a multipurpose function. Like the feedback loop, sorce travels from one person to the next, except it isn't amplified over time, and is instead consistent throughout. A proper flow chain keeps whatever is placed inside of it the same way it entered, without overtaxing or overloading the vessels that carry the chain. A flow chain takes concentration to uphold, and if it's not maintained properly can easily become a feedback loop. That's what happened to me during my demonstration.

After planning out how to setup the flow chain, I start by launching a dart into one crystal, then having it jump to another. After it gets halfway through, I send another dart into the chain, increasing the number of darts which increases the strength. The crystals in the Crystal Fields are setup to release their sorce before it gets to dangerous levels, so I can practice freely without putting myself in too much danger. The flow chain is working properly, but I haven't added myself to it yet. I'm going to try and create a sporadic connection; a flow chain that doesn't have a...flow. Like the world's most intense game of hot potato.

Without overloading the flow chain, I add a few more darts to it, then incorporate myself into the chain. A torrential rush hits me from inside, as the flow chain successfully pulls me into it, as if I'm one of the crystals. This...this feeling of power is amazing! Coursing through me like an ocean unleashed, the sorce within me feels like it's actually coursing through my veins. Then, I feel that surge hit me tenfold. Echo is now doubling my input, and now that torrential power becomes an overwhelming sensation. This is overloading. Luckily for me, the ring was re-crafted to stop me from overloading, so after a short time, the ring releases a flow of gold waves and mist pour into the air around my hand.

"It's working!" I shout.

With the ring regulating my input, I weave the flow chain back together. The six crystals around me are being kept just below their breaking point, but how much can I stress this new ring? Creating a flow chain is a decent way to practice sorce manipulation and control, not very useful as anything other than a practice tool. That's what my class's first assignment here was, and everyone else made it look so easy the first day, but this is difficult. I'm even starting to break into a sweat. Granted, everyone else was using one crystal, whereas I'm using six... they also didn't have an entity living inside them with a mind of its own trying to kill them from the inside out.

<Hey!>

Okay, okay. *Passively* killing them, from the inside out.

<Thank you.>

"You're not going to blow me up again, are you?" I hear Jessie say.

Jessie stands a few feet away from the circle of crystals. With Jessie startling me, I ended up losing my concentration, causing the flow chain to stop. Normally that would probably have turned out really bad, but with the ring I was able to immediately disperse all of it without hurting anyone. Well, besides myself that is. I collapse to the ground in an exhausted haze, staring up at the blue sky.

"Charlie? You, okay?" Jessie says.

Jessie rushes over to see if I'm still breathing. I put a thumb up in the air as she leans over me, blocking out the sun.

"Hey...w-what's.... up?" I say, panting like a dog.

"Is that *my* rotator ring?"

"No...yes...Master Uphraeus...reforged it..."

"Reforged it? To do what?" Jessie asks.

The fact that I borrowed this ring from Jessie completely

slipped my mind. Even after it came out damaged from the fight. I feel like a dick. It's her ring and here I was basically keeping and having Master Uphraeus reforge it.

"To help release some of the excess sorce I use. I'm sorry, I should've asked before I made changes to it. Do you want it back?"

I extend my hand towards Jessie with the ring still on my finger. She grabs and examines my hand like it's not even attached to me.

"Hmm…This is some next level stuff! I can see tiny runes inscribed onto the inner and outer rings," Jessie says.

I'm not sure if she's talking to me or making observations, so I look around awkwardly, avoiding eye contact.

"You can keep it. I never intended on taking it back anyway," Jessie says.

"Thanks, I appreciate it," I say, standing back up to my feet. "I still feel exhausted for some reason."

"Should the ring still be…turning?"

I look at my hand and notice the ring is still spinning but very slowly and its glow is barely visible.

"Oh. Probably not?" I say, as the ring comes to a stop.

"You should be careful; you don't want that thing to overtax you. Ever have a mystical hangover?"

"A 'mystical' hangover?"

"Sorce impairment is the technical term. Overtaxing is when your body uses too much sorce, sorce impairment is what happens afterwards."

"Right, that's coming up on next week's exam, isn't it?"

"Correct. Though, the exams are mostly practical, so you'll probably still fail if that makes you feel any better," Jessie says, laughing while rubbing my hair.

<She's annoying.>

"No, she's not," I say, out loud by mistake.

"What?" Jessie asks, giving me an odd look.

"Nothing, it's just Echo."

"Echo? You mean that thing you and Master Uphraeus were trying to figure out? It can talk?!"

Crap…I'm not supposed to say anything to anyone about this, but I just blurted it out right to Jessie. I look around the fields to see if anyone is nearby, luckily no one is out here for the weekend. Why would they be?

"Keep it down! I wasn't supposed to talk to anyone about this. I can't let any rumors getting out," I say.

Jessie mimes herself zipping her mouth shut and throwing away a key.

"I'm serious Jessie. I could get into a lot of trouble."

"You mean more trouble than stealing something from Master Uphraeus?" Jessie says.

Her face changes from curious to serious, as if she's in deep thought. Her eyes dart around as she thinks, before I can say anything she's ranting in a hushed tone.

"Wait, unless that was a cover up for last night? Master Uphraeus showed up and singled you out, meaning you did something you weren't supposed to. You were fighting and all of a sudden you turned into a different kind of person against Sanderon. Then, against Rhody you looked like you just about gave up, then came back with a vengeance. You were using that…'echo' thing? You took off the ring! Or you must've broken it, which is why Master Uphraeus had to reforge it… Why would he want to cover that up? Unless he suspects that—"

I cut Jessie off before she can finish. "Jessie! Seriously, you can't tell a soul. This is a lot more complicated than you think. I'll leave the rest to your imagination, but you're pretty much spot on with that analysis. You're a lot smarter than you let on."

"Smarter than I let on?! Tell me, Charlie, what exactly does that mean?" Jessie scowls at me. She holds a finger at my head, with whatever spell she's got at the end of it.

"I meant, you're smart. I just didn't realize you were *that*—and I'm just going to stop talking." My face feels flush.

Jessie and I spend the next hour practicing on a single crystal. We never were able to actually finish our first assignment here.

"Good. See? You're getting it!" Jessie exclaims.

The crystal we're weaving our hands around is shining like a prism. The colors move in and out of the crystals like ocean waves. A small tingling sensation moves through my hands. The key is to match each other's sorce output while maintaining a steady flow into the crystal. This exercise is about control and sustainability. Taking and sustaining control are vital to a Sorce's offense and defense.

"This is it? This is easy!" I say, laughing.

"Yeah, a wonder how you screwed it up the first time!" Jessie winks.

"Now let me try it on my own," I say.

"Okay, let's see what you got." Jessie steps back from the crystal to watch me.

I gesture her to move back further then move to the center of the hexagon again.

"Wait, seriously?" Jessie says.

I flick the rotator ring to spin left while giving Jessie a smile. Having only a little doubt in my abilities, I shoot all six crystals with a small amount of sorce. Then, I perform a juggling act of charging the crystals with more sorce and pulling it back. As the crystals light up, I feel the overwhelming surge between myself and the crystals. Then I flick my ring to the right, not losing any momentum, to start getting rid of some of the excess sorce. It almost feels like I'm dancing with the crystals. At that moment, I start acting on instinct and close my eyes to start feeling the sorce around me instead of watching.

Just like my fight with Noira, with my eyes closed, I can locate the crystals around me using Echo. I see six tethered lines connecting me to them, a gorgeous symphony of light and power. Jessie stands just outside the circle; I can see Jessie clearly with an added blue outline and a small tether between her and myself. Wait, no, not me; the ring. She still has a connection to the ring, even after being reforged? She must have a strong bond with it or the materials used to make it?

For five minutes straight I'm able to maintain a stable amount of sorce going into all six sorce crystals and back into myself. The iridescent glow from them is bright and flows through the air in flares. This is too much fun! My eyes are still closed, I haven't had a single reason to open them, it's like I can see everything around me that has sorce in it and more. The moment is nice, but brief, as I lose most of my concentration and fall to the ground. Luckily, I fell on beat with the timing so that all the sorce energy was channeled outward to the crystals and not me. I let out a laugh as I open my eyes to the sky and my arms spread across the grass.

"Woo!" I cheer. "Did you see that?!"

"Yeah, Charlie, I saw that. What the heck was that?" Jessie's tone sounds annoyed, or confused. Maybe both? "You struggled lighting up one of these crystals at the start of the semester; now you have six of them lighting up like fireworks! And you did it with your eyes closed!…What the heck was that?!"

I roll my head to the side, blocking the sunlight beaming down on me with my hand and smile in her direction.

"It's this new thing that's been happening because of Echo. If I close my eyes, and focus, I can sense the sorce around me. Like standing in a dark room and the only light I can see is sorce. I was using it a lot during the tournament."

"You can *see* sorce? When you close your eyes? Like, you could see me even though I wasn't casting a spell? So, was I like…naked?" Jessie says, giving me a side eye.

My face is probably a bright red now. "No! No, I could see you; fully clothed. You just had like a blue filter on you—and yes, I can see people, spells, constructs. If it's using sorce, or has it stored. I can see it."

I left out the part where she was still tethered to the ring.

"I've never heard of anything like that before. Someone

being able to *see* sorce with their eyes closed. It's like sorce ocularity! Or...sorce-vision! Sorce-sight!" Jessie says enthusiastically.

"I...kinda already have a name for it," I reply

"Can't be cooler than *sorce-sight*. What do *you* call it?"

"Echo Location."

LAURIE
PART II

I'd never seen Charlie the way I did at the games. Remembering his face and the way he looked during his fight with Rhody. I couldn't look at him or watch the fight, he looked hurt both physically and emotionally; it killed me inside. It's been a few weeks since then and I've watched Charlie from afar with that girl…Jessie? I've woken up with nightmares in the middle of the night, dreams of Charlie dying, Rhody dying, and shadows reaching out for me. The worst ones are when I'm the one killed…by Charlie. I know he'd never do something like that, at least, I think he wouldn't. I'd like to think that everything we'd been through would count for something. It's been about a month and a half since the games. Two months since I last spoke to Charlie in-person, and I feel something stirring in the air.

Rhody and I are part of the Queen's Wraiths, an Alignment that's set on helping people around the world by uniting Sorces under one rule and government. People think we're extremists, but they pretend not to see the world around them and the things that make it worse. There are people who don't practice sorce and those that do. Some are sorce impaired, meaning they don't have the ability to practice, some don't have the potential required to reach even the bare minimum, and others are scared of being challenged or killed for simply becoming one.

For these people, the world is a terrifying place; they work normal jobs with normal lives. Meanwhile, Sorces fight for territory, money, fame, or glory. Schools, like Sirrus? They remain neutral; teach and train Sorces, Artís, and Fencers. The Alignments: groups of sorce users with common goals. And Acquisitors: sorce users who only use their gifts for profit. There is no law, no government, no leader to keep them in line. They're all free to do as they please and it's been that way for centuries. In all of sorce history there's only been one record of a ruler, one who united all sorce users under a single banner, the first Legend; Tressia.

Legends; the unofficial title given to those who have surpassed the rank and title of Master. Legends, like Masters, are recognized by their seniors before gaining their title. For a Master to recognize you as someone on their level is not only an honor, but the rite of passage to call yourself one. Legends are almost the same, but require you to achieve a feat so great that the world will remember your name. Legends are usually addressed by their first name and a title fitting of their abilities. Brashier, Father of the Sun; "He Who Holds the World"; Ku'muaina, Judicator of the Ocean. To name the three off the top of my head.

Tressia, Queen of the Slain, Sovereign of the Sorces, Matriarch of the Lost, The first Legend. Tressia's knowledge was unparalleled, she ruled over the Sorces of the world with compassion and ruthlessness. Those who followed under her reign knew only peace, and those who refused her, knew only war. After she died, there was nothing to keep the Sorces united under a single rule, and so they separated and created their own factions and started the first Sorce Wars.

I've always wanted to help others, but I never knew how with how much the world needs. Now, I see a clear path, the resurrection of Tressia's ideals. The Queen's Wraiths aims to do just that. Master Krain, our leader, has tasked us with finding others throughout Sirrus that may want to join our cause. Nathan has been our most recent recruit. He's not very bright, but he has a knack for collecting information. Charlie would've been a great addition, but I knew if I told him about any of this, he'd try to pull me out, or worse, try to stop the whole thing and get himself killed.

I've noticed that Charlie has been getting better in classes. A few days ago, he gave a demonstration on how to properly deflect a basic sorce attack. Then he wanted to go further and block basic elements. Master Uphraeus was quite impressed, as if even he hadn't expected Charlie to have gotten the hang of things so quickly. I can tell that some of us are progressing faster than our peers and we're ready for more advanced teachings. Master Sindra has been paying more attention to my artifact prowess. Though she teaches at the school, I wonder if Krain would mind if I asked her about joining the Queen's Wraiths. We could use her knowledge in the coming discourse.

<h1 style="text-align:center">XI</h1>

The past three months feel like they've flown by. Only a month left before the first semester is over. Class demonstrations are beginning and each caste gets its own week for them.

Jessie and I are walking to Zach's Artí demonstration. Artí demonstrations are some of the coolest in my opinion. Artís specialize in the creation and use of artifacts like rings, coins, mirrors, staffs, glasses, gloves, sometimes even earrings. They're nicknamed the "Accessory Sorces" or "Accessories" but most of them find that title offensive and disrespectful. Masters of artifacts are capable of turning inanimate objects into weapons of destruction since they primarily use sorce fusion. Sorce fusion is pretty straightforward; take an object, fuse it with sorce. Though, as an Artís' abilities get better, they can preprogram multiple spells into a single artifact.

You want glasses that can enhance your eyesight to that of an aerial predator, while also having the capacity to dissolve anything made of brick? Talk to an Artí. Want a necktie that gives the illusion of being a vampire, that can also curse an unauthorized wearer to go mute? Artí. But they have the worst process between the three castes. In order for an Artí to create one of these things, it has to be built very specifically. I mean one *millimeter* out of line could break the whole artifact after a single use, or backfire the spell entirely and woe to whoever used it. At least, that's how Zach explained it. To me, the way they work, is divine.

"You think Zach is gonna make something out of fire?" Jessie says.

"Well, I would be shocked if he didn't, but surprised if he did too. His imagination always keeps me on my toes. He zigs when I think he's gonna zag, and zags when I think he's gonna zig," I say.

"Oh, so he hasn't told you?"

"Told me what?"

"Never mind, if he hasn't said anything, maybe it's a surprise?"

"Jessie, you can't just say that and then not expect me to interrogate you."

Jessie flashes me her signature deviously playful smile and giggles as she outpaces me walking backwards. She always pulls this "aloof girl" persona when she knows she's got a hold on one of my buttons, one that is vastly different from her normal tomboy side. It's annoyingly cute. But I'll never admit that.

The Artí demonstrations are being held at the Artícionado Theater, on the East side of the school. When the school added Artís to their caste list, they carved out the nearby mountain for them to practice. I always forget how big the school grounds are, much less that we're a floating island flying above the ocean. The mountains were eventually added onto and carved more, to the point where it's hard to tell which parts are school and which are still mountain.

Jessie and I grab our seats towards the front row, just two before the "reserved" section for Administrators and Masters. Administrators are the ones who run the technical side of Sirrus. Hiring Masters for specific positions, deciding what curriculums are taught or cut, etc. They're Masters with bureaucratic titles. I've noticed whenever there's bound to be Admins and Masters there's a nice hefty gap between them and other students attending. I assume it's because no one wants to gain any unwanted attention. The only students brave enough to squeeze in there are students on the Admin track and Versed students who're buddy-buddy with one or a few of the Masters.

The building is beautifully lit by floating cylinders that rotate and twirl in place around the room. More than likely built by the Apprentice level Artís to get their feet wet. The auditorium is fairly empty, but starting to fill quickly with students also trying to grab good seats in support of their friends. I spot Mat searching for us as he walks down the aisle.

"Mat! Over here!" I say, waving my hand to flag him down.

Mat sees me and his walk turns into a slight jog. He and I embrace and clasp hands before Mat takes his seat to my right.

"What's up, Jessie?" Mat says.

"Hey, Mat," she says.

"Miss I-Like-Pressing-Charlie's-Buttons over here apparently knows something about Zach's demonstration that I don't and won't spill. Do you know anything about this?" I ask.

Mat looks over at Jessie and shrugs. "No clue," he says.

I glare at Mat out of the corner of my eye. "Did she tell you not to say anything?"

"What? No, I honestly have no idea what either of you are talking about," Mat says.

I look at Jessie who turns into that "aloof" thing again and rolls her eyes into a shrug. I can tell she's holding back a laugh.

"This better not be a surprise. I don't think I'm in the right headspace for a surprise," I say.

Both of them remain silent.

"So, what's he planning?" I say.

"I don't know!" Mat says.

The lights dim as the auditorium's last few seats fill up. A short man with a large black beard walks onto the stage holding a small rod that couldn't be more than four inches long. He holds the rod in front of his face and it glows with a pink light. He taps the top of it, causing a loud popping sound throughout the room.

"Hello?" The bearded man says. His voice booming through the auditorium. "Hello, everyone. To those of you who don't recognize me, I am Lead Master Woodrain of the Artí caste. To those of you that do, unlike your other Masters, I have been keeping up with projects so, yes, they are due after this weekend."

A hushed groan leaves the mouths of many students. One or two of them immediately get up and leave the auditorium in a rush.

"This afternoon, we welcome all students from all castes to witness the accomplishments of our first year Apprentices and the artifacts they've created," Master Woodrain says.

The auditorium erupts in applause and cheers throughout. Some students even shouting specific names.

"These Apprentices have been hard at work with their studies, so please give them your support and praise. Remember; Protégés, Tertiaries, and Versed students will be having their demonstrations in the coming weeks, so be sure to show them support as well. This is perhaps the largest student assembly the Artícionado Theater has seen in years, and we Masters of Artifacts are pleased to have you. Please, no casting spells for the duration of the demonstrations, no flash photography, and please silence all organic and sorce communications. Thank you. So, without further ado, I present to you the Apprentice demonstrations!"

Throwing his small microphone in the air, it explodes into bright pink flower petals that cascade down onto the stage and slowly disintegrate. The crowd goes wild as Master Woodrain also disappears with the petals. His entrance was "meh" but that man knows how to make an exit. I wonder if pink is his theme or the petals? Maybe both?

"I hear Master Woodrain is the one who founded the illuminated petal theory," Jessie whispers in my ear.

"Really? I have no idea what that is but I like it," I say.

Jessie rolls her eyes and focuses her attention back on the stage. Master Woodrain's voice echoes out like before, announcing the first demonstrator to the audience.

"Please, welcome to the stage, our first demonstration by Apprentice Noira O'Caster!"

Mat leans over and whispers to me. "Isn't that the girl you fought in the games?"

"Yeah. She almost crushed me inside of a box. She's pretty good."

"I wonder how she'd like being trapped in a cage," Jessie says.

Noira walks out onto the stage to thunderous applause. Noira's deep red hair is curled, making it look like ocean waves, wearing a dark green cardigan with a black and grey striped kilt, with a pair of black heels. Noira definitely came prepared to be seen. She gracefully bows towards the audience, before stepping back to the center. A small ball floats from above down into her hand and she speaks softly into it.

"Thank ya, Master Woodrain, fer the lovely introduction," Noira says, her voice heard clearly throughout the auditorium. "Greetins, fellow students, and Masters. I'm Noira O'Caster, from Piquer Island, an Apprentice Artí wh'll be demonstratin' somethin' at's not been done 'ere before. At least, no' in a long while. Me father was a trapper. Made an honest living from it. Comin' to Sirrus, I thought that trapping spells 'ad to be rigid, built like squares and circles. But I've learned to be more flexible from the help of the Masters."

She walks towards the back of the stage to a black sheet draped over something large. Pulling away the sheet, it reveals small table next to some cages holding rabbits. The crowd is charmed by the sight of the small furry animals. Noira picks something up from the table, then shows it to the audience. It looks like a metallic butterfly that takes up the size of her palm.

"This is my demonstration. The Red Admiral."

She taps the butterfly and it fills with a red glow. As if coming to life in her hands, the wings flutter and the mechanical butterfly flies around Noira's head. She then pulls up her left sleeve and reveals a small bracelet that she rotates, unlocking the rabbit cages.

As the cages open the rabbits begin running free across the stage. Without missing a beat, the "Red Admiral" creates a red apparition of itself, then another, and another, until there's an equal amount to the rabbits. Each copy of the butterfly appears harmless until they attach themselves to the rabbits almost all at the same time. Each rabbit is immediately paralyzed and the butterflies are blown away as they turn to dust. Noira then gathers all of the rabbits and puts them back in separate cages. Then she returns to the front of the stage pulling the ball from above her head to speak into again.

"The Red Admiral is crafted from a sorce metal known for its retainability, and preprogrammed with an enchantment that creates duplicates, combined with a paralysis stone—this artifact that can be used for trapping and paralyzing your targets in a subtle and less confrontational way. Thank you for attending my demonstration." Noira gives the audience a bow.

The crowd cheers, claps, whistles. I bet Noira is feeling pretty good about it, and she should, it was impressive for an Apprentice and I can tell she worked hard. Though, I do wonder if she switched up her tactics because of our fight during the games. The thought makes me laugh.

"What's so funny?" Jessie asks.

"I think Noira may have gone with a different strategy based on our fight. She used a box to trap me, now she's using a more spread-out approach," I say.

"Oh," Jessie says. "Yeah, okay, that is kind of funny."

We watch as Noira leaves the stage, there's about a one to

three-minute wait between demonstrations. As time goes on, we witness Apprentices demonstrate some pretty crazy things. One Apprentice shows off his psychic watch that can influence others' decisions for ten minutes or mind control a single target for one minute. I was under the impression that artifacts were created out of only metals or stones, with very little mechanical components; boy, was I wrong. Many Artís showcase artifacts made from bio-material as well. Roses that can form barriers of thorns or use vines to constrict an object, vials of different elements that cause illusions, bones carved into creature figurines that can control their living counterparts.

Mat lets out a long yawn and checks his watch. "When does this loser get on stage? I'm getting bored," Mat whispers to me.

"I'm not sure. How can you possibly be bored watching this? These demonstrations are amazing," I say.

Someone from behind us gives me a decent shushing.

"It's really cool, I was impressed for a while, but now I want to get back to my project so I don't fall behind these people," Mat says, in a slightly more hushed tone.

"I get that. I'm getting antsy just thinking about some new things I want to try." I attempt to match Mat's volume.

Another "shush" comes from behind us. There's no way anyone can hear us, so now I'm irritated. I turn to look behind us and identical twins are looking at us. Mat turns to look as well. The twins shake their heads and both lean in opposite directions to reveal who's sitting behind them; it's Rhody and Sanderon. Both of them with stupid grins.

A barrage of Echo's thoughts fill my head, overlapping one another.

<Now.>

<We can end this. Here.>

<Release.>

<Take.>

<They're mocking us. They can see. Us. We won't lose.>

<Me.>

<They think we can't win. Never again.>

<Off.>

<Sanderon, first. Feedback him. No, Rhody. As long as they die. Watch him boil from the inside. You're too weak. What would Laurie think? She's watching>.

<The Ring.>

<Let me out.>

<I won't lose.>

<I'll bury them underneath this mountain.>

<I just need control.>

<Them, and whoever else gets in my way.>

I feel a hit to my shoulder. Mat's looking at me and slowly shaking his head. Someone grabs my other arm. I reflexively pull away and look towards whatever wants trouble. It's Jessie. She has a look of concern on her face.

"Charlie, what's wrong?"

I'm fine.

<Are you?>

We're fine.

<I'm not.>

You need to calm down. We're not doing this, not here.
<We should attack. Before they do.>
The games are over. We have no reason to fight them!
<She would hate to lose them. They die, she hurts.>
Laurie? What does she have to do with this?
<EVERYTHING!>

"Charlie," Jessie says, clenching my arm and trying not to draw attention to the people seated around.

A sharp sound pierces my ears, snapping me back into the moment. I slouch back into my seat, rubbing my eyes with one hand.

"I'm sorry Jessie, I got lost in thought," I say.

"That wasn't just getting lost in thought. You almost had another meltdown," Jessie says, concern on her face.

"What?"

Mat grabs my shoulder, pulling my attention to him.

"Dude, what was that with your eyes? Is that a Sorce thing? Do you need to see a doctor?" Mat asks.

"My...eyes?" I say.

I feel Jessie's hand grab my chin. She turns my head back towards her. "Crystal Fields. Except this time, it wasn't your hands, it was your eyes."

Crystal Fields? What the hell is she...? Oh shit! I rub my eyes then cup my hands over my face to check if I can see the glow. No luck. I turn to Mat.

"I'm fine, yeah, it's a...Sorce thing," I say, turning back to Jessie. "Are they still glowing?!" I say, my eyes darting back and forth looking directly into Jessie's eyes.

"No, no, you're fine," Jessie says, looking around the auditorium. "What were you looking at?"

"I saw Rhody and Sanderon."

"Was that, Echo?"

"Yeah, he was going nuts in my head," I say.

"What's up with your head? Are you okay? I can't really hear you guys," Mat says.

"I'm fine Mat, thank you. It's nothing."

None of us had been paying attention to the stage. The white noise of demonstrations becomes clear when a familiar voice is amplified from the stage.

"My name is Zachery Otterden. This is my demonstration, the Fencer. Artí. Sorce. Transformative. Caster. Or FAST Caster," Zach says.

Zach wheels a table from behind him to the center of the stage. On the table, there are three metallic shapes; a sphere, a box, and a cylinder. Each one large enough to hold in your hands. Zach picks up the cylinder first.

"Each discipline—each caste is unique. In order to become a better Artí, I thought to myself; I must learn how Fencers and Sorces work. Though to 'master' any of the castes takes a lifetime, I wondered if I could…borrow the techniques of my sister castes."

Zach twists the cylinder, separating it into two pieces then points both ends at the sphere and box. The sphere and box float towards him and take positions at his sides. The box floats in front of Zach as he attaches both cylinder pieces to the box. The pieces morph and shift like a 3D-puzzle into a handle.

"Fencer," Zach says.

The handle shimmers with a glow and from one end a broad blade extends, lit around the edges. Zach lifts the sword above his head and bolts of lightning pour from it onto the stage. With a bit of a struggle, Zach swings the sword in arcs around himself. Each arc of the blade creates a wave in the air that ripples like water.

"Though the weapon isn't as meticulously crafted as Fencer's would be, it can potentially protect against an opposing Fencer's weapon, if only for a short amount of time," Zach says, resting the sword on its point.

"Reshape!"

The blade fades away and the hilt reconfigures itself back into the box then ejecting the two cylinder pieces. Zach pulls the two pieces from the box and moves his attention to the sphere still floating next to him. He gestures with the pieces for the sphere to move in front of him then, like the box, he inserts the two pieces but this time from the top. The sphere spins and clicks, opening from different sides. The sphere finishes transforming itself into floating metallic hands.

"Sorce."

Zach reaches out and the metallic figures wrap themselves around the back of his hands, forming like gloves. Putting his hands out in front of him, Zach starts channeling sorce into his palms. He claps his hands together and separates them to form a sorce field around himself. Using his gloves again, Zach punches through the sorce field, shattering and dissolving it.

"Not as strong as a Sorce's field, but still enough to get the point across."

Zach calls out his "Reshape" command once again and the gloves lift off his hands and convert back into the sphere and two pieces. Zach grabs the pieces, gestures for the sphere and box to return to the table, then twists the two pieces back together.

"Thank you," Zach says, closing his demonstration and giving the audience a bow.

I realize that I haven't moved an inch since I heard Zach's voice. The crowd is silent as we are all still in awe of what just happened. Then all at once everyone erupts into cheers and praise.

———

Me, Jessie, Zach, and Mat are all walking back to my room after watching all the demonstrations.

"So? What did you get for your demonstration?" Mat asks.

"Seventy-eight points," Zach says, dejected.

"What?!" Jessie, Mat, and I say at once.

"Yeah, apparently incorporating Fencer and Sorce techniques wasn't a good idea. It was an Artí demonstration, so they wanted all of us to emphasize Artí 'uniqueness' or whatever," Zach says.

"Bullshit! You created all those things with an artifact. How is that not 'Artí uniqueness'?" Jessie says.

"I guess it makes sense in a very stupid way? Castes have a lot of pride for their craft, you basically tried to showcase a peace treaty between three warring nations," I say.

"Well, at least your demonstration went over well with the crowd," Mat says.

We all make it back to my room and relax on beanbag chairs, pillows, and blankets. We start discussing different things we've learned since the semester started. Mat talks about the tedious things Fencers have to know and do to forge weapons. Apparently, Fencers don't get to forge their own weapons until they're at a Tertiary level so all of their learning is theoretical and until then they practice with school standard weapons and making light repairs to them.

Zach explains his theory behind the FAST Caster. He says it's going to be a lifelong project and the goal is to be able to utilize key aspects from all three castes to fit any situation that may come up. He also says that what he demonstrated wasn't what he actually wanted to accomplish. He basically taped two knives together and called it a pair of scissors, which probably didn't go over the Master's heads and that brought his performance down.

Jessie goes on to talk about what she's thinking about specializing in and is heavily considering going into potion making and relic hunting.

"Really? Relic hunting?" Zach asks.

"Yeah?" Jessie says.

"I mean, it's not a problem, I'm just shocked since no one chooses that path usually," Zach says.

"Is that still a thing? I'm just saying, the odds of finding one are already low and finding one that people actually want is something else," Mat says.

"Well, Mat, not everything is about how much you can make. I guess I should say hunter/collector. To be more accurate," Jessie says.

"Why relic hunting and potions?" I ask.

"Potions and relics are neglected," Jessie says. "Mostly because people don't see a use for them anymore. People tend to work like that; just throwing things away. So, those two things got my interest. I think people just gave up on those things before they saw their true potential."

"Wow," Zach says.

"Yeah, wow," Mat says.

"That seems, very…personal," I say.

"What about you Charlie? What're you planning on specializing in?" Jessie says, putting me on the spot.

"Oh! Uhh…yeah, well…I mean I've thought about some things," I say, lying my ass off.

I haven't actually thought about what it is I want to specialize in. I've always wanted to get up there in titles, possibly even be a private teacher in my retirement, but I never actually thought about specializing in something. I only came to this school and pursued becoming a Sorce because Laurie was doing it. There're so many things to choose from; Alchemy, Potions, Relics, Illusions, Elements, Enchanting, Necromancy, Blood, Shadows, Voodoo, if you're lucky maybe Divination. There's also Transmogrification, Conjuration, Shapeshifting, and Taming. Those are the only ones that come to mind, but there's more.

"Like what?" Jessie says.

"Don't want to make a hasty decision, it's only our first semester," I say.

"Uh huh," Zach says, clearly not buying any of my bullshit.

"Wow! You have no idea, do you?" Jessie asks.

"Laurie really did just drag you here, huh?" Mat says. Mat catches glares from both me and Jessie.

"O...kay. I think I'll get another drink," Zach says, getting up from his sunken bean chair.

"Grab me a bag of chips while you're at it," Mat says. Zach responds with a middle finger.

"I'm sure you'll find...*something* to specialize in," Jessie says.

With that, Mat gets up and brushes the crumbs of whatever he was eating onto the floor.

"Welp! It's getting late, I think I'm going to go work on my project so Zach doesn't show me up in demonstrations," Mat says, going for a bag of chips.

"Seriously? It's not even that late?" I say.

"Zach, you coming?" Mat asks.

"Nah, I think I'm going to chill for a bit," Zach says, popping open his drink.

"The moon is almost gone," Mat says, clearing his throat.

"Oh! Uhh...*is it*? Alright, yeah, I'll head out with you," Zach says.

The moon is almost gone. I know that code phrase...I came up with that code phrase. That was something the three of us used to tell each other it was time to leave in case...we were suddenly *"busy"* with something and had to focus on matters at...hand. But the problem is that there was nobody around except the four of us, and the person who uses the phrase is usually the one who stays, yet Mat used it and he's leaving —*ohmygod*. No. They can't be serious. They're leaving me with Jessie. All she said was I'll find "something" to specialize in —*ohhhshit*.

That couldn't be what she meant. She was just using emphasis to make a point, that's how casual conversation works.

Is my heart pounding? It's pounding.

Zach and Mat both walk to the door. Jessie has a perplexed look on her face.

"Alright, we'll catch you guys later!" Zach says.

"Yeah, we'll—" Mat coughs on the chips he'd began munching on from eating too fast. "We'll see you two later," Mat continues.

"See you guys soon!" Jessie waves goodbye.

"Ye-Ah?" my voice cracks.

The door slams shut leaving nothing but Jessie, myself, and a wave of awkward silence. This isn't actually happening. Those two read into something that wasn't actually there, what if people find out? Who cares if people find out? Wait. What if Laurie finds out?...I don't...I don't think I particularly care. Maybe a little. Not entirely.

"Charlie!" Jessie says.

"Huh? Yeah?"

"Dude, you've been zoning out since I asked you what you wanted to specialize in. Had I known it was going to melt your brain, I wouldn't have asked."

"No, it didn't fry anything. I've never felt better."

"Sure..."

Jessie is laying down on her side directly across from me. She gets up and sits cross-legged, looking at me intently.

"Zach and Mat got out of here in a hurry. It wasn't anything I said right?" Jessie says.

"What? No. They just have their own stuff to deal with, we have this dumb code phrase that—"

"They're just being...them. I guess?"

"Well, someone hasn't really been...'them' if you ask me."

"W-what do you mean?"

Jessie scoots herself across the floor right in front of me. Her grey eyes practically piercing through my own in stark contrast with her black hair.

"Your eyes," Jessie says.

Is this happening? Is this actually happening right now? I

don't even know that much about Jessie…Aside from her favorite color being wolf silver, her favorite subject being History of Ancients, the way she puts her hair in a messy bun when she's stressed or angry, the laid-back tough-girl attitude she has through life, and her determination to prove something to people that don't even exist.

"My eyes?"

"Yeah, your eyes," Jessie says, using her hands to grab and hold my face, looking deep into my eyes.

"I…uh."

"The same thing happened to your hands at the Crystal Fields before you overloaded that crystal and blew us almost to particles. What was happening?"

"I-I'm not sure. This time when I heard Echo it was far more intense. Usually, it's one voice going back and forth with me, but this time it felt like an army in my head trying to escape. I was still in control, I think. It felt like I was focused on not transferring control, but in those moments, I guess the line between us blurs."

Jessie snaps her fingers and her eyes widen.

"That explains the Crystal Fields, the first time. You've been battling Echo since then? So, you must've gotten him at Sirrus. Or maybe just before?"

"We still don't know," I admit. "But we're thinking it may have been at a young age. I've been trying to think of early signs of Echo, but nothing sticks out to me. Shit. I don't think I was supposed to tell you all of that."

"Oh come on Charlie, who am I gonna tell? I pretty much only talk to four people at this school. Six if you count Mat and Zach, but that's only if you're there, really."

"Six? Who're the other three?"

"Two other girls from my history class and Nathan."

"Nathan? I thought you hated him?"

"No, that's you. He's a pompous ass, sure, but he also has good advice for exams that I happily take."

"I don't necessarily hate him; he just always seems to have a problem with me."

"Yeah, I think it's because he gets sweaty at night thinking of me and sees you as a threat. Either way, he has as much a chance as an ice cube in a dragon's mouth."

"Well, with Echo, I could be a threat to everyone. Still, he doesn't have to be such a dick about it."

"I meant a *romantic* threat, Charlie."

Jessie summersaults backwards and pops up on her feet. "Maybe you should focus more on finding a specialization instead of your Echo for a few days."

"Wait…Maybe *that's* it!"

"What?"

"*Echoes*…I'll specialize in Echoes."

XII

Jessie stands in my doorway getting ready to leave.

"How's the roommate?" I ask.

"Ugh. Still annoying as always. She has her friends over until midnight and then they all leave a mess behind," Jessie says.

"Oof, and she doesn't clean up?"

"She leaves with them!"

"I don't think you've even told me her name? Jinny?"

"Abigail."

"Abigail? You...wouldn't be talking about Abigail Mason?"

"Yes! You know her? What about Sia, Oni, and Lias?"

"Yeah, I know all of them. But let's not forget their most notable members: Sanderon, Rhody, and Laurie."

"No shit! Okay, those three are never in my dorm but I have noticed them together all the time. Wow..."

A chill runs up my spine and I shudder. Something is coming.

<No, something is here.>

"Charlie? Is everything okay?" Jessie says.

"Come back inside," I say.

Jessie, looking confused, listens and steps back through the door. I immediately shut the door behind her and lock it.

"Something is happening. I feel something out there," I say.

"Is it Echo? Is he trying to tell you something?" Jessie asks.

"Faintly, I haven't heard much of him since I got the new ring."

"Maybe we should call Master Uphraeus?"

"I'm not sure if that's a good idea. I think I'm still technically on probation, and Master Uphraeus hasn't said anything about contacting him since the cover story."

"Cover story?"

"Yeah, the whole me 'stealing an artifact' thing?"

"That was a *cover* story?!"

"Didn't I tell you that at the Crystal Fields?"

"No! All you revealed was Echo. Now you're telling me there's a whole conspiracy around you?!"

"Legends, help me…"

Suddenly, I hear what sounds like a melody on the wind.

"Do you hear that?" I ask.

Jessie looks around trying to listen. "Hear what?"

"It's like something is calling out, barely a whisper."

"Charlie, just a second ago you were freaking out, now you're calm and I'm freaking out."

"I have to find out what that is. Maybe it was Echo, maybe he's trying to show me something?"

I rush over to where Zach, Mat, Jessie, and I were sitting to put on my shoes.

"*Echo Location*. Let's find out where it's coming from," I say.

"Charlie."

I flick my rotator ring and close my eyes, taking a deep breath to focus on where the melody is coming from. I see Jessie's outline, then the outlines of other students. This is actually weird, and I'm seeing outlines of things I could've lived without. The melody isn't showing up, but I can still hear it. Then, another wave comes from the Southwest. It's not just any wave, it's clearly a sorce wave, yet different enough to be... something else?

"I got it. It's coming from the Southwest. Let's go," I say, grabbing a jacket from the hook off the wall next to the door.

"Charlie."

"Jessie, come on. What if there's something out there that we can't afford to miss out on? Where's your sense of adventure?"

"I...fine, but if I have to leave you behind to save my own life, I won't hesitate."

"I wouldn't have it any other way."

Jessie and I walk out of the dorm building and start heading Southwest towards the origin of the melody. It's past midnight so there aren't many people out and around, making it a bit easier for Jessie and I to walk around unnoticed. We get to the Crystal Fields and go around the sorce field, towards the forest behind it.

"How much further?" Jessie groans.

"We're definitely getting closer. Hang on, let me try something."

I place my hand against a tree and close my eyes, trying to get a sense of everything using Echo Location. I can see a bit more detail than usual, the roots of the trees, the leaves moving with the wind, all in beautiful outlines and colors. I wait for the pulse that's been pulling me closer to come again...There it is.

"So? Do you see anything?" Jessie asks.

"Hang on. Just got the pulse. Need to concentrate."

I pick up on the direction of the pulse, but I want to see if I can pinpoint the exact spot. Each time the pulse comes I try to follow it through the trees that it passes through. I'm able to see a bit further each time until I can see exactly where it's coming from. There's a small alter where it's originating from, and eight people standing around it. Before I can see any more details, I collapse to the ground.

"Charlie?" Jessie says, rushing over to me.

"What happened?" I ask.

"I don't know, you tell me? You were concentrating, then you started staggering and collapsed."

Jessie places her hand on my forehead.

"Well, that's new. I'm not used to using Echo Location. Must've pushed it too far."

"We should head back to the dorms."

"No. It's fine. I'm fine. There's something over there. Someone. Something there with people. An altar with a bunch of people standing around it."

"Your mouth is barely keeping up with your brain. Please, can we turn back?"

I manage to get on my feet and stand up.

"If you want to turn back here that's fine, but there's no way I'm turning back. I have to find out what those people are doing."

Jessie looks pissed, yet concerned.

"Fine," Jessie says.

"Jessie—"

"It's fine. Let's go."

"Maybe—"

"Lead the way."

"Okay."

Any other day I'd probably give in to the guilt trip, but this feels far more important. Passing through trees, brush, and avoiding whatever insects that we don't recognize, Jessie and I make our way further through the labyrinth of foliage. As we approach the point of the pulse and melody, I tap Jessie on the shoulder and silently tell her to slow down so they don't hear us coming. After passing a few trees the area is within eyesight. Jessie and I crouch low and walk slowly towards the mysterious group to get within earshot.

"If he had it he would be here by now," one of the figures says.

"Maybe Rhody and Sanderon were wrong. Maybe they didn't find anything interesting after all," another figure says.

"Those voices sound familiar," Jessie whispers.

"Sounds like Rhody and Sanderon are here. Must mean the whole gang is here; including Laurie," I whisper back.

"Or maybe you should all shut up and wait," a familiar voice responds.

"Yup, that's Rhody. I'd know his irritating voice anywhere," I say.

"Patience, everyone…Patience," A deep voice says.

I don't recognize the deeper voice as any of Laurie's friends. It sounds much older, like a man in his forties.

"Rhody's only mad because the kid almost beat him during the games," one voice laughs.

"He didn't almost beat me, I had him until that bastard Uphraeus showed up," Rhody says.

Jessie puts a hand on my shoulder, stopping me from moving any further forward. My jaw clenched up and I ball my fists in a fit of rage.

"Sure. Then why did Sanderon surrender against him?" A light voice says, probably Abigail.

"Were you dumbasses not watching? I surrendered because Rhody told me to," Sanderon says.

"Quiet!" The man says.

A moment of silence passes. Jessie and I exchange glances. She looks scared and mouths to me "we need to leave" but I shake my head, defiantly.

"Charlie, is it?" The man says.

My heart skips a beat. Did he just call to me? He definitely said my name just now. I can see everyone else around him looking around and searching. The figure with the deep voice raises a hand to calm them.

"No one here is going to hurt you, Charlie," the man says. "I know you're here. The shard picked up on your presence."

I can't see the shard behind the man. I close my eyes to concentrate and see if I can visualize what he's talking about. Jessie notices and shakes her head at me. I ignore her implied suggestion. Using Echo Location, I can see a bit more clearly. Eight people, and a single shard above an altar. The shard is outlined in a yellowish-orange, and I can see the pulses it's still generating.

"You and this shard are cut from the same cloth…It reaches out and calls to its own."

I stop using Echo Location and notice I've broken out into a cold sweat.

"I'm here to help you, Charlie. I'm here to change the world. My name is Master Krain. You may not know me, so addressing me by that title is optional. If you want, you can just call me Krain," the man says.

"We. *Need*—to get out of here," Jessie whispers.

"If we move or make another sound, he'll find us, if he hasn't already," I say.

Krain walks in circles looking out towards the trees, occasionally looking in our direction. I can tell he's wearing a long robe, along with the others, but his shimmers in the moonlight. Their faces aren't human, they look like they're wearing masks, but I can't make out exactly what they look like.

"I know you must have *a lot* of questions. About who *I* am. Who *you* are. What an *echo* actually is?" Train says.

I take a deep gulp of air as Jessie and I exchange looks.

Krain continues to pace around as if speaking to a large audience. "Yes, I know. Do you feel an excess amount of sorce flowing through you? Perhaps, *whispers* from people you can't see, or maybe you feel as if you have an entirely separate *person* inside you?" Krain has a hint of glee in his voice. He continues.

"I bet Uphraeus has told you many terrifying things about it; it's dangerous. Don't use it. He's probably thought he can, with what little power he actually has, suppress it for you I bet he hasn't even explained the *actual* effect it's having on you."

"Actual" effect? What's that supposed to mean? My ring begins to spin on its own, the whistling sound it makes can be heard very faintly. I cover it with my hand trying to get it to stop. I look back over at Krain but something is off about where he is now…There's no one else around him. Laurie and the others are gone. Jessie tugs on my sleeve and points at a cloaked figure off to the North of us.

"Like I said Charlie, no one is going to hurt you. I've deemed it so. There is something that *will* hurt you. And it talks to you as if your body is not your own," Krain says.

Jessie and I move slowly away from the cloaked figure. It could be any of the eight, but I'm hoping it's Laurie and maybe she can explain herself.

"It's time for you to come out now," Krain says.

A dome of purple mist explodes outward from Krain, disintegrating trees down to their stumps. Jessie and I are feeling exposed as we look around and see we're in-between two of the cloaked figures. I pull Jessie up by her arm.

"Run!"

The cloaked figures hear me and begin their pursuit. Jessie and I move our way through the now desecrated forest towards the east where we came from. Flanked from both sides, we dodge sorce attacks of pulses, darts, and conjured ropes.

"Charlie!" Jessie screams out to me.

I turn to see her legs wrapped together in translucent glowing ropes. The two cloaked figures begin to converge on us, with another six headed our way. I stop for a moment, trying to decide if I should go back for Jessie or not. I spin my ring and launch my own sorce pulse at one of the cloaked figures. It smacks them across the face, stunning them. I run towards Jessie and try to help her untie her bindings. The second cloaked figure gets within ten feet of us and I send dart at him, this one charged with more intent…and anger. The cloaked figure swiftly deflects it with a zapier, a very *familiar* zapier.

"Ch-Charlie, just go. Leave me here, get help," Jessie says.

"I'm not leaving you."

Jessie's eyes are starting to water, I've never seen her like this; scared, and it's my fault. I dragged her into this. Now it's up to me to get her out. I charge another pulse in my hand, except this time, I'm overloading the next son of a bitch I hit. The pulse swirls around in my hands like waves being ripped and torn apart by hurricane winds. Growing in size, sparking, and shifting colors. Before I launch the pulse, I feel my body start to tense up, causing me to lose concentration and the pulse to dispell. A silver mist slowly wraps itself around my body, making it almost impossible to move. The same mist Master Sindra put me in the first day I was late to her class, but not as strong, not as potent.

I slowly turn my head with what little control I have left, to see the other six cloaked figures gathered. Now, I can see all seven of them. Each one wearing a mask of some demon possessed animal with twisted gold antlers. A vulture, rat, snake, cat, crow, owl, and a bird. All of them painted black with gold markings. The one in the middle, wearing the cat mask, has their hands around a locket artifact that's creating the mist.

"Laurie?" I ask.

Their hands around the locket cringe. The vulture masked individual roughly nudges the one with the cat mask. The mist takes hold of me and Jessie. I collapse to the ground next to her.

"I can only assume that means the dickhead with the rat mask is Sanderon?" I say.

"He shouldn't be able to talk," the rat masked figure says, raising his zapier and pointing it at the person in the cat mask.

"Shut up, Sanderon! This is a rushed artifact; do you want any of use to be permanently paralyzed?"

There's no question. That's Laurie's voice.

"Are you an idiot? We're masked for a reason!" Sanderon says.

"Watch your mouth," the bird masked figure says.

"He already knows who we are. There's no point," Laurie says.

"Yeah, but she doesn't," Sanderon says, looking at Jessie.

"She's not stupid, and probably picked up on my voice by now too," Laurie says.

"Who is she?" the crow asks.

"Jessie Zirdi," the bird says.

"Great," the vulture says. "You've been practicing for weeks Laurie. Stop fucking around and shut'em up."

I feel the mist wrap around my throat. I look at Jessie, she can't speak, but her eyes tell me everything; "I'm scared, Charlie. I'm scared and I don't want to die."

I know, Jessie.

<I won't let that happen.>

The seven of them gather around us and cast a levitation spell to lift Jessie and me. We float through the air as they slowly walk us back towards Krain. Once there, they lower us onto the ground in front of Krain, his back turned looking out towards the ocean. I was so caught up in finding this place I hadn't noticed we were on the edge of the school's floating island. The breeze is cold, and the faint sound of waves crashing underneath us is the only thing breaking the silence.

Krain turns around in his black cloak that shimmers with gold swirls across the fabric. His mask is the face of a demon-like bat, and gold antlers on the side, but his was different from the others; white instead of black. He walks over to us, still bound in mist.

"Who is our special guest?" Krain says.

"Abigail's roommate. Her name is Jessie," the owl says.

"We're using our real names now?" Krain says.

"We're all aware of who they are, and Charlie already guessed Laurie and Sanderon's identity," the bird says.

"So, you confirm their suspicions? Did you find anyone else?" Krain sounds annoyed.

"We didn't see anyone else. And I thought you said there were only two people around here anyway?" The vulture says.

I couldn't pick up on it before, but now that I'm focusing on his voice, I can tell; that's Rhody.

"Believe it or not, there are people at this institution that can barely rival my power but it's still enough to put everything at risk," Krain says.

"Well, I—"

"Silence! My patience with you is starting to fall. Not a word out of any of you from here on out unless called upon."

With a wave of his hand, Krain removes the silver mist from me and Jessie. We both inhale deeply; it feels like having a weight lifted off my chest. I roll over onto my side, legs and wrists still bound together to check on Jessie.

"You almost suffocated them, Cat," Krain says.

"Now, Charlie, I'm sorry we had to meet like this, but I was getting the feeling that you weren't going to be coming to me on your own."

Krain makes a gesture with his hand, pulling Jessie and me up, and onto our knees. He walks up to us and kneels down to our eye level.

"Nice to finally meet you, Charlie," Krain says, extending a hand out to shake mine.

I thought it may be a sarcastic gesture with my hands still bound together, but as he extends his hand, my binds disappear. My first reaction is to try blasting him to hell, but I know he's far more powerful than I am, regardless of the validity of his "Master" title. I look around to see where the other seven are standing. All of them, in a half circle several feet back, stand watching. I put my focus back on Krain, his hand still out. His mask, the white bat, has a mouth carved into it that looks like a smile and a frown depending on how you look at it. I extend my hand out and shake his.

"Krain, was it?" I say.

"*Master* Krain!" The snake corrects me.

Krain's mask hides his entire face, so I can't tell where he's looking, but the bat's eyes are still locked on me. There's a cold silence, one that made the hairs on my neck stand up. His hand hasn't released mine from the shake, the stillness and calm before a storm. Without a word, Krain points at the snake-masked Sanderon with a steady hand. I hear a scream, and flash. I turn my head to see there's only six people with masks now.

"I-is he dead?" I ask.

"Would you like him to be?" Krain replies.

No answer. I just look at the ground contemplating his question.

"Well, something inside you does."

That triggers a thought in my head about something Krain said earlier.

"W-what did you mean when you said the echo would hurt me?" I ask.

"Before I answer that, let me ask you this: what has Uphraeus told you?" Krain asks.

"Echoes are rare things. Most knowledge comes from myths and legends. It stays with you until you die," I say.

Krain lets out a hearty laugh.

"That's definitely one way to put it. But to be blunt; you're going to die," Krain says.

"*What?!*" Jessie cries.

"Y-you're lying. Master Uphraeus would've told me that," I say.

"I have no reason to lie to you Charlie. I'm trying to help you. You see, I'm trying to forge a better world, and you can help with that. At the same time, if you help me, I'll make sure that echo of yours doesn't get the chance to do what it's supposed to," Krain says.

"What makes you an expert in echoes? How do I know you're even telling the truth, that you won't use me to gain whatever you're after and toss me to the side like you just did to Sanderon?" I say.

"I lead you here, didn't I? Using a shard from a place where I believe echoes are born. It's more information than you have now. I'm also not the one who lied to you in the first place. That would be Uphraeus. Meanwhile, I've been very forthcoming with you. And to address your last question, Sanderon is fine. He was disobedient, so I had to make sure his actions had consequences, as all actions do. You understand right? Like when Uphraeus told you not to take off that ring, so a cover story was made to make you look like a thief? Seems like Uphraeus has caused you more harm than good at this point," Krain says.

Contemplating his words, I have to admit it...he's right. Though, I can't prove Master Uphraeus lied about echoes killing the Sorces they're attached to, it makes sense with the way he and Master Sindra were talking. He did also come up with a fairly convincing cover story for me in a short amount of time. I don't want to believe him, but there's also no reason for him to lie. He has me and Jessie tied up and useless. Whatever he wanted from me he could get, through direct or indirect force. He hasn't laid a finger on Jessie or myself, so he's willing to be reasonable.

"I can see it in your eyes. You're piecing things together. Am I right?"

"Even if I believe you, being tied up alongside my friend isn't exactly giving me any reassurance," I say.

"Look at it from my point of view: two very promising young Sorces, one with a very unique trait that could level a small stadium, have been convinced that their teacher is a righteous hero. But I take your point," Krain says.

With a wave of his hand, Krain dispells the restraints from around our wrists and legs. We stand to our feet, and Jessie's first instinct is to try and fight, but I grab her wrist. Jessie looks at me with a very confused expression.

"I'm here with you. We wouldn't get very far anyway. Let's just hear him out," I say.

Jessie takes a deep breath and nods. "I trust you."

"Let's have a real conversation. How many of you are there?

Who are you? What do you ultimately want, and how do I fit into your picture?" I ask.

Krain notices the change in my posture now that I'm standing, making him stand up and take a step back. Krain stands well over six feet tall, so his intimidating factor hasn't changed much. He chuckles behind the mask.

"I like this version of you. It's confident; suits you well," Krain says.

Turning to the shard, Krain takes it in his hand and places it in a pocket inside his cloak. The same shard that called me here in the first place. After which he claps his hands together and the small alter it was floating on turns to a pile of rocks. He then pulls his hands apart and makes hand gestures that turn the pile of stones into a chair and pulls it over to sit in front of Jessie and I.

"I was raised in a small town that exported minerals to Alignments and institutions. My father made an honest living as a miner, until one day, an Alignment came to our town. They were called the Serpent's Scepters. They'd been known to go from town to town, pillaging and taking resources. We didn't live close enough to any city-states or more benevolent Alignments for them to be concerned about us. The Serpents had apparently suffered a defeat during a turf war, and they found that their enemies had recently traded with us. So, we were obviously the ones to blame for their crushing defeat. The people pleaded for them to have mercy, no one was strong enough to stand against them, so we offered them free supplies. They surely took the offerings, but felt they had to send a message; they killed my father, and half the town. No one cared, no one was there to help."

"That's…very unfortunate. I'm sorry about your father, and your town. You were victims of an unforgivable crime," I say.

"Oh, but I'm not. Don't get me wrong, the issue devastated me and my mother, but that event triggered me to become the Sorce I am today. I used to be a student at this very school, just like you two. I graduated, as most do, with the title of Versed, then went out into the world, hopeful, strong, and determined to make a name for myself."

A student at this school? That's how Master Uphraeus and Master Sindra must know him. He must be the same age as them, if not somewhere around there.

"Me and my...*colleagues* were excited to change the world," Krain continues. "Start our own Alignment, and unite everyone together. No more city-states, no more rogue Alignments, a utopia. We went on a quest to find answers, to study the history of Sorces more in depth, from places all over. In Eclipsys we discovered more about about the history of the first Sorce War, and eventually pieced together a more coherent history of the first Legend; Tressia. You're familiar, yes?"

"The ancient queen of Eclipsys. She ruled a long time, and changed our understanding of sorce forever," I say.

"The history books tell you that she was a powerful Sorce had unimaginable armies at her disposal. That she was a Sorce, a queen, a conqueror, who eventually lost her claims and faded away to history. What they *don't* tell you, is that she created a country where all were bound under one rule. That she did what was necessary to create a peaceful and prosperous world. Without proper rule, Sorces run wild with no restraint. To answer your question, Charlie; ultimately, I am someone who once sought glory, but now I only seek the betterment of my people. Using the power of your echo, we can bring to life Tressia's temple and unlock her knowledge for us to unite Sorces across the world."

"So your name is Krain, you ultimately want to govern your own nation, and in order to do that you need Echo. You still haven't answered how many of you are in this...Alignment?"

Krain laughs.

"Detail oriented as well? You're going to be great Charlie. It's not just an Alignment, it's an ideal. We are known as The Queen's Wraiths, and we are legion," Krain says.

XIII

"Can I have a moment with Jessie alone?" I ask.

Krain and I have been talking for what feels like hours. Could just be my nerves, but I honestly don't know what to think anymore, especially if everything he says is true about himself, Master Uphraeus, and the Queen's Wraiths.

"You can stand by the cliffs behind me. Be quick," Krain says.

"Thank you."

"Take this with you." He hands me a tiny glass ball no bigger than a marble. "In case our conversation must end short."

I nod and take the mysterious ball and put it in my pocket. Jessie and I calmly walk to the edge of the island, looking over the black ocean where it blends seamlessly with the night's horizon. Before I speak a word, Jessie hugs onto me tightly. I can feel her trembling as I return her embrace.

"I think we're going to be okay," I say.

Jessie is silent for a moment then breaks away and wipes her eyes.

"I really hate crying," Jessie says.

"I told you it would be an adventure," I say. "So, what do you think?"

"I think we're dead. But we're not going down without a fight."

"Not if I join him."

"You can't be serious?" she says.

"You heard our conversation. I can't necessarily verify everything, but it lines up enough. He doesn't strike me as the type to lie, at least not right now, when he's trying to make a deal. He's very careful with his choice of words. Means he doesn't want me to call him out on any false information."

"Which also means he has something to hide; the truth," Jessie says. "You're seriously thinking about trusting the guy with the evil bat-mask, who is currently leading a group of people, *two* of which kicked your ass and almost killed you, the other being your *ex* who kicked your heart in the ass and left you for one of the aforementioned?"

"Look, even if we had another option, maybe learning more about Krain and the Queen's Wraiths will give us more information about Echo."

"Oh yeah, thanks for telling me about your magical terminal illness, friend. When were you going to tell me there was a high probability of you dying?"

"Uphraeus said it would be with me till I was dead, he didn't say I was actually *dying*. Krain is the one who said I was going to die. I don't know who to believe."

"*Master* Uphraeus. You're practically initiated with the way you're talking. Wait, did you say Master Sindra too? *She's* in on this?!"

"Jessie, please. Be quiet."

"Quite frankly, I don't think it matters at this point. All of this is bullshit. There's a guy with a mask, other students following his orders, we're trapped, Master Uphraeus and Sindra are involved and possibly lying about it, there're multiple conspiracies behind *everything*, you're *dying* and it hasn't even been four months since this whole thing started."

Jessie puts her hands her face and releases a deep breath. I reach out and hold her hands to comfort her.

"Jessie, everything is going to be alright."

"You don't know that."

"Will you trust me?"

Jessie takes a deep breath, then exhales. She squeezes my hand and nods slowly.

"Yes. I will trust you. It's just *them* I don't trust."

"Leave them to me."

"Am I about to join a cult? Are *we* about to join a cult?"

"*We* aren't going to do anything. *I* am going to get you out of this mess, and—with any luck, myself."

I hold up my right hand and look at what's being held in my fingers. Jessie looks and sees my rotator ring. She raises an eyebrow.

"I know I said I was going to trust you Charlie...but I don't think that even with the ring off you can do anything about this."

"Yeah, but I'm banking on what happened last time I took it off. I have a feeling that the sneaky Master who reforged this ring also put a small enchantment on it. How else would he have known to get me at the Sorce Games?"

A huge sorce pulse erupts from the trees towards the North, where Rhody, Laurie, and the others are standing. The intensity of the light makes Jessie and I shield our eyes. At that moment a very familiar, but much angrier voice comes from the same direction as the light.

"KRAIN!!" Master Uphraeus roars.

Master Uphraeus comes through the trees with a fury, blasting two masked students and knocking them to the ground. Krain, unphased by Master Uphraeus' entrance, simply turns his body a quarter way towards me and Jessie. Master

Uphraeus ignites in green flames. The flames move to cover his arms and forehead, forming two emerald bracers around his fists and forearms and a pair of ox horns on his forehead. Master Uphraeus extends a finger out to Krain.

"You. I swear if—" Master Uphraeus notices Jessie and me standing by the cliffs.

"I can assure you everyone here *was* safe, until you showed up blasting away as always," Krain says.

Krain snaps his fingers, opening seven portals circling Master Uphraeus and the other masked wraiths.

"It's time to leave. I'll handle this," Krain says.

The masked students flee through the portals, except one; Laurie. Her cat mask looks back at me before stepping through. What has she gotten herself into?

<She needs our help.>

Echo, no, whatever it is you're thinking, stop.

<*I want to know what Master Uphraeus is hiding, and if Krain is telling the truth.*>

Wow, you seem a lot more docile now. The new ring have anything to do with it?

<*No. As you change, so do I. You've had a paradigm shift, and so have I.*>

And what is that?

<*We both want answers and we both don't want to die.*>

Something we can finally agree on.

"You and me Krain...Let the young ones go, then we can settle this once and for all," Master Uphraeus says.

"I haven't been keeping them hostage, nor threatened their lives. We were having a civil conversation. I know that's not something you're familiar with, William," Krain says.

Master Uphraeus charges at Krain, leaving a trail of green flames behind him. He launches into the air with his fist aiming straight at Krain's head. Without flinching, or moving an inch, Krain steps to the side and grabs Master Uphraeus' free-hand, using his momentum to catch him in mid-air, spinning, and throwing Master Uphraeus back in the direction he came. Master Uphraeus tumbles through the air, landing on his feet which are now covered in the same emerald light as his hands and horns on his head, resembling an ox's hind legs and tail.

"That's always been your problem, William; you never evolved, never changed. Decades ago, I told you how you could improve your strength, but you ignored it even to this day. You're too stubborn," Krain says.

"No. I have always stuck to a code, a moral compass, staples that make me who I am. Unlike you, I don't abandon my principles when they no longer suit me."

"I never abandoned my principles. You just never took the time to understand them."

Master Uphraeus kneels to the ground with his arms stretched out and his palms facing the ground. The green constructs around his arms glowing brighter as emerald flames pour from his hands. As the flames grow and warp around, two green ox spirits come to life from the flames. Master Uphraeus begins another charge, this time with his ox companions, weaving and moving with them in sync. Master Uphraeus approaches from the center, then crosses with the ox on the left, then with the one on the right, changing his position until the last second.

Krain blocks one ox with his hand, stopping its momentum.

The ox digs its hooves into the ground trying to push against Krain, with no progress. Master Uphraeus approaches from behind the ox and throws a kick at Krain's chest, which Krain blocks just as easily. At the same time the second ox approaches from Krain's flanks at full speed. Krain slaps Master Uphraeus' foot away to catch the other ox. With his attention divided, the oxen pin Krain in a stalemate between them, using their long horns to keep him from moving.

From the sky, Master Uphraeus lets out a roar with two fists coming down on Krain. The attack connects with Krain's mask, shattering it into pieces and causing a small detonation. The knock-back pushes Master Uphraeus back and dispells his oxen. Jessie and I shield our eyes from the brightness and the dust. Looking at the aftermath of the attack, we see Master Uphraeus; no Krain. Then, out of the ground, giant purple and black tendrils erupt from the ground with thorns the size of spears creating a circular cage that enclosed me, Jessie, and Master Uphraeus.

"Out of respect for the past, I give you a warning Uphraeus: You have one month."

Krain's voice reverberates through the giant vines. "Come out and fight me coward!" Master Uphraeus bellows.

The tendril vines crack and splinter with a purple light, exploding into a violet mist. The trees that were once cut down are back as if they never left. The tendrils gone and the craters they made vanished as well. The entire area looked as if nothing had ever happened. I notice Jessie and I have been holding hands since Master Uphraeus first showed up. We walk together to get closer to the epicenter of the fight to speak to Master Uphraeus.

"Are you okay?" I ask.

Master Uphraeus brushes off his coat, still looking for signs of an attack.

"Fine, my son. I assume Krain cast an illusion when I shattered his mask, offering a time for escape. He's always been a deceiver, makes sense he specialized in the illusive arts. But we have no time for a history lesson, I have to get you two to safety."

"I assume you got my message?"

"Yes, smart thinking taking off the ring. I half expected to have to fight you, if you'd been alone."

"Seriously? Why?"

"Taking off that ring meant you either didn't listen to me,

again, or you lost control. Either way, it meant you and I were going to have to start lessons again."

He pulls a small glass ball from his vest pocket; it looks similar to the one Krain gave me. It floats above his hand as he speaks to it.

"Eve. I have them. Portal on my location," Master Uphraeus says.

"Them? Who else is there? Don't tell me you found Krain?" Sindra says, through the ball.

"No, well, yes. Long story, I just need a portal for three. High chance there're illusionists around so, make it specific. Me, Charlie, and Jessie," Master Uphraeus says.

"Jessie? Miss Zirdi?" Master Sindra says.

"Affirmative," Master Uphraeus responds.

"Portal incoming."

Master Uphraeus gestures for us to stand back as he leaves the glass ball floating in the air. White wisps of light flow from the now glowing ball as they expand and move to create a portal. Master Uphraeus nods his head in the direction of the portal.

"You two first. I'm right behind you," Master Uphraeus says.

I nod at Jessie and she walks through first. I walk up to the portal and stop just short of walking through to the other side.

"Have you been lying to me?" I ask him.

"Now's not the time or place. It's not that simple," Master Uphraeus says, his eyes still searching the area.

"Am I dying?"

"…Yes."

I walk through the portal. On the other side is a room I've never seen before. Elegant chairs sit in a circle near a fireplace, no, not a fireplace exactly; there's a waterfall where the flames should be and a tiny ecosystem within in it. Drapes of glimmering stone move with a subtle wave, like silk. Jessie sits in one of the chairs near the…waterplace—that's what I'm calling it—with Master Sindra standing a few feet away from where I emerged.

"Come in Charlie, hurry!" Master Sindra says.

I rush over to the chairs then realize that the room is just a single part of what looks like a much bigger building with connecting rooms and hallways. Master Uphraeus shortly follows me through the portal. Master Sindra, standing at the ready, closes the portal behind him. The portal collapses in a spiral and returns to its glass ball form. Master Sindra takes the ball and hands it to Mater Uphraeus.

"Are you injured?" Master Sindra says.

"He got a few good counters on me, but didn't leave a scratch. Next time, will be the last time. Unfortunately, I was more focused on getting Charlie and Jessie to safety."

Is that how he saw it? I don't know about Jessie, but from my perspective it looked a lot more like Master Uphraeus had a grudge match with an old enemy and we just happened to be in the way at the time. Then again, Krain was getting in my head.

"How are you two doing?" Master Uphraeus says.

"*When* were you two going to tell me, I was *dying*?!" I say. "You told me yourself you don't have a lot of information on echoes, so when the *hell* were you going to tell me that this... this *thing* inside my head is *terminal*?!"

"Charlie..." Master Uphraeus says, extending a hand towards me cautiously.

"*No!* I'm *not* going to calm down! Krain said you were lying, I trusted you, and now I find out from that psychopath that I'm *dying* and the one person I trusted at this school has been lying to me! All of this, after I just figured out something I'm good at, pretty sure I'm over my ex, I made new friends, and I got settled on a specialization a few hours ago!"

I feel lightheaded and almost collapse on the floor before Master Sindra gestures a chair to move underneath me to catch my fall. A second later I feel Jessie's hand on my shoulder.

"Are you done?" Master Uphraeus says.

With my head cradled in one of my hands I nod in response.

"He's right. You should've been more honest with him," Jessie says.

"It's not that simple Ms. Zirdi," Master Sindra says.

"Never have I heard of a sound and calming way to tell another that they're going to die. Though it may have been an oversight, I felt that it was not my place. No one here has been in an ideal situation. I'm sorry you thought—I'm sorry that I deceived you, Charlie," Master Uphraeus says.

I peer down at my hand looking at the ring. It's starting to <aggravate me> with it on.

"What does this ring do exactly? Because the way I see it now, it's more than just a tool to help me control Echo. It's starting to look like a tracking collar," I say.

Master Sindra looks at Master Uphraeus and lets out a large sigh, shaking her head. She walks towards an archway leading to another room.

"I'm going to get beverages for everyone. William, stop being stubborn and secretive. It only leads to more problems," Master Sindra says, walking out of the room.

Master Uphraeus takes in a deep breath and exhales. Taking off his glasses and rubbing them with a cloth he pulls from his jacket pocket. He reaches out for one of the chairs and the nearest one flies into his grasp. Fixing the chair to face me, Master Uphraeus sits down, looking straight at my face. His expression is very somber.

"The ring is a means to help you control echo," Master Uphraeus says, staring at the ring.

"It is also a tracker, in case something…dangerous were to happen. In that case, the ring is also there to stop you as a last line of defense if it ever comes to that."

"What do you mean: 'Last line of defense'?" I ask.

"If the ring is taken off, or destroyed, it suggests that you've been compromised. If your echo were to become unstable, the ring would do its best to mitigate the damage. Much like a sorce field does against an inside threat," Master Uphraeus says.

"So, it's supposed to stop anyone else from getting hurt if Charlie does end up dying?" Jessie asks.

"Exactly. It acts as a container and a warning. If the ring is destroyed along with Charlie, then the ring did what it was supposed to do. If the ring is destroyed and not Charlie, then the ring failed," Master Uphraeus says.

"And at no point did you think to tell me?" I ask.

"I wanted to tell you, Charlie, honest I did. But how could I without knowing what exactly might happen?" Master Uphraeus says.

Jessie and I exchange looks.

"Since you're aware of the issues now, I'll fill you in on what I hid from you in my research," Master Uphraeus continues.

Jessie walks over to pull a chair next to me so we can both face Master Uphraeus.

"I have no hard proof or evidence of what is actually happening to you, but based on legends, myths, folklore, and tales from other countries, I have put together enough information to give a rough estimate of the risks and dangers. At least enough, in hopes that we are not *completely* blind," Master Uphraeus says.

Master Sindra walks back into the room holding a tray of drinks.

"Here's what I assume: echoes are entities that are tied to an individual and their sorce. How they develop is beyond me, but it appears that it happens at an early stage, possibly even at birth. There also seems to be events that trigger or activate the echo, in which the echo then manifests as something physical. These manifestations vary but seem to be mostly physical at the beginning—like distorted eyes, concentrated points of sorce on the body, in one script, even horns. Though I'm unsure of that being a cultural depiction or literal," Master Uphraeus says.

"It can develop at birth? So, I've been screwed from the start?" I ask.

"Is there any mention of a cure? Something that can stop it? Someone must've come up with something by now, right?" Jessie says.

"After the physical manifestations begin, things start to become unclear. Which is why I've been trying to study Charlie discretely. In the images and writings, it seems that echoes start reaching their final stages as spirits or become part of one's soul. With an echo having fully formed, it fights for control from the host. This creates a power-grabbing dynamic that ends with both sides losing," Master Uphraeus answers.

"Is it possible to convince an echo to not do that? What I mean is that, as of right now, it doesn't seem like Echo is trying to take control, he does *want* control but it seems like it's more for his pride, maybe even to our benefit…I'm not sure which."

"Your echo is speaking to you; which means it's evolving. Have you noticed any changes in your thoughts or behavior? Perhaps a shift in his?" Master Uphraeus says.

"Actually, yes. He seems calmer now."

"Was that with the ring on or off?" Master Uphraeus says.

"On," I confirm.

Master Uphraeus strokes his beard, staring off into space. "I'm going to be honest with you Charlie."

"That'd be a nice change for once," I say.

"This is not something it can control—" Master Uphraeus says.

"Echo. His name is Echo." <I say adamantly.>

"You *named* it?

"Well, it—ugh, *he*—has a mind of his own now. So, yes, his name is Echo."

"*Echo* can't control what he's doing to you. It's in his nature. If there was a way to separate you two, then maybe. But there are many complications with that theory. We don't know what would happen to either of you or if it's even possible."

"What led you to study echoes? If these things are so rare, obscure, and barely researched, what made you start looking for them?"

"Krain. Krain was obsessed with his studies, he was thinking of specializing in the unexplained and relics. He came across the myths of echoes, actually, he's the one who coined the term. I joined him and we uncovered many things."

"If I remember correctly, it involved *me* too, William," Master Sindra says.

"Yes, of course," Master Uphraeus says.

"So, you all knew each other in the past?" I say.

"Yes, we were all students at Sirrus some years ago. William and Krain were always testing the limits and patience of the Administration, while I was busy keeping them out of trouble," Master Sindra says.

"If I recall, you also had your fair share of...*trouble*," Master Uphraeus says with his eyebrows raised.

"Back to the main topic?" Master Sindra says.

"Krain believed he could resurrect Tressia, the first known Legend among Sorces, but in order to do so he had to have enough power to do so. Echoes may have the potential to provide enough sorce to complete his plan. He wants to rule the world, and bring it to its knees," Master Uphraeus says.

"Was that the shard?"

"What?"

"The shard he used. It called to me, to Echo. That's how Krain was able to lure me there."

"What did the shard look like?" Master Uphraeus says.

"I'm not sure, I didn't get a great look at it before he put it away. But I think it was giving off the same sorce as Echo," I say.

Master Uphraeus nods his head in thought, stroking his beard intently.

"What did you and Krain discuss before I arrived?" Master Uphraeus says.

"Well, he knows I have an echo. He told me that you'd been lying to me. And that's pretty much it,"

"Did he say anything specific about how he was going to utilize you or Echo?"

"He spoke about possibly helping me, but before I could ask him what he meant, you showed up."

"Hmm…That is unfortunate. I would like to know what he plans to do with you. Now that he knows you have an echo, he most certainly will make you a primary target. What about the other masked people there? Did you recognize any of them? Was I right about Smill or Barian?"

"You mean Laurie and Rhody?" inquires Jessie.

"Yeah, we couldn't confirm any identities," I say.

"Well, yeah. I thought I may have heard one of their voices but we weren't close enough to *really* hear," Jessie says.

Good recovery Jessie.

"I may need the both you to testify to Head Master Anidas," Master Uphraeus says.

"Head Master Anidas? I didn't realize Sirrus had a Head Master," I say.

"Every school has a Head Master, child. That's how the schools were built; Head Masters are the ones who dedicate their lives to maintaining the conduit that powers the school grounds. You would know this by now if you'd been paying attention in your classes," Master Sindra says.

"I'm sorry Master Sindra. I knew about Head Masters, and I did read about Head Master Anidas before coming to Sirrus, I just haven't heard much else or even seen him around. I started to wonder if he actually existed," I say.

"Head Master Anidas is…a difficult person to track down. Which is another reason I've been trying to keep things under the table. Prior to your class's arrival, Head Master Anidas was far more involved around the school and now suddenly he's only contacted the rest of the Administration through letters or secondhand talks," Master Uphraeus says.

"William, are you implying that Head Master Anidas is also part of this?" Master Sindra says, laughing at the suggestion.

"I think it's a possibility," Master Uphraeus says.

"That doesn't make a lot of sense. Schools are and have almost always been neutral grounds for any conflict. They were built to be self-sustaining, run by Masters, and there's no strategic benefit to take them," Master Sindra says.

"Unless your first objective is to take the neutral grounds and start from there," Master Uphraeus says.

Master Sindra, Jessie and I all shift a bit in our seats as we listen to Master Uphraeus' theory.

"Imagine your goal is to establish a new rule, government, or empire; do you attack fully armed nations, or do you take the neutral and weaker parties first? If I were trying to establish a new rule, I'd bank on the neutral parties and their need to remain neutral," Master Uphraeus says.

"What's your plan then? Find Krain and take him out?" I say.

"If I can. I'm unsure how far his influence has traveled so I can't say for certain where he is or what his plans are. My only lead, at this point, is you," Master Uphraeus says.

"I guess we just have to wait and see?" Jessie says.

"Sadly, yes. I think it would be best to keep Charlie hidden away here though," Master Uphraeus says.

"Where is here? Is this a secret location on Sirrus?" I ask, curiously.

"No. This place isn't in Sirrus," Master Sindra says.

"Where are we?"

"I'll transport you two back to school grounds," Master Sindra says.

Master Sindra and Master Uphraeus rise from their seats and gesture Jessie and I to get up with them.

"I have a question. What was that small glass ball you used earlier?" I ask.

"Ah, that. It was a crystal ball. Old technology, made practical," Master Uphraeus says.

"How does it work?" I ask.

"You'll learn about it later, not much to be said about them, but it's not something that should concern you right now," Master Uphraeus says.

"Understood."

Master Sindra walks over to where we first entered through the portal. She rolls up her sleeves to reveal a charm bracelet, plucking one of the charms off and tossing it into the air. The charm then turns into a portal that shows the Crystal Fields.

"You should both make your way back to your rooms. No one should see you here so it shouldn't draw any suspicion," Master Sindra says.

"Do be careful," adds Master Uphraeus.

Jessie and I walk up to the portal and Jessie walks in first. "Charlie."

I turn back to Master Uphraeus.

"If you remember anything. Let me know?" Master Uphraeus says.

I nod. "Sure."

I step through the portal behind Jessie and the portal closes.

———

I walk Jessie to her dorm and proceed to walk back to mine. I dig into my pocket and grab the small crystal ball Krain gave me. Holding it in my hand, I find myself thinking about what Krain said about helping me. If Krain isn't lying, if he's telling the truth, then maybe he can help me. Master Uphraeus said himself he doesn't know how to help me, but Krain has been studying echoes for years. There might be a cure for me, or at the very least, there might be a way for me to help me live just a bit longer.

"Krain?" I say.

I tap the crystal ball with my finger, hoping to make it glow or turn on or something.

"Krain? Is this working?"

A dim light appears in the middle of the ball.

"Hello, Charlie. Have you given thought to my offer?" Krain's voice says, through the ball.

"I have."

"And?"

"What do I have to do?"

XIV

"Sounds like you know as much as Master Uphraeus does. Which, by the way, isn't much," I say.

Master Krain is sitting across from me at a long table. I can tell by the craftsmanship that none of the furniture in this place is cheap, which means Krain either has a lot of resources or he's good at getting what he wants. He ported me here after my classes today.

"I have much more than just theories, child. The shard I used to call you to meet me last night is proof enough of that," Krain says.

He stands up from the table and walks over to a large round table, with runes carved into the top and sides where the table is rounded off. He gestures for me to come forward.

"Echoes are intricate things. They have a way with sorce that I've not seen in any textbook, article, scroll, or historian's archives. Do you know why I called them 'echoes' in the first place?" Krain says.

I shake my head, watching him as the runes on the table shift and turn. Krain motions with his hands for the runes to rise up. As they light up, the runes project a representation of the world.

"This world is in shambles. Has been for quite some time. When I was your age, I had dreams of becoming a great Master, a Legend even. One who solved many of the world's problems and did it with other likeminded individuals," Krain says.

The projection of the world slowly decayed, rivers dried, forests burned, and then restored itself.

"What changed?" I ask.

"Nothing. That's still my goal. I've come to realize that I can't do it through good will alone. I may become famous or infamous. Hailed as a hero or a tyrant. But one thing I will be known for is creating order in this world."

"So where do I, and or Echo, come in?"

With a wave of Krain's hand the projection morphs into a polyhedron made of black stone that shines like glass. floating just above the top is a crown made of white mist, with a gold jewel in the middle.

"Are you familiar with this?" Krain asks.

"Doesn't look like anything I recognize."

"Tressia's Tomb; the origin of her legacy. Tressia ruled over her own nation from this base of operations. It is massive in size, holds her army of the dead, and acts as a beacon for her crypts. When Tressia fell, her tomb was displaced into fragments, making sure her tomb wouldn't be used again."

The polyhedron split into diamond shaped pieces then became highlighted points around the globe as the world reappeared.

"What a statement: *If I can't rule, no one can,*" I say.

"Her will was absolute."

"Her spite more like it."

"The fragments were fought over for the better half of a century. When her rule ended, the first Sorce War began. The Sorce Wars created chaos. Different nations and tribes across the world sought the shards that Tressia's Tomb left behind in hopes of recovering their power."

"I thought the Sorce Wars started because of the Cataclysm?"

"The Sorce Wars *caused* the Cataclysm."

"Why does history tell a different story?"

"The fragments of Tressia's Tomb were found by different Alignments, yet none of them could use the fragments. People thought that they could be used to gain some semblance of her power, but the shards had no real power of their own. Some collected multiple fragments, yet they did nothing."

As Krain speaks, the projection of the fragments dance around the air.

"There was a temporary truce between all the castes and Alignments who'd collected the fragments. There was no need in the senseless killing if there was nothing to be won," Krain continues.

"So, let's all come together and figure out what it does, then decide if we should keep killing each other. Sums it up?" I suggest.

"You see it, right?"

I nod.

"They gathered the shards, and began experimenting on them. Without any prior knowledge of Tressia's real power, the fools caused a reaction from the fragments that created what we know today as the Cataclysm. After that, it was agreed among the new leaders that they would destroy the fragments to stop it from happening again. They couldn't destroy them, so they separated and buried them."

"That doesn't sound like it'd end well: We're going to bury something we don't understand that has immense power. Judging by the way this story goes, I'd imagine someone wasn't happy about it."

"You're catching on quickly," Krain smirks.

"Look, I might not be the best Apprentice, but that doesn't mean I'm slow."

"I'm starting to see that. Glad to know you stand with me now."

"The history lesson has been nice and all, but what does this have to do with today, me, Echo, and you?"

"Many tried to keep what fragments they had, but they were quickly disposed of along with their fragments. This continued the Sorce Wars until all the fragments they were aware of were gone. After the Cataclysm is when echoes started rising in myths and folklore."

The projection of fragments on the table morph into crude artistic depictions of echoes. Some painted on intricate vases, rocks, paper, or clay. Each one displaying a person with a shadow behind them that looks wicked in nature and resembles them in some way.

"I believe that the fragments of Tressia's Tomb, the Cataclysm, and the echoes are all connected. There're too many coincidences for them not to be intertwined. Years of research point to Tressia's Tomb and its revival, but I don't think it's possible without an echo. My running theory is that Tressia was able to rule with almost limitless power because she had an echo, maybe even the first echo."

"Echo has appeared as a shadow before. He was standing behind Rhody when I first met him at the Crystal Fields," I say.

"Was the shadow doing anything in particular? What did it look like? Can you see it all the time?"

"It wasn't clear, it was almost like the spots you see after staring at a bright light for too long? I don't see him all the time, I've only seen him standing behind Rhody. I thought maybe it was Rhody doing it. Makes more sense now."

Krain's shoulders relax as he exhales in relief. He waves his hand again, changing the projection to a faceless person.

"There are steps—er, signs of stages. Some happen out of order but they usually have the same end."

Krain looks up at the projection to avoid eye contact. "They die."

"These entities seem to be tethered to their host. Making it impossible to remove them."

"Like a parasite or virus?"

"That's exactly what I thought! But, it gets trickier than that," He says.

The projection creates a human figure with a purple outline. "They are simultaneously foreign and organic in nature. Once attached to a host, it mirrors them and subtlety copies their habits, feelings, thoughts, and emotions."

The purple outline separates from the figure, positioned directly behind it.

"At the same time, they are trying to create their own sense of self, creating an image that closely resembles whoever they're attached to. It begins as a formless thing, but the closer it gets to becoming whole, the more stable it becomes. Many voices sound like one, shadowy figures become solid, etc. Then the fight for control happens and that's when…"

The purple outline fills in and becomes a separate human figure, now both the figures struggle against each other until they both disappear.

"The host dies…" I say.

"Unless, we find something to contain it," Krain says.

"Using Tressia's Tomb?"

"Oh, my boy, you're ambitious and I like that. No, Tressia's Tomb isn't accessible. The fragments have to be reforged, and there has to be a Sorce strong enough to power it. At least, that's my running theory. Which is why I've been looking for another like you. I think echoes are the key to unlocking the mysteries and power that Tressia left behind."

"You said…<another like me?>"

Krain hesitates, his eyes slowly bouncing around as if he'd just confessed to a crime.

"Yes, another. I met someone years ago who also had an echo. Sadly, I wasn't able to test any of my theories as the echo consumed his mind first, and eventually he decayed in his own conjured flames."

"How old was he?"

"A lot older than you."

"*Older?* How is that possible? I thought people died at a young age?"

"He had it for about six months. In other words—he wasn't born with it."

"So, what's your plan for separating Echo?"

"The foundations of our society were built on Tressia's reign," Train says. All nine major schools of sorce have a cornerstone that powers and protects their sorce network. These cornerstones are much like the fragments of Tressia's Tomb; created by Tressia using the same materials as the fragments, but they aren't dormant. If we can access the cornerstone on Sirrus, we might be able to use it to separate you and your echo."

"I get the feeling that the Head Master wouldn't be too thrilled to have us poking around the school's cornerstone, let alone the other Masters, and even then, I'm sure there are security measures in place to stop anyone from getting near it."

"I have many people within the Queen's Wraiths that have access to Sirrus. Getting to the cornerstone won't be a problem. All I need from you is to be prepared when the time comes. Things will move quickly, and if you want any chance of removing the echo you'll have to do as I say and act swiftly."

"Understood. How long before your people are ready?"

"Trust is a two-way street, Charlie. Though I don't think of you as an untrustworthy person I—"

"Don't trust me enough to tell me *all* of your secret plans?

"Fair enough. And I'm not too sure that—" Krain pauses, then continues. "I'm not trying to *kill* you and everyone at this school? Agreed. One step at a time then? Keep the crystal ball, I'll contact you with more information when necessary," He says.

Krain turns away from the table, deactivating it and removing the projections.

"Who is part of the Queen's Wraiths?" I ask.

"The ones here on Sirrus? I have a feeling you already know exactly who; Laurie, Rhody, Sanderon, Abigail, just to name a few. But there're more, and I'd prefer their identities remain anonymous. Uphraeus is not to hear a *single* word of this, not even the possibility of you finding a cure for your echo."

"You trust that I won't?"

"I'll trust you not to discuss anything we've said outside of this room, and you'll have to trust that I won't forget about you and leave you to die."

"Pretty grim deal there, don't you think?"

"I like you Charlie, but my patience is wearing thin," Krain says, waving a hand and recalling the crystal ball he gave me.

He holds it in between his thumb and index finger; looking at me through it. Krain paces slowly for a moment, then takes a deep breath.

"This is how we communicate. Keep it on you at all times, but don't let anyone know you have it or where you got it. Someone at your level shouldn't own one," Krain says, throwing the crystal ball back at me.

"Okay. Don't tell anyone, wait for your call. Do the others know I'm...?"

"No, they don't. Though useful as they may be, they're still children. Your...*personal* issues are sure to get in the way of the bigger picture. I do have others around to keep you in line if something like that were to occur, but I'd rather not have to use them."

Krain throws the crystal ball behind me, turning it into a portal.

"You're free to go," he says.

I turn to the portal, getting ready to leave without thinking. I pause just at the entrance and turn back to see Krain watching me.

"Does this mean I'm part of the Queen's Wraiths now?" I ask.

"Not now…but if you so choose to, you can later," he says.

I nod, and turn back to the portal. Taking a deep breath, I enter it, and instantly I'm back in my dorm room. The lights are off, the portal transforms into the tiny crystal ball and returns to my hand. As I stand there in the cold of my room, there's a silence, but a silence that feels unfamiliar. As my eyes adjust to the dark of the room, I notice a silhouetted figure sitting on my bed. Rhody? Sanderon? Maybe, Nathan? No. None of those would make any sense. Their posture is very relaxed, like they've been waiting for me. Master Uphraeus? No. Too short. They look so familiar, like I've seen them before, I know this person. My mind is racing as I stand in my room, in the silence, paralyzed by fear and fear of the unknown. I can only mutter one question:

"W-who?" I say, trying my best not to sound afraid of the answer, but failing.

"You already know." <He> says.

That voice…that voice is…The sudden adrenaline rush hits my chest like a battle-hammer. I know that voice, I know who it is, I knew the moment I saw them, I just didn't want to believe it. My throat is dry, and my eyes are moist. Is this what it feels like just before you die? Am I afraid of death?

<"You should be. It might be closer than you think.">

Hearing his voice again makes me fall back onto the floor. Immediately, I scurry backwards out into the living room. I stand to my feet, turn to look at the darkness in my room, but the dark figure is gone.

<"Charlie.">

That voice…*my* voice. Calls from behind me. I turn around, slowly. What I see when I turn around is an almost perfect copy of myself. Same height, same black curly hair, same voice, same face. It even has my smile, the smile I get when I know I've got someone by their ankles. But his irises shimmer with a subtle golden light, and his skin is much paler than mine. As if someone almost made the perfect copy…but not quite.

"E…Echo?"

<"Who else?">

His grin grows larger as he gives a slight courtesy bow, opening his arms to present himself.

"H-how? W-wh-what?"

<"Time's running out. You're getting stronger, but so am I, and now we both know what that means.">

I must be going mad. This isn't real, is it? Echo? Echo is in my head. He can't be here; he'd only be here if he was separated from me. Right? I need to take off this ring to—

<"No need in taking off the ring. Don't want Uphraeus asking questions after we just got back from Krain's and getting all suspicious. Not that he'd be able to see me anyway.">

"*Master* Uphraeus—"

<"He's your Master…not mine.">

"Are you here to kill me? Absorb my body and take over?"

<"I don't really have a choice in that matter, do I? But no, I'm not. Even if I wanted to, I wouldn't know how.">

"So then how are you here? What are you?"

<"It's ironic. You treat me like a stranger, but we've been together since we were children.">

"What?"

<"We've been together for a long time, you know? I can remember now, I wasn't conscious at the time, but I held on to your anger and anguish for years; made it more than what it was. I enhanced your existence so to speak. I started as thoughts and ideas, eventually becoming strong enough to periodically influence behaviors. I had no idea what I was doing at the time, I just…I felt so many things as we grew up.">

Echo paces around the room.

<"Then, I was just barely a whisper. I couldn't say or do much, but the best thing you could've done for me was come to this school. You've been going through it physically, emotion-

ally, and your sorce capabilities have simultaneously been improving and in complete chaos. I'll take responsibility for the chaos.">

Echo laughs.

"So, you've been feeding on me like a *parasite*? Since I was a *kid*?!"

<"I'm not a parasite. I've been helping you, as you've been helping me. At least, I've been trying to, but Uphraeus keeps getting in the way.">

"How have you been helping me?"

<"Who got us out of the tournament? Sanderon was about to kill us, I stopped him. Would've killed him and Rhody too if you hadn't put the ring back on.">

"Sanderon wasn't going to kill us, Krain wouldn't have allowed that."

I don't think Sanderon would've killed us, but if I hadn't let Echo take over what would've happened?

"If you want to continue living then why don't we work together?"

<"How long do you think that'll last? You and I have very different ways of handling situations.">

"We can make compromises. When it comes to everyday life, you can make the decisions, but when it comes to survival and fighting, that's where I come in. Sound good?"

<"You're not stupid, but you are in shock, so I'll let that slide. You handle your friends; I'll take care of our enemies.">

It's the way he says *enemies*, while staring into my soul that makes me nauseous.

"So, you're saying we're a team?" I ask, extending my hand towards him.

Echo frowns as he looks at my hand then back up at me.

<"Clever. Let's call this a temporary alliance.">

Echo shakes my hand. Though I don't feel another hand shaking mine.

"Am I the only one who can hear and see you?"

<"Unless someone has access to your mind, otherwise yes."
>

"So what now?"

<"Now? Now we wait for Krain's call.">

LAURIE
PART III

"Do you think I could borrow a few tomes from you? For more research of course. I think I'm getting the hang of some of these spells," I ask, looking through Master Sindra's collection of scrolls and books she has in her office.

Master Sindra and I have been spending a lot of time together during her office hours. She's been helping me with my techniques. Though I'm not specializing in her field, Master Sindra thinks that I can handle more advanced spells if I practice reading and writing them.

"You haven't returned the last three you took," Master Sindra says, looking at me through the magnifying glass on her desk.

She stands from her desk and walks over to me, holding a stack of papers in her hand.

"Laurie, you've been doing a lot of…research, lately. I'm always excited to see students learning, but this seems more like an obsession or, if I'm being honest, a preparation for battle."

Usually, I'm a very good liar, but that's under circumstances where I know I'm going to have to lie. Master Sindra asking that question suddenly puts me at a disadvantage. Have I let on more than I intended to? Perhaps I let something slip? No.

Master Uphraeus must've tipped her off. That wouldn't make sense either, if they knew, if Charlie had told them, I would be having a very different conversation with her or the Administration behind a fortified sorce field.

Maybe I'm just being paranoid.

"Well, our final presentations are coming up. That might as well be a battle, am I right?"

I let out a half chuckle. Smooth, Laurie...smooth. Master Sindra nods with a closed smile.

"Indeed. I remember going from an Apprentice to Protégé, it was something special. As a Sorce who specialized as a scribe I was top of my class, well, all of my classes," Master Sindra says, pointing at a small shelf with many books, scrolls, and stone tablets that looked old.

"I know, you and I are from the same city. I grew up in New Skyway, New Shelltar."

"My, I haven't been there in ages. So much has changed, I'm sure. Is the Draxolotl Pier still there?"

A pleasant, memory-laden smile spreads across her cheeks. "Yes! It's beautiful as always. I used to go there all the time with Char—with people—*friends*, all the time."

Master Sindra stares at me with an analytical eye and tilts her head to two chairs separated by a small table. I reluctantly follow her and take the seat opposite her.

"Charlie, hm? I've noticed the tension between some of my students. You and he have the most I might say," Master Sindra says, placing her small framed glasses on the table.

"I'd rather not talk about it. Please?"

"I'm curious, Ms. Barian. How did you know I was from New Skyway?"

"You're practically a Legend back home. Even the smallest accomplishment of yours is heard. At the local school they have a tribute to you. You're the main reason I chose to come to Sirrus. I always wondered why you started teaching instead of going out into the world, doing amazing things, starting a library, or joining an Alignment." I gesture at the pens, quills, and other memorabilia around her office.

"Well, I'll try to take that slight at my academic career as a compliment."

She glares at me slightly.

"I'm sorry, I didn't mean—"

"Not to worry my child, I know what you meant." She sighs.

"The headlines don't tell the whole story. I did start teaching at a young age, but there were many adventures before that. When I graduated as a Versed, skipping the Tertiary level, I was ready to take on the world! I had two of my closest friends at my side and I could do no wrong."

"What happened?"

"Me and my two closest friends, William and Bastion, decided to take on a project together. The project was to dig into more research on a myth of sorts. A sorce anomaly, if you will, that could potentially lead to a breakthrough in how we understand sorce. That's what I thought anyway. Turned out, Bastion had…other ideas, and I wanted no part in them."

"Is that how you became a Master? With the project?"

"No, my dear. After the three of us graduated, we embarked on adventure after adventure in hopes of obtaining more research. Many times, we almost died. We went from the sunsets of New Shelltar to the rains of Piquer, from the blizzards in Berixe to the capes of Bū Té'Val. In between different leads to the next piece of research, we would help around the world with burning forests, melting glaciers—floods from melting glaciers, and in some cases, we had to fight of an Alignment or two."

"It almost sounds like you three were on the road to be Legends!" I say.

"We thought we were!" Master Sindra sighs.

"We at least acted like it. None of us said it loud, but we all truly believed it. Eventually, though, Bastion showed his true colors. The lengths he was willing to go for power. The people he was willing to sacrifice for what he deemed the greater good."

"The three of us ended up in Eclipsys. Are you familiar with Tressia?" Master Sindra asks.

"The Legend? Yes! I did a whole paper on her in foundation school. I admire her greatly; I hope to one day be recognized on her level."

"Well, Bastion had thought that Tressia was somehow linked to this project of ours and figured there was a breakthrough underneath one of Eclipsys' temples. The only issue was that the temple was cursed. Without mine or William's knowledge, Bastion had recruited nearby Sorce tribes to help us on our excavation to be bait for the horrible things we found inside that wretched place."

"This…Bastion. He sacrificed these Sorces to the curses without you knowing? How?"

"We'd all agreed that it was going to be dangerous, but we had a few Fencers and Artís with us, so we covered our bases and were prepared for any situation. Bastion failed to mention at the time, that the curses in this temple required lives to break them. William and I didn't know until it was only the three of us. Then, to make matters worse, Bastion also omitted the fact that the thing we were after would cause a sorce rift and destroy the neighboring Sorce tribe's homes."

"That's awful. Who would go that far and why?"

"Bastion would. He said it was necessary to save the rest of the world. I knew Bastion always had a passion for leadership, he and William constantly bickered about it, and he also had a heart for wanting to do the right thing. The right thing usually meant creating a more violent solution to correct the wrong one. If an insect queen was mistreating her brood, Bastion wouldn't remove the queen, he'd burn down the nest."

"Did you have to…*kill* Bastion?" I ask.

"By the heavens, I didn't want to! But it was either put down our best friend, or try to save as many people outside as we could. It was a hard decision. William and I got out of the temple and we saved a lot of people. There was a Sorce there, his name was Master Ujahta. He helped us secure the tribes, and evacuate the ones in danger. That day, Master Ujahta recognized William and I as Masters. When the dust settled, Bastion was gone. We never heard from him again."

"Wow...I'm sorry about your friend Bastion. You and your friend William sound like an amazing pair."

Master Sindra lets out a small chuckle through her sniffles. "Well, don't tell *him* that. William Uphraeus is not a man who likes to relive those days."

"Master Uphraeus?! That's who William is?"

"Indeed."

"There aren't a lot of people who could've done what you two did, or made the choices you had to."

"Bastion used to think the same thing. He'd always say: *My glory shines to the next world.* It was his motto, never caught on with William and I, but he loved it. It made him and his ideas seem more esoteric. That's what I think."

"...My glory shines to the next world?"

No...It couldn't be.

"Master Sindra? Did Bastion ever become a Master?"

"No, not to my knowledge. Bastion was never a Master, nor did his name ever come up around others I've stayed in touch with."

"If you don't mind me asking, what was Bastion's full name?"

"Bastion Krain."

Master Krain...I don't believe it...

"A lovely story Master Sindra, but I should probably get going. Lots of studying to get done."

I stand to my feet and give Master Sindra a bow before turning for the door.

"Laurie."

I turn around to watch Master Sindra slowly rise from her chair. Her expression tells me she knows.

"Yes, Master Sindra?"

"Krain is a very dangerous individual. He would often intimidate or persuade people to get what he wanted. Though we chose not to, Master Uphraeus and I could've wiped his name from the scrolls of time...If he were to return, and or threaten any of my students, I wouldn't stand for it. I would protect them."

"Understood, Master Sindra. I surely hope someone like that doesn't return, ever. It would be disastrous for everyone involved."

"Indeed. Many lives would be at risk. Including your own."

"Have a good rest of your afternoon, Master Sindra."

"Be wise, Laurie."

———

I'm in my dorm bathroom throwing up, my hands shaking, and heart beating through my chest. I thought about telling Master Sindra everything, but I couldn't, Master Krain would probably *kill* me, if her story was true. Extreme measures for extreme results; this is what we signed up for. It's what *I* signed up for.

Wait...how does she know? I knew going into this we'd have to do some drastic things, but if Master Sindra was telling the *truth*, then...Maybe that's it. She must've been lying. Master Krain wouldn't kill us to achieve his goal, he *needs* us. Right? It doesn't matter, I took an oath, I made a promise, and I intend on keeping it.

———

Using the crystal ball given to me by Master Krain, I call an emergency meeting.

Concealing our identity is the first rule of emergency meetings, all of us are given masks to hide our faces. I was given the mask of a cat. Abigail, a bear. Oni, a black bird. Rhody, a vulture. Lias, a crow. Sia, an owl. Sanderon, a rat. And Krain, a bat. Each mask is pitch black with red eyes and golden antlers. The animal's faces are contorted and appear possessed.

We all must arrive alone. No one is allowed to walk through their portal with anyone, even if that person is also part of the Queen's Wraiths. If you arrive with someone else, it is assumed that you and your identity have been compromised and you will be expelled from the meeting. Though, now I assume "expelled" means killed.

We're all given half of a passphrase. No two phrases are the same, and each half is given to someone specific. Rhody and I share each other's halves, where Abigail and Oni have a separate one. You're not allowed to speak until all passphrases are spoken aloud and verified by both parties. Once all three of these checks are met and everyone is present, then the meeting can continue.

Rhody appears within the first three minutes, wearing his vulture mask.

"Death is a curse," I say, standing ready as Rhody walks through the portal.

"Curses can be broken," Rhody responds.

Rhody and I nod at each other, then take our seats. The location we're in is a circular room with chairs all facing the center of the room where the portals open. Abigail and Oni come through their respective portals next, exchanging their phrases and taking seats on the other side of Rhody. Sanderon and Lias show up after a few minutes, then Sia shows up last. For an hour, we all remain silent, waiting for Krain to arrive before I can explain why the meeting is being called. Finally, Krain arrives and exchanges his phrase with Sia.

"This emergency meeting will now be called to order. The Cat has called the meeting; Cat, you have the floor," Master Krain says.

Krain steps away from the center of the room and stands to the side. I rise to my feet and walk to the center to address everyone.

"Master Sindra of Sirrus has discovered my association with the Queen's Wraiths," I say.

"She wasn't forward with her accusation, but the subtlety in her words gave me more than enough confidence to assume that she's aware of the Bat's presence on school grounds, *and* my involvement in the matter," I continue.

Master Krain rubs his chin under his mask and nods slowly after hearing my words.

"If the plans of our order are to be completed, I motion that our plans be moved forward. Our attack should be soon, and without hesitation."

"Motion heard, Cat. Please, sit down," Master Krain says.

I leave the center of the room; my hands are visibly shaking. "Has anyone else's identities been compromised that they're aware?" Master Krain asks the room.

Everyone shakes their head no.

"This is troubling. No doubt because of Uphraeus and our fight on the ridge. I second the motion that the Cat has proposed. We'll move swiftly within the coming month. There are still others that need to be...introduced, to our cause," Master Krain says.

We all nod our heads in agreement. "What say you all?"

"Agreed," the rest of us respond.

"This doesn't put us at a substantial disadvantage, but it does make things complicated. Are there any foreseeable issues with moving forward ahead of schedule that should be made aware to the group?" Master Krain asks.

Rhody raises his hand.

"Yes, Vulture?" Master Krain says.

"Charlie; we aren't sure of his location, or if he's given up our element of surprise. I assume he's the reason Master Sindra is aware of our plans? Should we deal with him before we proceed?" Rhody asks.

"No, Charlie is not to be involved for now. I can tell you, that as of now, Charlie is a neutral party. Though I'm certain I can get him to choose a side, even if we move the window forward," Master Krain says.

I raise my hand.

"Cat?" Master Krain says.

"Master, how can you be sure of Charlie's position?" I ask.

"Let me worry about that. From this point forward you are not allowed to engage with or hinder Charlie in any way. You've all done great work so far, I'll handle Charlie and any other opposition from here on out. We have what we need to get started. By this month's end, we initiate our mission. Are there any other questions?" Master Krain says.

We all shake our heads.

"Good. Meeting adjourned. My freedom will be afterlife," Master Krain calls.

"My allegiance is hereafter."

XV

Three weeks since Krain and I spoke and I haven't heard a word from him. In those three weeks, Jessie, Mat, and Zach have had all kinds of questions. Mat and Zach have been asking about our kidnapping. Both of them want to fight someone and do some investigating. They immediately assumed Laurie and Rhody were behind it. They're not wrong, but I denied the credibility of their accusations. Jessie has been asking if I've heard or seen Krain since the incident, but I haven't told her the truth.

Classes were normal for the most part, aside from the fact that Jessie and I have been increasing the distance between Laurie and her friends. They all sit in the front row, where they've been in all our shared classes since the beginning of this semester. Jessie and I have been sitting in the farthest rows we can. Nathan including himself when he can. When Nathan can't sit next to Jessie, he shares a row with Laurie, Rhody, and the rest of their group. A part of me has thought about telling Nathan who they really are. <Another part of me> hopes they <kill him> or maybe that's Echo.

Speaking of Echo, he's been relatively silent lately and I've felt my sorce manipulation changing. I don't know what Echo's been up to, but I can tell he's been slowly <changing> me.

<Changing us.> To this day, I haven't fully comprehended that I'm sharing a mind, body, and possibly soul with another entity. I've been increasingly paranoid that he's going to take over when I'm asleep or not paying attention. Luckily, I haven't woken up in random places like people with lycan-syndrome. The thought of being a Sorce with lycan-syndrome, or something <even worse>, sends a chill down my spine.

I've noticed that <I've changed a lot> since the beginning of the semester. The training with Master Uphraeus, focusing on my studies, help from Jessie, all of it has been making me a better Sorce. I notice the small and big improvements to my abilities. <I've gotten better> at utilizing the sorce available to me and I've also gotten used to Echo's power and I can feel us intertwined in our practices. I now know the basics of elemental sorce manipulation and general enchanting, though I don't know how much that'll help in <the coming plan.>

Although I haven't heard Echo in a while, I swear I can see him from time-to-time in the corner of my eye. Walking through hallways, passing reflective surfaces, even in dreams. A different kind of fear possesses you when you see an image of yourself that isn't quite you—even if it is just for a split second. Echo and I still share thoughts, <conflicting> thoughts that don't make sense.

Sometimes in the middle of the day I'll see images in my mind, images of people in my life lying on the ground, bloodied and <dead.> I also see images of the people in my life gleefully living in bliss around me, and we're all relaxing as we watch the stars. The strangest images are the ones where I sit on a makeshift throne. Each time the only difference is the people. People are either <kneeling to me> and pledging their loyalty, or they're waiting for <their execution.>

The mental toll this is taking on me…two different people living in <my mind>…two people living in <my body>…Sometimes I think about removing myself from the equation, if I'm not here I can't see any of those dreams come true, especially the darker ones, but I know <that won't solve my problems.> But, if I didn't exist, then I wouldn't have to have these dreams...or are they visions? Either way, I don't think I'm the one to stop them or make them happen. I didn't ask for any of this, I don't want to be <like this.> If I'm going to survive, if I'm going to <beat this> thing, if I'm going to beat Echo, then <I have to fight> and <fight anyone in my way. No matter the cost.>

XVI

The crystal ball that Krain gifted me gives off a sonic ringing that pierces my ears through my sleep. When my eyes open, I see the ball shining on my nightstand. I pick the ball up and shake it, thinking that will make it stop, or answer what or whoever is calling me. I check the clock on the nightstand and it reads 1:13AM. Suddenly, the ringing stops and I hear Krain's voice on the other side.

"Charlie?" Krain's voice, through the ball.

"Yeah, I'm here."

"Good. It's almost time. You have three days until we make our presence known to Sirrus."

"Three days?" I say, rubbing my eyes as I try to wake up.

"Yes, is that a problem for you?"

"No. Just seems sooner than expected. Thought you'd wait until the students left Sirrus."

"That was the original plan, but it has come to my attention that we don't have much time. Some of the Masters are catching on to our plan. Like I said, when this begins it will move fast."

"What's the plan to get to the cornerstone?"

"Lucky for us, Sirrus is planning to make a stop to exchange its resources. The next destination is Eclipsys."

I boarded Sirrus back when it was in New Shelltar. I remember packing my things and almost not making it the last day. Laurie was packed and ready to go two days prior, but I procrastinated. Sometimes I wonder if <things would've been different> if I hadn't.

"I thought we were scheduled to stop somewhere else a few months from now?"

I throw the covers off and head towards my bathroom to start getting ready. The crust in my eyes is still fresh, and Krain is hitting me with too much information.

"This is an emergency stop. Don't be concerned with the specifics, just be prepared on day three. Everything will go smoothly. Just do as I say and we can avoid any and all trouble."

"I thought this was going to be discreet?"

"It will be. Any developments on the echo?"

I pause for a moment, arguing with <myself> on whether or not I should tell him.

"Echo has manifested as a copy of myself. In my mind. I'm not sure what it means, but I assume it's not good?"

Krain goes silent for a moment. Long enough for me to wonder if the connection is still active. "Then three days is a hard deadline. We can't wait any longer."

"Is there anything I can do in the meantime?"

The crystal ball dims and goes back to its usual glass look.

<"Krain?">

Silence.

I put the crystal ball down on my bathroom sink. Only three days left till <I can be free> of Echo. I still don't know what the plan is and it makes me wonder what Krain might actually do. Thinking about it, I don't know who Krain is—not like Master Uphraeus, apparently. I'm only half way done brushing my teeth when there's a loud knocking at my door.

BOOM-BOOM-BOOM

"CHARLIE?!"

BOOM-BOOM-BOOM

"CHARLIE ARE YOU AWAKE?"

Wait, it's almost two in the morning. Why am I brushing my teeth? Why is someone knocking at my door? It sounds like Master Uphraeus, but what in the world is he doing here at this hour? My brain is still foggy.

BOOM-BOOM-BOOM

"CHARLIE!!"

I rush to the door and open it. Master Uphraeus, Master Sindra, and Jessie are standing on the other side. Master Uphraeus clears his throat.

"Hello, Charlie. We uhm, we have urgent things to discuss," Master Uphraeus says.

"What's going on? I mean—Hi, Jessie. Hello, Master Sindra," I say, giving Master Sindra a bow.

At this moment I realize I'm standing there without a shirt, or pants on; only boxers.

"Would you all excuse me for a moment?" I ask.

Master Sindra and Uphraeus give me a stiff nod and Jessie just laughs, staring straight at me.

"You're welcome to come in!" I say, rushing through my living room to my bedroom.

A moment later, I walk back into my living room fully dressed, where Jessie sits on one of my bean-bag chairs. Master Uphraeus and Master Sindra are standing on either side of her. Before I get a word out Master Uphraeus speaks.

"We've got confirmation that Laurie Barian, and by association, her friends, are working for Krain. Master Sindra spoke with Ms. Barian yesterday, looking for any evidence and came across something interesting," Master Uphraeus says, gesturing for Master Sindra to take over.

"I told her about Krain and how I knew him. Though she remained calm, she made it very clear she was hiding something, so I placed a small artifact on one of the books she borrowed. It allowed me to track her location across Sirrus," Master Sindra says.

Keeping track of a student is a direct violation of the rules on Sirrus and could get Master Sindra fired or worse.

"I monitored her location for a few hours before she disappeared from my map of Sirrus, and ended up on my world map. That's when I saw her location had been teleported to Eclipsys. William and I had our last encounter with Krain in Eclipsys. Things are lining up too perfectly at this point, so something must be done," Master Sindra continues.

"What's that something?" I ask.

"If everything we've been assuming is right—then we have to take you into hiding, Charlie," Master Uphraeus says.

"Go <into>—? No. I'm not going into hiding. I have—"

<A splitting pain> shoots through my skull and down my spine, causing me keel over.

"*Charlie?!*" Jessie says, rushing over to me to help us up.

"<We> aren't <running. Krain> might be able <to keep us alive.>"

We say.

"What?" Master Sindra says.

"Who is *we*, Charlie? Are you talking about Echo? Is he in control right now?" Master Uphraeus asks.

"I'm here," I say.

<"What happened to we?">

Echo has never spoken to anyone else. Echo has never used my—<our body>...no *my* body to speak out loud before. <Sharing a mind>, or at the very least, sharing a body with someone else is not fun.

"Charlie, let me see the ring," Master Uphraeus says, rushing over and kneeling down to inspect the ring on my hand.

Reacting out of fear, I launch a dart at Master Uphraeus, the sudden attack causes him to fly backwards onto the floor. Master Sindra immediately creates a small sorce field between me and the rest of the group. Jessie looks at me with absolute <fear in her eyes>.

"*What* has gotten into you, child?!" Master Sindra says.

<I look down at the ring> and notice that it's slowly rotating and is glowing an unusual white and gold. Master Uphraeus rises to his feet, <still shaken from the preemptive strike.>

"Echo, I presume?" Master Uphraeus brushes off his coat.

"You're far worse than I thought. Charlie, if you can still hear me, you don't have much ti—" <He continues.>

<I'm here too. Is that a problem?>

"It's still Charlie, but Echo will apparently be joining us for the duration. <Hope you don't mind?>"

Master Sindra exchanges looks with Uphraeus. Jessie is quietly watching from behind Master Sindra's sorce field. Figures, she probably thinks we're out of our mind.

"You and Echo are joining forces now? When did *this* start?" Master Uphraeus asks.

"<Not long after the Krain incident.> Echo began projecting himself in my mind. He's become his own entity. <Now, we're working together to stop what's happening to us.> It's a means to an <end.>"

"You do realize, that this means any day now, you will consume each other and neither of you will exist? What is your plan here, boy?" Master Uphraeus asks.

"Maybe we should all take a deep breath and calm down. We're here to help you Charlie, not put you in a cage," Jessie says.

<Help us? They don't know anything! They can't help us even if they wanted to!>

"<Help me?> How can *any* of you help me? *None* of you even knew about this until <*we*> did! None of you have a single idea as to what can help me! <But I'll find someone who does.>"

"Charlie, the girl is right, we want to help you! William believes he may have found a way to prolong the effects. We're not sure for how long, but if we can stop it from killing you now then we can find a permanent solution later!" <Sindra urges.>

"No one else you can trust right now, Charlie. Krain is looking for you, and the fates only know what might come of you then. You're running out of time and options." <Uphraeus says.>

<"And what if I refuse?">

A puzzled expression crosses all three of their faces.

"<What if we>—I decide not to trust you, <or take Krain up on his offer?>"

We slowly back away from the sorce field to put more distance between us.

"What offer?" Master Uphraeus asks, taking a step toward the sorce field.

Shit.

"<I mean what if Krain wants to help me?> What if he removes Echo? <Problem> solved."

"Charlie, has Krain reached out to you? After that night?" Master Uphraeus asks, putting his palm on the sorce field.

"<You didn't answer my question.> What if Echo gets removed?"

"Whatever poison he's putting in your head, he's lying or has some sort of angle. He's trying to use Echo's power for himself, whether that means turning you into a puppet, ripping Echo out of you and leaving you for dead, or worse—destroying both of you so no one can have it," Master Uphraeus says.

"Well as far as lies go you're 0 and 1 to Krain. <I'm not letting people make decisions for me anymore.>"

"Charlie, whatever you feel is right, I'm with you. Please, hear them out, and if you don't like it, you don't have to go," Jessie says.

<Why her?>

"Why are you even here? What are you getting out of this?"

"They asked me to be here to comfort you, or at least convince you to go with them. I don't know exactly what's happening to you, but I want to help. I'd rather you not end up *dead*…if that's any consolation," Jessie says.

<"Comfort me? Why would I need you to comfort me? We barely even know each other. How long has it been, a few months? You're practically a stranger.">

Jessie nods and slowly blinks.

"I'm sad to hear that, *Echo*. Charlie, are you with me?" Jessie says.

"It is…me? <It's both of us.> He's looking out for me; <he doesn't want> to kill me."

"Even if that were true, it's out of his control. It must be, because if it wasn't, then why won't he let you go?" Master Sindra says.

"<Stop it!> You're trying to get in my head. I'm not going anywhere with you. Any of you." we say.

Master Uphraeus removes his coat and rolls up his sleeves as sorce energy moves around his body, giving him feline arms and legs with the tail and horns of a large horned mammal.

"I'm not giving you much of a choice here, boy; you can either surrender, or I can bring you in. I won't allow your arrogance or misconceptions to jeopardize the lives of everyone else. I'm sorry." Master Uphraeus says.

<"If you think you can stop me old man, then please try.">
Master Uphraeus looks to Master Sindra.

"Drop the field, Eve."

"William. Maybe we should give the boy some space; come back another time."

"And wait for him to signal Krain, or Krain to take him under our noses?" Master Uphraeus inquires.

Master Sindra shakes her head in disapproval before lowering her hands. The sorce field slowly fades away. Master Uphraeus still locking eyes with <us.>

"Last chance boy." Master Uphraeus says.

I flick my thumb against my rotator ring and it begins spinning both outer rings. The top ring glowing gold and the bottom ring a bright white.

<Sorce Field. Now.>

Echo advises me and I throw a sorce field out in front of me, I immediately follow with two sorce blasts. Master Uphraeus charges through and breaks my sorce field with ease, as I expected, and is hit by the following sorce blast. He takes a direct hit, but the animal cloak around his body doubles as a shield so he's unaffected.

"I believe Echo has overstayed his welcome, but I'll be sure to excuse him." Master Uphraeus cracks his knuckles.

<"How sure?">

I need to escape to a bigger area. Master Uphraeus is better at close combat, I'm at a clear disadvantage. I create two DISCs on either side of me and make a break for my room. Master Uphraeus uses his arms to shield whatever I've programmed the DISCs with and runs after me. I knew whatever attack I put up wouldn't work, so I programmed them to make anything that interferes with their connection light as a feather, causing Master Uphraeus to lose his footing and slightly lift into the air. It doesn't last long because a few seconds later I hear large footsteps coming for my room.

With no time to think, I charge my ring and with the help of Echo, we create a small feedback loop to blast my window open. I turn back to see Master Uphraeus charging through my door, so I jump through the giant hole in my room that *used* to be my window. I live on the third floor of my building, not an ideal place to escape from. Thinking fast, I try to create a sorce field around myself to brace the impact, hitting the ground and shattering the shield around me while taking most of the brunt of the fall.

I get to my feet and look back up at my room. Master Uphraeus stands in the frame of the hole and kicks the rest of the wall out, avoiding having to climb through. For some reason my first thought is, "I'm not paying for that." I take a few steps back as he leaps from the third floor onto the ground without taking so much as a scratch. I figure that's my queue to run, so I do. I run straight for the Crystal Fields since it's surrounded by a forest, and hopefully I can find a way inside and use the crystals to my advantage. I turn my head to see where Master Uphraeus is and he's gaining on me.

<"Charlie! Over here!">

I look to see myself—actually, Echo, standing and waving his hands about fifty feet away and ahead of me.

<"Come over here!">

"He's about to catch us! What're you doing over there?!"

<"There's a tether between us; grab it!">

There's a long distance between Echo and myself and I can see a faint tether between us. Reaching out with my hand, I grab the tether and feel a jolt and vibration throughout my body. Without stopping, I keep running head first into a tree that wasn't there a few seconds ago. I rub my stinging face and assume I'm caught. Looking behind me, I see a bigger gap between Master Uphraeus and me, though he's still moving fast and headed towards me.

"How did we do that?"

<*That's* my *version of* Echo Location.>

"*Your* version? Okay? Let's try that again, this time somewhere a bit further?"

<*This time focus on where the tether is taking you.*>

"Got it."

Echo appears further away, standing inside the sorce field that surrounds the Crystal Fields. I can barely see him waving his arms over his head. Duh, I don't have to *see* him, I have to look at the tether. I stop running to take a moment to focus on the tether, the sound of Master Uphraeus' footsteps closing in on me. The feeling of the tether becomes stronger the more I focus, but I can feel it fade the further away it leads.

<*You have to focus, Charlie.*>

I know.

<He's almost here. Hurry!>

It would help if you weren't screaming in my ear—or head!

<It's do or die. He's here.>

Blocking out the noise of Master Uphraeus' charging towards me, and Echo's voice, I rotate my ring to focus on the tether once more.

"I've got you, boy," Master Uphraeus says.

His voice is right behind me, and I feel his hand closing in on my shoulder. As I open my eyes, I see I'm standing in the Crystal Fields, where Echo was standing. I turn back to try and see where Master Uphraeus is, but it's too dark to see clearly.

That was amazing Echo!

<You're welcome.>

Let's keep moving. Master Uphraeus might've noticed where we ported off to.

<Why are you guessing? Use Echo Location.>

To teleport?

<To sense where he is, idiot.>

Hey, be nice!

Using Echo's advice, I kneel down to catch my breath and stabilize myself. I can sense the crystals, the sorce field, and myself.

I don't see Master Uphraeus.

<Well, he didn't just disappear.>

Maybe he teleported, with us?

<If he could do that, he would've caught us a while ago.>

Fair point. Then we should keep moving. Maybe we lost hi—

DONG!

A loud sound fills the air. I look around to see what it might be but don't see anything, I turn off Echo Location.

DONG!

Again, this time with a slight cracking sound behind it. I use Echo Location again to get sense of my surroundings.

DONG!

The sound and the wave of sorce behind it ripples through the sorce field and the ground where the field meets. I see the origin now; it's Master Uphraeus, standing on top of the sorce field and smashing it with his fists.

<We should leave now.>

Agreed.

Master Uphraeus slams down onto the sorce field from above, causing fractals in its design and cracking its frame. I begin to leave towards the South of the fields, and I notice a crystal just off-center of where Master Uphraeus is.

<We should leave…NOW!>

Hang on. I have an idea. One time I overloaded one of these crystals, I'm thinking we can use that to our advantage.

<You mean one time I overloaded one of those crystals?>

Wait, that was you?!

<It's always been me.>

Right…

I put my hands on either side of the crystal, channeling as much sorce as I can into it. As usual the crystal crackles and sparks, with light bouncing within it.

DONG!

I hear the cracking and chipping of the sorce field above about to shatter.

<Charlie?!>

Just a little bit more.

The crystal shines brightly, followed by a whining sound as it overloads.

Now, we can leave!

I immediately turn and run for the South end of the Crystal Fields. Echo once again projects himself through my mind several feet ahead of me, allowing me to use Echo Location to teleport to him. Just as I teleport, I hear Master Uphraeus break through the sorce field, the fractals ripple through, seeing the after effects ahead. A second after the crashing, I hear the crystal explode all the sorce that's been built inside with an appropriate

BOOM!!! The safeguards on the crystals make sure the blast isn't lethal, but it does knock you on your ass—I know from experience.

After the explosion I hear only the wind in the night. Shouldn't he be groaning, or cursing my name? I expected it to give me time, but I didn't think…It couldn't possibly have done anything critical…I don't see him. Did I just kill Master Uphraeus by accident?

<There's no turning back now.> I have to commit to this. How did all of this happen? How did I get here—more importantly, <how do I get out?> I've done everything I was told to do up to this moment. I've followed other people and *their* wants, *their* needs, and *their* expectations. For the first time, that I'm actually aware of—I'm making my own decisions, I'm taking my life into my own hands…<and that includes the consequences.>

I reach the edge of the sorce field on the Southside of the Crystal Fields, and take one more glance back. Master Uphraeus isn't there. I try to use Echo Location, but the only thing I can sense are the crystals. That can't be right. The blast shouldn't have killed him, at most it would've knocked him unconscious. Right? <I guess it doesn't matter, I have to go to Krain now.> There's no one else. So, I grab the crystal ball that Krain gave me out of my pocket.

"<Krain?> Can you hear me?" I say. Silence.

"Krain?"

Silence still. I still don't know how these things work.

"I'm at the end of my rope here…Master Krain if you can hear me, please get me out of here."

I collapse to my knees.

"I'm here, Charlie. I'm here." Master Krain's voice emanates from the crystal ball.

The ball flies away from my hand and creates a portal in front of me. I rise to my feet, and take another look back at the Crystal Fields. I use Echo Location to sense what's going on, and I see multiple traces of sorce gathering around the fields. No doubt the other Masters have gotten word of the incident at my dorm and have come to investigate.

"Are you ready to join the Queen's Wraiths?" Master Krain's voice comes through the portal.

<"Yes.">

XVII

Stepping through the portal that the crystal ball had opened, I shield my eyes from the light on the other side. The portal closes immediately behind me, my eyes still adjusting to the change from the pitch black of night, to the now well-lit room that Master Krain ported me to. Once my eyes adjust, I see Master Krain walking over to me, he places a hand on my shoulder.

"You're safe, son. You're here," Master Krain says.

"Where is *here*?" I ask.

Pulling my hand away from my eyes, I see the room with more clarity, I see we're in the room where Master Krain and I had our conversation about the origins of echoes. The only difference being that one of walls was half glass.

"Welcome back, to the Crypt," Master Krain says.

I walk over to the glass and see a circular room below, with about fifty chairs facing inward at the center all around, and every seat is filled with people in cloaks and animal masks.

"The Crypt? Seems pretty grim for a guy who wants to *save* the world?" I say.

"Tressia has her Tomb. Krain has his Crypt," Master Krain says.

"Poetic. Seems to be your MO."

"If pictures are worth a thousand words, then a poem is worth a million."

"I don't recognize that quote?"

"I just said it."

I nod my head, still observing the people below us. "So, these are the Queen's Wraiths?"

"Yes, and they're waiting for you."

<"They look like demons.">

<Master Krain walks over to the glass to stand next to me.>

"To conceal their identity," Master Krain says.

<"Wait. Why are they waiting for me?">

"Because I told them we would initiate our plan as soon as you arrived."

"I thought you said it was happening in three days?"

"A precaution I took, in case Uphraeus was able to capture you tonight and take you into questioning. Sirrus docks at Eclipsys at daybreak. If all goes well, we'll have the cornerstone by then and we can avoid any major conflict."

"And if all *doesn't* go well?"

"Then, come daybreak, the students will have a place to evacuate."

"Why Eclipsys? And why now?"

"It's where I'm planning on rebuilding Tressia's Tomb. The Queen's Wraiths are everywhere, including Administration."

"Master Uphraeus assumed that the Head Master was involved in your plans. So, is he?"

"No. The Head Master of Sirrus is a lazy and incompetent man who doesn't think highly of the Queen's Wraiths. That's why we're striking discretely."

"He hasn't been around much, from what I've heard. Does that have anything to do with the Queen's Wraiths?"

"We've been sending him on wild goose chases. He believes the Queen's Wraiths are setting up an ambush at a different school, so his advisors suggested he figure out the validity of the rumors while they made an unofficial stop in Eclipsys."

"I thought the attack was in three days. Everything is happening tonight?"

"To summarize it; yes."

"Intricate web of lies. If any one of them breaks, it all falls apart."

"Webs are built with purpose and reason. Lies have to be built the same way. If your lies are scattered around, they get messy, and annoying."

"Should I be writing this down?"

"Let's go down and meet the rest of the group," Master Krain says, holding out a cloak and a white bat mask, with gold fangs.

Master Krain and I walk through the chamber above, down the winding staircase, into the circular room where everyone else is seated. As I follow behind Master Krain, both of us in white and gold cloaks and matching animal masks, I look at the crowd and try to find Laurie. Everyone's eyes are on us, the room holds a chilled silence as we approach the center of the room.

"My allegiance is hereafter!" Master Krain says, from the center of the room, with myself standing to his right.

"My allegiance is hereafter!" The Queen's Wraith responds.

"The wait is almost over. Tonight, we strike against Sirrus, to capture the cornerstone and begin the finalization of Tressia's Tomb," Master Krain says.

The crowd claps in unison.

"With our newest recruit to the Queen's Wraiths, who bears the mask of the golden bat, he shall unlock the cornerstone from its position, and guide us through."

The crowd claps once again. "Everyone knows their parts?" The crowd nods in silence. "Good!"

Master Krain leans over and whispers in my ear. "Would you like to say anything?"

I just got here and I feel like I might've just joined the most dangerous cult in the world, on top of killing my favorite Master, which means the best-case scenario is that I'm a Sorce on the run for the rest of my life.

<"Failure. Is not an option!"> The crowd claps and cheers.

"Well done, my boy." Master Krain pats me on the shoulder. "You heard him! Tonight! Our kingdom will come of age!" Master Krain says, waving his hand outward toward the crowd, releasing crystal balls that fly to the back the rows of the room, opening portals.

Everyone rises from their seats, leaving out through the portals created by Master Krain. Everyone except two people, the Vulture masked person, and the Cat. Standing next to each other.

"Is there a question?" Master Krain asks. The Vulture points at me.

"Why him? I was supposed to be the one to wear the golden bat, not Charlie!" It's Rhody's voice.

Master Krain whispers into his fingertips and reaches out to Rhody, lifting him in the air and restraining his hands and feet.

"It's that *ignorance,* that *arrogance,* and that *incessant need* to be more than you're capable of, that holds you back. Give me *one* good reason not to remove your mask and give it to someone else!"

An ethereal pair of purple tendrils creeps around Rhody's neck, choking him, causing small breaths to leave his lips. The Cat, who is has to be Laurie, raises her hand immediately.

"Speak," Master Krain says.

"Master, please, forgive him. His devotion to the cause is the only reason he seems irredeemable. But I can assure you that he knows his mission, and he'll carry it out without question," Laurie says.

Master Krain looks at Laurie, then Rhody, and finally at me. "What say you? Does the Vulture live...or is he too much of a problem?" Master Krain asks.

<That kill…is mine.>

"He…should *live*? I'm not sure we have the resources to spare? And…despite his…*overeager* nature, he's still a decent Sorce," I answer.

Master Krain then releases Rhody and his body falls to the ground. Laurie rushes to him to console him, but he pushes her away and stands to his feet. Though his face is covered by a mask, <we can feel the look of resentment coming from his posture and breathing.>

"He's right; we don't have the people to spare. Which equally means that we don't have room for mistakes Get to your positions and execute your part of the plan as instructed. No more, no less."

"Yes, Master Krain," Laurie says, urging Rhody to come with her.

Laurie walks down one of the aisles towards the last open portal. Rhody stares at Master Krain and me, no—<he stares at *me*.> I can feel <the tension and rage building in him.> After a moment, he turns and follows Laurie down the aisle through the portal, leaving Master Krain and I alone in the chamber.

"He's going to be a problem for you," Master Krain says.

"He'll only be a problem for himself. <His style of combat is nothing compared to mine.>"

Master Krain gives a small chuckle.

"If my informants are even slightly accurate, you don't have a specialization, let alone a style," Master Krain says.

I don't have a specialization, <but I've been working on my own style.> Styles are a Sorce's crutch, when all else fails your style is the only thing you have to rely on. Although, a style can only help you for as long as your opponent doesn't know or understand it. After that, your style becomes a weak point in combat.

"True; I haven't really learned much about styles. I'm still just an Apprentice, so combat isn't something we've covered.

But, if you need me to explain the history and fundamentals of sorce to save your life, I'm your guy."

Master Krain has his secrets, and I have mine.

"I'll keep that in mind," Master Krain says.

Looking around the room, Master Krain opens another portal in the center of the room.

"Let's begin our part of the process. Stay close to me, and do as you're told. With a bit of luck, we'll have you cured in no time," Master Krain says.

I'll find *a way to free us both, Echo.*

<*What if you can't?*>

I will, I promise.

<"Where are we going?">

"This portal leads to the courtyard. From there, we'll enter the Head Master's chambers, and find out where he's holding the cornerstone," Master Krain says.

Master Krain and I walk through the portal. We reach the other side at Sirrus, arriving in the main plaza, where most ceremonies happen. Wind blows steadily, not too strong, but still enough to give a calming yet stressful silence. The courtyard is made of extravagant marble with lights that float around tall pillars. The pillars stand almost as a gate leading up to the main doors of the Administration building. It's only a couple hours after midnight, so it's still dark throughout the island. Master Krain walks out in front of me.

"Come," he says.

<I follow him through the courtyard, his pace is steady but slightly faster than mine. As we approach the steps, the main doors open. Master Krain holds his hand out to the side, telling me to stop where I am. Three people step out, wearing Masters' robes and tunics, dress that is commonly only worn during large events...or battles for distinction between sides. Sirrus has a specific crest that its Master's wear, designed into their clothing. Usually, close to the crest, is a sigil of their caste; Sorce, Artí, or Fencer.>

Master Krain's hands light up for a moment, until the three Masters are only a few feet away from us. Standing in the middle is a Master Fencer, standing on his left is a Master Sorce, and on his right a Master Artí. The Fencer draws a deck of metallic cards from his tunic, the Artí takes a stance with large beaded bracelets on each wrist, and the Sorce ignites his fingertips.

"Hello, friends! What seems to be the trouble?" Master Krain asks, cheerily. Master Krain moves in front of me.

"Masters of Sirrus don't usually wear masks, and your robes don't look familiar," the Master Fencer says.

"You should've been alerted of the incident; a curfew is being put into effect for students, and Masters should be searching their respective areas. What caste and area are you from?" The Master Artí says.

"Incident?" Master Krain asks.

"There was an attack at the Crystal Fields involving an intruder and Master Uphraeus." The Master Sorce moves his head to look at me behind Master Krain.

Master Krain looks over his shoulder and back at me.

"Really? I wasn't made aware of any incident. I assume this message came through our crystals?" Master Krain asks.

"Yes, your crystal should've relayed the message from the Administration. Would you mind handing over your crystal and telling us who you are?" The Master Fencer holds out his hand.

The Sorce Master and Artí Master move to position themselves at our flanks.

"I don't have it with me at the moment. Perhaps I could retrieve a temporary one in the meantime?" Master Krain shrugs.

"How about you two take off your masks, and identify yourselves first?" The Master Artí says.

"And then answer my question; tell us who you are." The

Master Fencer's cards move around him and meet at eye level with Master Krain.

"Well, I wish we could've used a more diplomatic way around this, but what can you do?" Master Krain says.

In a swift motion, Master Krain grabs the cards in front of him and creates a sorce field blocking the immediate counterattack from the Master Fencer's remaining cards, and the Master Sorce's detonation blasts. At the same time, the Master Artí who is standing closest, targets me with his beads and they swarm like insects. I try to shield myself with a sorce field but the beads break through immediately, pelting me in the chest, blowing me backwards and then moving around to tie up my wrists like handcuffs, suspending me in mid-air.

Master Krain notices my ongoing predicament and throws the cards at my bindings, cutting me free. While distracted, the Master Fencer uses his cards in a full stack to puncture through Master Krain's sorce field, allowing the Master Sorce to use the cards as a tip to a spear and launches an enchanted pole right behind the cards, shattering the sorce field.

<Well, all of that is what would have happened. If Master Krain and I were actually still there. The moment Master Krain's hands started glowing, a wall of illusion was cast, I wasn't sure what was happening as my vision had a slightly tinted color to it. Master Krain slowly stepped away and pulled me off to the side. Adding me to the illusion allowed me to see what was fake and what wasn't. I saw a version of Master Krain and myself standing in our places that looked tinted in a dark blue. As the conversation began between the illusion and the three Masters, Master Krain and I walked past them, up the side of the long steps.

It looked as if my copy was going to get Master Krain's copy captured by not even putting up a fight. I'm not sure if that's to sell the illusion or drop their guard. Perhaps both? As Master Krain and I reach the top of the stairs, he turns around to observe the ongoing struggle. They're still trapped in the spell, but the Master Fencer is about to reveal it.>

"Now, let's see who you are," the Master Fencer says, as he pulls off the mask of Master Krain's copy.

It reveals a faceless man. "Copy-trap! Ru—"

Before the Master Fencer can finish warning his colleagues, both illusions of myself and Master Krain explode in a bright blue flame, killing all three Masters instantly. Their bodies scatter on the newly scorched steps.

"Well, that didn't go as planned," Master Krain says.

"Y-you d-didn't mean to k-kill them?!"

"No. I'm talking about you getting into a fight with Uphraeus and alerting the whole Administration about our presence," he says with a glare.

Still looking at the bodies of the three Masters, I open my mouth to respond, but I can't. Three Masters are dead...now... Master Krain killed them, because of me. No. He killed them because he wanted to. He didn't have to. I flinch as Master Krain grabs my shoulder.

"They didn't give us a choice. It was them, or you. If we don't find that cornerstone, you'll end up just like them. Most likely worse," Master Krain says, tilting his head towards the bodies.

"Couldn't you have—"

"We don't have time to argue. I'll be taking you to the cornerstone, with or without your conscious consent. Let's move."

Master Krain moves past me and through the giant doors into the Administration building. I stand there, staring out into night sky, wondering what I've done. What I signed up for, how things got here, if I'm going to survive, and what life would it be? Suddenly, I feel a gripping sensation around my body and neck. It pulls me through the doors, and they violently shut.

"I won't ask again, boy. Move," Master Krain says.

<In that moment, I realize that this is no longer a mutually beneficial relationship. This only ends with Krain getting what he wants at all costs.>

<"Yes, Krain.">

XVIII

"Queen's Wraiths; now is the time. We're inside the Administration building." Krain gives instruction to his crystal ball.

"Master Krain, they've already begun sweeping the school for intruders. It looks like they may be headed towards you after that flame in front of the building," Laurie's voice says from the crystal.

"Yes, sadly our presence was revealed before we got here. Everyone, keep the other Masters at bay while we search the building. The only thing that has changed is the amount of time we have, everything else remains the same. Understood?"

"Understood."

"Roger that."

"My loyalty lies in the great beyond."

"Heard."

"For the Queen's Wraiths!"

"We serve in death!"

"My allegiance is hereafter!"

Multiple voices confirm Krain's commands.

"The Administration building is where the Head Master

conducts most of his business. Luckily, without him here, it's one less obstacle," Krain says.

"So, we're headed to his office?" I ask.

"Perhaps. Though I'm sure something as secure as the cornerstone won't be above the surface of the island," Krain says, looking around the interior.

The ceiling is forty-feet tall with pillars positioned along the walls. There's a circle in the center of the room, with different colored stones and symbols engraved on top. Krain looks at the ground, touching it with an open palm.

"Do you know what an illusion is, Charlie?"

Krain stands to his feet and points up. Both of us recline our heads to see a giant, beautiful, and powerful looking object. A triangular shaped thing, suspended in the air, giving off what looks like fog and radiant light.

"Is that the cornerstone?" I say.

"No. It's fake. Something that big and powerful, yet you don't *feel* anything do you?"

Strange, I *don't* feel anything. Sorce on that scale should give off *some* presence.

"Illusions aren't what you're seeing; it's what you *aren't* seeing. Not opposite the truth, but...inversions," Krain says, looking up at the fake cornerstone suspended in the air.

He moves to the center of the room right underneath the not-cornerstone. Looking down at the flat ground, Krain weaves his hands around, as if using them to feel the air around him. He fires a bolt from his fingertips, into the ground, revealing an unrecognizable crest hidden in the architecture.

"This is it. Use Echo to overload the lock here," Krain demands.

<"What? Why can't you do it?">

"You see that crest?"

<"Yes?">

Krain opens the top of his robe, pulling off the right side of his runic underneath to show part of his chest. A smaller version of the crest is tattooed on the right side of his chest, the ink giving off a gold and green shine.

"It's the symbol of the Queen's Wraiths," Krain says.

"H-how deep does…all of this go?" I ask.

"I told you; Tressia built the foundations of everything we know today."

"How am I connected to all of this?"

"Whatever this lock is, I'm sure you can figure it out."

I reluctantly walk towards the center where the crest is, cursing under my breath. Placing one foot steadily on the tiles, a shock zaps my foot.

"Ow! This thing is rigged, what if it kills me?"

"It's not going to kill you. If you're quick enough."

"I'm assuming at this point that I don't have a choice?"

"No. No, not really."

"And here I thought you were reasonable man."

Okay, let's do this Echo.

<I don't like him.>

You don't like anybody.

Pushing my hands down onto the crest again, gritting through the pain of the crest fighting back, my hands start to go numb and I feel the energy moving up my arms as small vibrations. Echo creates a feedback loop, eventually causing us to match, then surpass the output of the crest itself and cracking it in half. Feeling the overwhelming amount of sorce coursing through my body, I have a split-second thought of using all the excess energy and blasting Krain with it. Only problem is that he hasn't brought me to the cornerstone, and knowing him, he's probably expecting it anyway.

Taking the ring, I aim it at one of the walls and expel the energy outward, destroying half of a pillar and cratering the wall behind. I look at Krain, and he nods in approval before vanishing into a mist. It was an illusion. Krain walks over to me and the now broken crest on the ground from the opposite direction.

"I wasn't sure if you'd try using the that charge against me, so I took a small precaution," Krain says.

<Figures.>

"Good to know we still don't trust each other," I confirm.

Krain waves me away from the crest and I move to let him examine it. Brushing away the chipped pieces, Krain pours his own sorce into the crest, causing a reaction of light throughout the floor. The ground beneath us turns into a marble iris that begins to open one section at a time. The transformation turning into a large winding staircase leading underneath the building.

"Now, the challenge begins," Krain says.

I follow Krain down the winding stairs, both of us holding lights in our hands to see the way. The darkness below us appears limitless. Our lights only reveal what's right in front of us. As I look back to see how far we've traveled down the stairs, I see no light from the top; only the last few steps I passed. As we continue, Krain's crystal begins communicating.

"Master Krain, we've reached the main building," an unrecognizable voice says. "But Masters from Sirrus have caught on to our positions. Many of us are caught in battle. This is going to turn into a bloodbath, *very* quickly. We're trying to establish a stronghold on the building, but it may not happen as expected. What should we do, in case of failure to protect the building?"

"There is no contingency. You all succeed, or you fail. And if you fail, you'll answer to me, and unlike Sirrus, I don't take prisoners," Krain says.

"Understood," the voice responds.

Krain and I make our way and find ourselves at the end of the stairway. Our only option moving forward is a long hallway, lit by white flames that stick loosely to the walls. Krain pulls a small artifact from his cloak and whispers into it, then throws it down the hallway. The artifact bounces and dings across the floor. A moment passes before a single hole appears from the ceiling of the hallway where the artifact lands, and blasts it with an unfamiliar gas.

"Hm. Rigged with enchantments and traps. That artifact was supposed to disable all of them, but I guess there are some that won't trigger so easily," Krain says.

"Maybe I can figure this out," I say, stepping into the door frame.

"What exactly are you going to do? If you die in this hallway, everything we've done will have been for nothing," Krain says.

"Just, don't distract me."

Krain takes a step back and remains silent. I look around the hallway; nothing out of the ordinary. I create a DISC sending it a foot in front of me. Then I use Echo Location, the one that allows me to sense sorce in the area. I'm almost overwhelmed by the amount coming from the double doors at the end of the hallway. I've never felt that much power coming from a single place. In my mind's eye I can't even see what's beyond the door, only the intense outline around the hinges, top, and bottom of it's frame. Using a tether to the DISC, I get a sense of the other spells and enchantments that might be ahead of us. There are a lot of traps, but it's hard to tell what they are, or how strong they are.

"The cornerstone must be on the other side of this door," I say.

The ground beneath us begins to tremble and shake. It sounds like the rumbling of a thunderstorm above us.

"Master Krain, we're at the Administration building, but many of us have had to retreat or have fallen! They've countered every move we've made! Someone must've tipped them off!" A voice cries out from Krain's crystal.

I wince at the thought of Krain blaming me for everything going wrong. I look back and see Krain staring at me as he continues to listen to the voice coming from his crystal. It wasn't me, was it you, Echo? <How would I have done something without you knowing?> I don't know, that's why I asked.

"WE'LL HOLD OUT AS LONG AS WE CAN! MY ALLE-GIANCE IS HEREAF—!" The voice cuts out.

<He never planned on helping. He's going to kill us both, or trap one and use the other.>

Or trap one and kill the other. My bet is that you're the one getting trapped.

<No. I'll kill him. We can do it right here. I won't let him! I don't like this. Laurie is up there. Right here, right now. I'm going to kill him, and everyone on this damn island. She needs our help. LET ME OUT!! We're not afraid! This ends NOW!>

A shrieking pain crawls up my spine, to my head. I can feel my body start to ache all over as Echo's thoughts pour and mix with my own. I no longer can tell which one is which, and his emotions blend with mine; <anger>, fear, <vindication>, anxi-ety, <betrayal>, grief.

"Echo, stop!" I scream out loud, holding my head.

"What is it boy? What's the echo doing? Is it taking control? Has it fully matured?" Krain asks.

Echo. I can't do this right now, please, I need you to calm down or we're both going to die down here.

<Let's go. I'm tired of his presence, his arrogance, and lack of respect for either of us. Especially me. Use Echo Location.>

"I'm fine, Krain. Just a bit of a head rush."

Standing to my feet and brushing off my clothes, I look down the end of the hall and see Echo. The projection of him is only in my mind, so Krain is unaware. A tether begins to mate-rialize between me and Echo, letting me visualize where I'll be teleporting.

"Well then hurry up and get us through this hallway. Laurie might not be alive when we surface, if we don't hurry," Krain says.

Echo and I lock eyes with each other, neither of us pleased by that comment. The tether couldn't be any clearer. I grab onto it and just like last time I feel a wave of vibrations through my body, but this time is much less horrible and feel like Echo and I were in sync for once. On the other side of the hallway standing in front of the door, I slam a charged fist into it to crack it open.

"How the hell?!" Krain gasps. He stands where I left him on the other side of the hallway still loaded with traps. "How did you…? Get me to that side now!"

"I'll find the cornerstone. Without you," I say, walking through the door.

In the next room is a person standing in front of a giant tetrahedron shape that resembles the image that Krain showed me of Tressia's Tomb. The white and gold light emitting from the shape lights the entire room, barely allowing me to see the face of who's standing there, but there's no doubt. The broad shoulders, the height, the pointed beard and formal dress, and the frame of his glasses.

"No way…" I whisper under my breath.

"Hello, Charlie," Master Uphraeus says. "Come to your senses yet?"

I break out into a sprint and rush Master Uphraeus. He grunts as my head hits his chest pulling him into a strong hug.

"I'll take that as a, yes?"

"I'm so sorry Master, I thought I killed you. I thought I was protecting myself. Now there's three Masters and—"

"HA! You thought you could kill *me*? Not on your life son. Save your breath. I've had time to think about what's been going on. I'm just glad that I didn't have to knock you around when you came through that door."

"How did you know? How did you get in here?"

"By the Legends, my boy. You're terrified, aren't you?"

Master Uphraeus looks at me. I let go of him and he taps the sides of my face a few times, knocking the tears on my cheeks off.

"It's good to uh…good to see you too," Master Uphraeus says.

Wiping the tears from my face and clearing my throat, I straighten my shoulders and give a quick nod to my Master.

"After you gave me the runaround, I figured Krain had gotten to you and the only thing that would be of importance was the cornerstone here at Sirrus. I haven't pieced it all together, but I had a hunch. Since Krain and I used to be partners I figured the cornerstone is where he'd be headed. I'm the one who tipped off the Administration and set up this plan."

"It was you! Oh man, I thought Krain was going to blame *me* for his plans going sideways. He's on the other side of the hallway. I assume he's trying to figure out how to get past the traps as we speak. Something about the cornerstone and Echo are linked. I don't know how or why, but that's Krain's theory," I continue.

"Hmm. It is a powerful relic, though I'm not sure how the two are linked. What were Krain's plans after you got here?"

"Do you hear that?"

"Hear what?"

The same sound Krain used to get me to find him on the cliffside of the island starts coming through the cornerstone. Calling to me, like a familiar voice.

<"It's asking for me…to come home?">

"Charlie, you're bleeding!"

I break my gaze from the cornerstone to look at Master Uphraeus. I feel the slightest bit of moisture on my lips. Wiping it away with my hands, I see the smeared blood coming from my nose. I hear a loud whisper come from the cornerstone that calls my name. I look back at the old relic that seems to be pulsating now.

Charlie. It whispers again.

"Laurie?" I call out to the cornerstone.

Charlie, come to me. Let me take the pain away.

It sounds like Laurie! Is she trapped inside, or calling to me from the cornerstone to find help? <She's in trouble. I have to help her; I have to try.> A sudden tug on my shoulder pulls me back, breaking me out of a trance. My hand is out, just couple feet away from touching the cornerstone.

"Charlie!" Master Uphraeus shouts. I turn back to look at him.

"What?"

"Charlie, whatever is happening I don't want you near that cornerstone. It's too dangerous to—"

A shrieking scream fills my ears.

<GRAB THE CORNERSTONE!>

A sudden explosion blows open the door leading to the hallway, distracting me from the strange voice inside my head. Two silhouettes enter the room through the smoke and dust. Krain and Rhody are now inside the room with us.

"William," Krain says.

"Bastion," Master Uphraeus responds.

"If you hand over the boy and the cornerstone, I'll give you a head start to run before I kill you," Krain says.

"Very funny, I was going to tell you the same thing. Except I was going to tell you to leave the boy and the cornerstone alone," Master Uphraeus cracks his knuckles.

"Grab the boy, I'll handle Uphraeus." Krain gestures for Rhody.

"Yes, Master Krain," Rhody says.

"And don't kill him, unless absolutely necessary. It would be a pain to kill him before having the chance to extract Echo," Krain says.

"You son of a bitch! You were going to kill me and take Echo?!" I shout.

I watch as Rhody slowly makes his way towards me.

"I told you I'd save you from Echo, I didn't say you'd survive," Krain says.

"Pretty dumb to—" I stop.

Remembering how Krain got us into the Administration building, I instinctively shut up and use Echo Location to get a sense of the sorce around me. There should only be five points: The Cornerstone, myself, Master Uphraeus, Krain, and Rhody, but I sense seven points in the room.

"Illusions!" I shout to Master Uphraeus.

I immediately throw a sorce field out in front of me, just barely blocking Rhody's electric attack.

"I knew Master Krain made a mistake, letting you join the Queen's Wraiths. You're a piece of shit, you know that? That's why Laurie left you," Rhody says.

Rhody is simply trying to get me to overreact and lose any sense of tact by making me emotional and angry...one out of three worked. Dropping the sorce field, I throw darts and bolts at him, forcing him on the defensive. Rhody responds by casting his own sorce field; blocking my attacks. Just like before, Rhody uses a spell to cover his body in that glitterscale armor he used at the Sorce Games. Rhody lets out a cocky, high-pitched laugh that pisses me off even further.

"I've been waiting for this; I've made some improvements since our last fight. I knew I should've killed you at the tournament, now I have a chance to do it slowly," Rhody says.

<Charlie.>

Yeah, Echo?

<We're probably going to die soon.>

Yeah, I can feel it too.

<Then before we go. Can we work together? Just this once? To show this son of a bitch what we can really do?>

Funny thing is, I was about to ask you the same thing.

"You're right, Rhody. Krain did make a mistake letting me join the Queen's Wraiths. You're all insane and joined a cult for power. Laurie did leave me, for reasons I'll probably never understand. But I'm doing just fine without her, and I have a goal now. And if you didn't want to die here tonight..." I say, pulling my rotator ring off of my finger.

<"You should have killed me at the tournament.">

Normally when taking off the ring, I feel a surge of pain and noise in my head. Not this time, this time all I can feel is a harmonization between me and Echo. The sorce coursing through my veins, ready to burst. Rhody charges at me, holding a lance made of lightning aimed right for my head. Rhody plants his feet onto the ground and leans in for the thrust, stabbing into a small sorce field I created. I grab the lance to try and force the weapon out of his hands and we get into a struggle.

"Is that it? All this time Master Krain talked about how powerful this 'echo' person would be. Never would've thought it'd be you, or that it would be so *weak!*" Rhody says.

Rhody breaks the lance in two, giving himself more agility and momentum to throw a spinning kick at me, sending me backwards. Rhody rushes me again, throwing the two electric lances at my feet forcing me to crawl backwards on my hands.

Rhody leaps into the air, turning his glitterscale hands into scythes that ignite into flames.

<Charlie, over here!>

I see Echo standing several feet behind Rhody with a tether that links us. I grab onto it right before Rhody lands his attack, his scythes penetrating the ground where I'd just sat. Using Echo Location to teleport behind him, I take the opportunity to create two DISCs and program them quickly. I throw the first one at Rhody, but he reflexively knocks it away, plunging it into the ground next to him. I take the other DISC and place it on the ground right between my feet, then wait for Rhody's next move.

"You're a coward. A traitor. And a child playing Sorce," Rhody says.

"The only Sorce I'm playing, is you," I say.

Rhody lets out an audible grunt and lunges towards me swinging his flaming scythe-like hands at me. Moving backwards, I weave and dodge his moves, being careful not to move too far from the DISCs that are now in the ground. I use Echo Location again to teleport to the first DISC that Rhody hit, increasing some of the distance between us. Then I create two more DISCs and again throw them at Rhody. Rhody knocks each of them away, sending them into the ground around him.

"Stop running and show me what Echo can do! fight me!" Rhody snarls.

In a flurry of swings, Rhody's scythes begin shooting arcs of fire and lightning at me. I put up a sorce field and block the incoming attacks, but each arc weakens the field.

<Now?>

Not yet, Echo.

"Is that *it?!* And here I thought you'd actually gotten stronger since the tournament. My mistake. Would you like to take a minute to rethink your strategy? I'll wait," I say.

I give a mocking laugh and smug grin. Rhody clasps his scythes together fusing them into one big blade, swinging it into the ground and creating a small fissure that cracks and arcs towards me, exploding in a fury of fire, stone, and lightning. It breaks through my sorce field, a direct hit, bringing me to my knees.

"That barely even…scratched me," I say, coughing through the pain.

A little dazed, I smell copper and there's a wet sensation on my face, I wipe the running blood from my mouth and nose. Rhody slowly walks towards me with an arrogant smirk. He summons a shining red spear in his hands and twirls it around, causing arcs of electricity to bounce around the floor and the spear.

"Hey, Rhody. If you think you can finish me off before I end this. Go ahead."

I clasp my hands together, and create another sorce field around me.

"Gladly," Rhody says.

Rhody rushes towards my sorce field, slashing away at it, making it crack and distort. Except this time, I'm repairing the field as fast as he's attacking it. Rhody slashes again, the field cracks, the crack fades, he slashes again, repeat. Using Echo Location, I highlight the DISCs and their placement in my vision.

<Now?>

Almost.

Rhody continues to slash away, then brings his hands together again forming a single blade.

"Die!" Rhody says.

Rhody thrusts his blade into the sorce field and much to the look of surprise on his face, it does nothing. Then the blade slowly starts to crumble, and his glitterscale armor cracks. He tries to concentrate to stop the slow decay but all he can do is let out exhausted gasps.

Okay, Echo. Now!

<"My turn."> I hear myself say as Echo takes over.

Breaking the sorce field, I stare at Rhody's splintering helmet. I launch a dart right into his chest, knocking him backwards onto the ground. I walk towards him as he tries to collect himself. Rhody stands to his feet and attempts to launch a spell at me, but it fizzles out in his hands.

"What the hell did you do to me?" Rhody says.

<"Your sorce belongs to me now," I say, pointing at the DISCs around the area.>

The DISCs I placed have been slowly draining Rhody's sorce from him. The more sorce he used, the more they took. When Rhody made contact with the DISCs, he unknowingly created a tether that linked them together. After enough of them were setup, his output became their input, and he worked against himself.

<I extend my hands to pull the DISCs towards me. They collect in the air around me, extending their sorce and adding it to my own. My hands look just as they did when Master Uphraeus pulled me away from Rhody at the Crystals Fields. My whole body is now an intense aura. All but one DISC drops to the ground and turns to dust. The one that remains is still charged. I take it into my hand, and toss it to Rhody. A confused look crosses his face.>

<"Take it. And get up.">

<Rhody immediately understands the challenge and pure hatred fills his eyes. He knows I'm taunting him, it's a direct insult. Allowing him a fighting chance when he knows I could've ended him right there. Rhody stands to his feet, brushes himself off and crushes the DISC in his hand, taking back some of his power. He encases both arms in glitterscale, then forms his left hand into a blade. Rhody and I take our stances.

Rhody charges at me, using sorce to increase his speed, swinging his blade in a downward arc. I block with my left hand and jab his right shoulder, causing a crack in his plating.

Rhody uses a foot to sweep my leg, causing me to lose balance and almost fall backwards. I see Rhody to my right and use Echo Location to reposition myself at Rhody's flank and immediately strike his spine. Crack. Rhody snarls, spinning to counterattack, the blade pierces my left shoulder. We lock into a struggle, holding each other in place.>

"You know what the funny thing is Charlie?" Rhody says.

<Our eyes locked, his blade slowly driving deeper into my shoulder. One hand on his blade, the other on his shoulder. Rhody twists the blade again slightly, the searing pain makes my knees weak, enough to give Rhody the upper hand. He pushes forward, forcing me backwards and leads me up against a wall.>

"I don't even care about Laurie as much as you do. She was just convenient. I recruited her to be fodder for this siege. She's definitely been more useful than I thought though. She ended up bringing you here, and she's not so bad in bed either." Rhody laughs.

<Charlie is standing behind Rhody, a tether appears but I can't grab it with both my hands occupied. I feel the subtle turning of the blade in my shoulder, I'd loosened my grip as I lost focus.>

"Who are you looking at kid? Huh? Echo? Is that how

you've been porting around? You have to concentrate?" Rhody says.

<Rhody's blade begins to glow with an intense heat that slowly crawls up towards the end that's lodged into my shoulder. As the blade heats, I can smell the wound cauterizing. I scream out in pain, still trying to pull the blade from my shoulder, and also keeping Rhody from driving it any further.>

<"I've just got one question, Rhody.">

Grunting through the pain, I put all my strength into the hand holding the blade and squeeze it until it snaps in half, cutting my hand in the process and immediately grabbing the tether. Now, standing behind Rhody, I restrain his arms.

<"You want to see what I can really do? Without Charlie?">

"What the hell?" Rhody spits.

<"Hi, Rhody. A pleasure to finally hurt you...in the flesh.">

Rhody breaks free of Echo's hold and about-turns, catching a fist to the jaw from Echo. Rhody lunges in an attempt to tackle Echo, but Echo teleports swiftly out of the way and counters with a strike to his ribs.

Crack.

<"Master Krain was looking for me. Not you.">

Rhody turns the glitterscale on his arms into fl and fires several fireballs at Echo. One fireball is dodged, another deflected with a sorce field, the next taken and thrown back to destroy another. Rhody continues a flurry of fireballs, causing a smokescreen around Echo. Rhody barely standing on his feet, panting like an animal, exasperated and low on morale, looks at the smoke trying to find a figure.

<"Are you done?">

Echo's voice comes from behind. Rhody turns around to a bright palm that Echo is holding directly at his face. The blast sends Rhody to the floor, sliding across the ground. As Rhody gathers himself, Echo approaches him with slow determination. Rhody attempts to attack, blue sparks fizzle out of his hands. He shouts curses and tries again, but to no avail. The fear in his eyes is something I will cherish forever as he turns to run and faceplants right into a sorce field. Echo has him trapped.

<"You wear the mask of an animal; you're as feral as one; now you're caged like one.">

Having Rhody trapped in a sorce field, Echo shrinks it down to a size that puts Rhody on his knees. Although Echo is in control, I can feel my body getting dizzy from the exertion; blood dripping from my nose and mouth. Echo is going to overtax us, or worse, we're almost at the end of our time.

As the sorce field around Rhody closes, Echo expends our remaining sorce, causing small detonations inside the field. The confined space closing slower around Rhody makes him feel every bit of pain. <His screams of pain make the process that much more enjoyable.>

<"What mask did you wear?">

Echo casts a bolt inside the field, inflicting more pain on Rhody. Rhody's screams ended after the first.

<"A vulture, was it?">

Another bolt.

<"They reek of death!">

Another bolt.

<"How fitting.">

Echo, enough. This is torture! He's been beaten, let it go!

<"Every opportunity to kill us, he's taken. How many chances does he get before he has to die?">

If he's stupid enough to attack us again, that's his death wish, but this is sick.

<"Every moment of grief, hatred, pain, and torment he's afflicted onto you has doubled on me. I know you want him dead, I'm the only one strong enough to carry it out!">

"What...who're you talking...what's your problem?" Rhody whimpers.

<"You're my problem...">

Echo. NO!

Echo extends a hand towards Rhody, closing the sorce field

tighter around him and causing several arcs of lightning to dance around the inside, stabbing Rhody with electricity as they move. Suddenly, I— Echo, is launched sideways, hitting the adjacent wall. I assume at first that it's Master Krain coming to save his Apprentice, buy it's Master Uphraeus.

"That's enough, Charlie!" Master Uphraeus says.

Uphraeus's tattered clothes and battles scars tell me that his fight with Krain hasn't been easy.

"You're losing control!" Uphraeus says.

I look down at my shaky and bruised hands; he's right. Master Uphraeus must've knocked Echo out of control, I don't feel like a passenger in my own body anymore.

<No! We're so close! We can end this now!>

No, Echo!

<He's MINE!>

Echo assumes control over my right hand and aims for Rhody's limp body on the ground in front of us. I use my left hand to hold back, but Echo struggles with me.

"Charlie! Where's the ring?!" Master Uphraeus asks.

The ring! That's right, if I can put that on, maybe– <it won't help.> But it might– <not.> Who am I? <I'm Charlie.> No, I'm Charlie. It's me! I'm the real one. <You're the fake, I've always been the real Charlie.> That's not true, you're trying to take over my body! <It was mine from the beginning! I'm finally taking back what's mine> The ring. Where's the ring? It's lost. I see it. <Rhody dies now. > Not today.

I can see the ring, it's on the ground near the cornerstone. I can see a faint tether between me and it. I release my right hand and quickly reach for the tether between myself and the ring, teleporting me to it just before Echo releases a bolt from my right hand that would've probably killed Rhody. Picking up the ring with my left hand, I attempt to put it on, but Echo refuses to give me control, fighting with my own body to put it on.

"Charlie, how can I— " Master Uphraeus is cut off by a

sudden wave of silver mist, leaving him paralyzed and unable to move.

"L-Laurie?" My mouth is barely able to form the word.

"Charlie? What…what's happened to you? Your eyes, they're glowing…you're bleeding and…" Laurie trails off as she looks around to see Krain and Rhody's bodies lying limp on the ground.

She gasps in horror.

"Laurie…Help me. <Help me, help you.">

Laurie looks at me in disbelief. "You're not Charlie," Laurie says.

Laurie rushes to Krain's body, leaving me to fend for myself as I struggle to put the ring on.

<*Failure! Worthless. You shouldn't be alive. All this pain, and for what? You have no reason to live. Why struggle? Even if you win. You've already lost. You have no one. Everything you ever wanted; gone. You'll have gained nothing. You still lose. Give in. Don't let the pain continue any longer. What do you have to live for? This agony won't end, even if you put on the ring. It only helps…for now. Who will you be without the anguish? Charlie. Charlie. Charlie. Charlie. Charlie. CHARLIE! CHARLIE!! CHARLIE!!! CHARLIE!!!!* >

<*CHARLIE!*>

XIX

Wake up, Charlie

The voice pulls me out of my head, like being pulled from underneath the water several feet under. It's Jessie's voice. I look around the room but I don't see her. I look back at the ring and remember that she's the one who gave it to me. Looking closer, I notice there are still inscriptions on the ring, and one on the inside that I hadn't noticed but was now faded, but it clearly spells her name:

JESSIE B. ZIRDI

B?

You want to know what the B stands for? Jessie's voice echoes through my head. *Then come back so I can tell you.*

With a newfound resolve, I take a deep breath and force the ring onto my hand, helping me gain control over my body. My ring is rotating and sparking, I can still feel Echo trying to erupt and break free. Hopefully, Krain was onto something and all of this wasn't for nothing. I approach the cornerstone and try to place a hand on it, like trying to force polar magnets together, it pushes against me. I can feel Echo fighting to take back control and the cornerstone feels as if it's pulling me in.

Fine. You want out? Then get. Out.

I let Echo take partial control and the cornerstone pulls me towards it. It lets out a large pulse and lifts me into the air. I can see a tether that covers my entire body connecting me to the cornerstone. Another pulse from the cornerstone hits my body like a sledgehammer, and ripples throughout my body. A brief image in my mind appears: I'm standing in a dark room with a swarm of people. As I look, I see each person is standing eerily still. To my immediate right is Echo, staring straight ahead at something. In unison, everyone in the room kneels, including Echo.

"Krain! Noooo!!" I hear Master Uphraeus' voice in the distance.

Pulled out of the vision, I see Krain reaching out to grab me.

I reflexively put both hands out to stop him from getting any closer. By touching me, Krain is now also connected to the cornerstone.

"This power is mine, boy! Give it to me!" Krain says.

"I don't want it!" I say, struggling to pull his hands free of me.

"I'm going to change the world! There will be peace in our time! Structure!" Krain says.

Another pulse surges through me, this time I feel it ripple through my hands, traveling to Krain. Krain's eyes stare past me and towards the cornerstone, his face in absolute awe, as if looking at someone or something behind me.

"By the tomb's light..." Krain says. A single tear falls from his eye. His eyes slowly fall on me. "...You'll be the death of us all, boy," Krain says.

Krain's eyes begin to emit a harsh light, cracks in his skin like fractured glass form and glow, his grip on me tightens. A flash of visions course through my mind. I see a city of white and gold with people building and constructing tall buildings, obelisks, and odd shaped alters. Then bodies of people and the city burning, with what looks like a giant cornerstone floating above the wreckage. I see gravestones of Sorces, Fencers, and Artís. I see war. I don't understand what any of it means, but it feels like a part of me knows what's happening, or what happened, and hints of what might happen.

In the middle of these visions, I find myself in a throne room, a dark, old one that looks deserted. On either side of me there are people holding their heads down and kneeling before me. No, not for me, for a woman sitting in the throne ahead, who's looking down at all of us; at me.

"Death exists in time, but there is no time for death." The woman's voice echoes through the throne room.

"Who are you? What is this place?" I ask.

<"It's where I'm from...">

My own distorted voice responds from Echo now standing to my right.

"What do you mean?"

<"She is our queen.">

Krain's comes from my left. I jump back.

"*Krain*?! What ar—"

As I prepare to counterattack whatever Krain is thinking of doing next, both of them keep their eyes on the woman in the throne, as if I'm not even there…or a threat. I notice that Krain's voice sounds different, the same way Echo's voice is a distortion of mine. His skin is much paler, his eyes are white, and gold fissures glisten in his skin.

"Queen? You mean *Tressia*?"

All at once, the people…or things that were kneeling and bow with their heads down, and glare at me with an ocean of white glowing eyes. As if I'd just threatened to murder their families.

"*Queen* Tressia, yes," Krain says.

"What's happening here, Krain? Where did you take us?" I ask.

"No, not Krain. Only a servant of Tressia," Krain says.

At his words, Krain kneels to Tressia and the other patrons of the throne room look to her as well. Tressia sits on her throne, made of some kind of black stone or glass. She hasn't moved or said a word but her eyes are locked onto the three of us who stand before her.

"Not Krain? You sure as hell sound like him, and *look* like him, albeit less…lively," I say.

<"He's like me."> Echo speaks up.

"Like you? You mean…This is Krain's *echo?!*"

As the words leave my lips the picture becomes clear. Krain's echo and mine have the same corrupted voice, paler skin than their counterparts, and eyes that have a faint golden glow. How does Krain now have an echo? What is this place? What significance does Tressia have in this place? As these thoughts race through my head, I'm startled by the loud and sudden shock of a woman's voice filling the throne room.

"You," Tressia says, pointing at Echo.

<"Yes, Queen Tressia."> Echo says.

"I do not recognize you. Come before me."

Echo obeys immediately, take steps towards Tressia. As he approaches the first step, Tressia holds out a finger to stop him. She points the finger down, and Echo kneels without hesitation with his head bowed. The eyes of the others focus on Echo.

"How have you come to be?" Tressia asks.

<"I.. I don't know."> Echo says.

"You know who I am?"

<"Yes.">

"But you don't know where you come from?"

<"No.">

"Do you know your purpose?"

<"…No.">

"Where is my tomb?"

Echo is silent. Does she not remember that her tomb was destroyed? Have we traveled to the past or did Tressia never die?

"Your tomb is under construction as we speak, your majesty," Krain says.

Tressia's eyes dart to Krain.

"Then how many of my wraiths are lost?" Tressia asks.

Krain walks up to kneel besides Echo at the steps of Tressia's throne, pointing at Echo.

"This one may be the last," Krain says.

"I see." Tressia nods. "To not know your origins, to not understand why you have desires, to be severed from your duties as a wraith. Your pain and grief must be unbearable."

Echo slowly nods.

"Those from the other side have no concept of what my tomb can do, or what its return would mean. Empires felled should stay that way. Resurrection is a path to destruction. I will give you clarity, then you will return from here and seek out my tomb."

Tressia extends her hand, conjuring a web of golden reeds of light that surround Echo. The gold tethers bind to Echo's skin, covering his wrists and neck. Echo is pulled up onto his feet, further into the air as this transformation continues.

"Back to my cornerstone. Fulfill your purpose."

As Tressia speaks these words, she rises from her throne and casts a blinding light that forces both me and Echo through the air. Echo and I are transported to another room, with the cornerstone I touched in the center. But this room is different, it's not the same as the one Krain, Master Uphraeus, and Rhody were in. I'm not entirely sure where I am anymore.

<"I know my purpose now."> Echo says standing across from me, the cornerstone between us.

"What purpose? What *was* that? How was that even *possible*? What did she do to you, what did she show you?"

<"You have to die. Now. That's what she showed me. I thought I was fighting to occupy the same space as someone else. I was confused, misguided, and lost. Same as you when you first arrived at Sirrus. Now I know that it was you who was in my way. We cannot exist as one, we cannot exist separately, you have to die, and I have to reclaim my birthright.">

"Are you going to try and kil—"

A sorce dart is hurled at me mid-sentence, sending me backwards and crashing hard onto the floor. He's lost his mind. Whatever Tressia did to him, it changed him. Now, I don't know what he's thinking or what he plans…I don't know what he's thinking…I don't know what he's thinking! Getting to my knees and spinning on my heels, I take a defensive stance and ready for another attack from Echo.

"Once I'm dead, what do you plan to do?" I ask.

Echo walks around to stand between me and the cornerstone. This surreal moment, looking at Echo, the plague on my mind, the parasite of my soul, and crux of my anguish—is now cursed by someone else.

<"Thank you, Charlie."> Echo says.

"What?" I say.

<"Thank you. For hosting me. For giving me life. For giving into your darkest thoughts. It made me stronger; it made me better. The cost was killing you softly, silently, and indefinitely. I couldn't have done it without you. You're going to die here and live on through me. I will hold onto your memories, and take care of Laurie, even Jessie if you want.">

You know what's funny? I mean the craziest irony that couldn't be made up? I didn't even want to come to this stupid school. Sirrus? Really? Very few, if any well-known Masters have ever come from here. Its most popular thing is that unlike other schools, Sirrus doesn't have a set location. It floats around the world across the ocean. That's it, it's not even in the top ten best schools. It's ranked what? Twelfth? I only came here because I didn't have any motivation to do anything else, that's the truth. I didn't want to be a teacher, I didn't want to help the planet, I didn't want glory, I didn't want *anything*. Every motivation I said I had was bullshit. I came here because of Laurie.

Looking back, I understand where Echo came from. He was right, he's been with me for a long time. Resentment, anger, frustration, fear, anguish. I fed those things over and over again, taking it out on myself more than anyone else. I felt neglected and alone, so much that I neglected myself and the seed called Echo growing inside. It grew until its thorns had my mind and soul in a grip that hurt to pull away. Now it's time to prune this thing.

I didn't feel I belonged anywhere, now I *know* my place is here at Sirrus. This is *my* school and if Master Uphraeus can teach me to become *half* as good a Sorce as he is, I'd be honored. If Laurie hadn't left me, I'd still have no direction. Now I have aim, and I'm not just going to be a Master, I'm going to be the greatest Master the world has ever seen. I never wanted anything to do with my family, now I'm going to make sure they know who I am.

Now I'm going to kick Echo's ass and walk out of here, so Jessie can tell me her middle name.

Echo approaches me with a calm and determined look, holding a sorce dart in his hand that gradually grows longer into a spear shape. I cast three darts at him and Echo deflects them easily, but it gives me some time to get to my feet. Echo launches the spear directly at my head, I take a side-step and catch the spear. The sorce made to use the spear feels strange, it glows with a mist like the eyes of the people who kneeled before Tressia's throne. I manipulate the spear and transform it into a shield. Echo forms two sorce blades in his hands and lunges at me. I parry one blade but fail to block the other before he cuts the left side of my rib cage.

<"The only thing you've been able to do is control how much of me you let out. All your strength came from me, and now that I'm free from you, you have nothing.">

Echo's blade is beginning to dig deeper into my shield. We no longer share a mind and body but he's still in my head., I can almost see the tether between us. Wait...no way...that *is* the tether! So we're still connected through sorce. Well, here goes nothing.

I grab the tether, forcing Echo to switch places with me, where he now holds the shield and I hold the glowing sorce blades. Having the advantage of shock and surprise, I don't lose momentum, and swing my free blade down onto Echo. With a forceful *crack* the shield I was once holding shatters and causes Echo to stumble backwards.

<"How did you—?">

Nope! I turn the sorce blades into a shockwave, cutting Echo off mid-sentence. No way I'm letting him think his way out of this or figure out what's going on. I tug the tether to catch Echo from falling backwards, followed by a sorce charged punch to his jaw. That felt great! That's for all the suffering I had to endure, the next kick to his ribs is for trying to take over my mind, then the sorce bolt going straight for his head is supposed to be for everything else…but he catches that one. Shit. Echo uses the momentum of the bolt to increase the distance between us.

<"Our tether?">

Echo tries to grab the wavy chord that binds us, but his hands pass through it like air.

In *Sorce Manipulation 103*, Master Uphraeus explained that using sorce creates a relationship between you and whatever you're using sorce with. These tethers are usually invisible to the naked eye, but with Echo, I was able to see them. I thought Echo Location was something I could only use with Echo, yet somehow this ability has remained without us being joined together. Echo can't use the tether apparently, maybe because it's mine? No, things that are tethered share a sorce connection, that means he should be able to use it. He can't use the tether because…

…If the tether is broken, the spell or object may disappear or lose its effect. As you learn how to control sorce you will learn to no longer need these connections and can remove them alto-gether. Luckily, only things that can manipulate sorce can use these tethers against you.

My thoughts race through Master Uphraeus' teachings, looking for answers. Echo can't manipulate sorce? As I'm trying to think, Echo charges at me in a rage that I can only describe as feral. He gets two good hits in before I counter with a sorce field to block any more attacks while I think. Echo thrashes at the sorce field violently.

<"Come on, Charlie! fight me…"> Echo's voice gurgles.

…The only things that can't manipulate sorce are things that are dead. Ms. Barian, hand down, hold your questions. Things

that are dead, inanimate, or illusions. Curses, enchantments, hexes, runes, and other sorce based utilities can be used to make these things act, but only in a way that is done by someone who made them. Only things that are truly alive can manipulate sorce.

Echo isn't alive. Echo isn't *using* sorce...he *is* sorce.

"I'm not going to fight you," I tell Echo. "I'm going to control you."

I drop the sorce field and watch as Echo seizes the opportunity to attack. He conjures another blade into his hands and swings it down, intending to slice me down the middle, but Echo stops in mid-attack, frozen. His eyes struggle, he grunts trying to move, but his hands and feet are frozen in place.

<"What is this?">

"Sorce Manipulation 103. Sorce is the essence that can be wielded through many different means." Like controlling a puppet on strings, I weave my hands around to force him to stand straight up with his hands to his side. "Sorces are users who prefer to wield it in its most raw form." I can feel Echo struggling against my hold on him. It feels like a pulsing heartbeat in my hands that reverberates through my body. He's like a feral animal wanting nothing more than to break free and make its captor pay.

"Sorce can be dangerous, as there are two ways it can kill you if you're not careful. Overtaxing: When the sorce of a person or thing is expelled beyond its limit, causing internal damage that often leads to death." I can see the look in Echo's eyes, he wants to say something, he wants to dismantle me, but I'm the one in control...not him...not anymore.

"The second one, I'm sure you're familiar with, is the one where I lost control and allowed you to almost hurt Jessie at the Crystal Fields. Overloading: When sorce is pooled or channeled beyond the maximum capacity of its container. As a result, it explodes and is destroyed."

Echo writhes as I lift him into the air, channeling sorce into him little by little. I've learned a lot from Master Uphraeus, I guess I actually *was* paying attention in class. As I continue to try and restrain Echo, I hear a word escape his lips through gritted teeth.

<"One way."> Echo says.

"What?" I ask.

<"There's only one way to get rid of me. You die.">

"Let's find out."

With one last push I launch a heavy sorce dart at Echo, which is too much. It's overloading him. Though, that doesn't have the effect that I thought it would. His eyes shined with the familiar white glow the people had in Tressia's throne room. And the cracks I saw in Krain's face appeared to be crawling across Echo's as well. As he explodes into what should be basically a sorce flare, he instead becomes a mix of silver and gold mist that screams like a twisted wraith come back from the dead. The mist swirls and becomes a face like mine—like Echo's, but more...dead...and vengeful. It was terrifying, honestly. The face slams itself into me, carrying me straight into the cornerstone and smashing me into it. The mist and I both touched the cornerstone, and my chest felt a flash of searing heat and pain that felt like I was being branded from front to back. That's the last thing I remember before everything went black.

———

"Charlie, are you okay?" I hear Master Uphraeus say.

I can hear Master Uphraeus, but I don't see anything, though my eyes are open.

"Yeah, I think so," I respond in a haze.

Suddenly, I feel arms on me, the shock is enough to make my adrenaline spike.

"Charlie!" The voices of Mat, Zach, and Jessie all cheer out.

"Thank the stars of Maethril," Master Sindra says.

"W-w-what? What're *you* guys doing here?" I ask.

The moment of surprise turns into a moment of absolute fear when I realize that these could be illusions of Krain. I try to use Echo Location, but I can't. I can't use any of my Echo abilities. I put my hands up to my face and feel the comfort of soft cloth over my eyes, and some parts of my hands and chest.

"What happened? Where am I? I was just—"

"Charlie, you've been out for a while." Master Uphraeus cuts me off to calm me down. "After you interacted with the cornerstone and Krain foolishly tried to pull you from it, he overloaded. If it was an illusion, it was a damn good one. I thought you were gone too, but I had a feeling I should wait."

"How long?" I ask.

"He was down there for half a day at least," Master Sindra says.

"Master Uphraeus brought you here to the nurse's office after the Masters of Sirrus fought back against the Queen's Wraiths," Jessie says.

Though I can't see her, hearing her voice again sends a warmth through my ears and the faintest tickle up my spine.

"Mat and I got here a couple hours ago, Jessie got here before us," Zach says.

"Honestly, we're a little mad you didn't call us in for backup sooner," Mat says.

Okay, even if these were illusions, Krain doesn't even know what Mat or Zach sound like.

"I'm not sure where Ms. Barian or Mr. Smill went, but they'd be foolish to show their faces on Sirrus again," Master Uphraeus says.

"So Krain is…?" I begin unwrapping the bandages when I feel a hand stop me.

"You can't take those off just yet, but here, I'll help you get oriented," Master Sindra says.

Though the bandages are still there, and I can feel them,

they've gone completely opaque, which is a very odd sensation for the skin and the eyes.

"As far as I can tell, yes. Krain is dead," Master Uphraeus says. "I can only assume the cornerstone overloaded him."

"I'm sorry," I say.

Though I'm not sure what I should say, if I should even mention Tressia, Krain's echo, or my final battle with my Echo, which felt as though it happened three minutes ago.

"We lost Krain a long time ago. Now, it's official, but we'll move on," Master Sindra says.

"That's right. This time, together...hopefully," Master Uphraeus says, locking eyes with Master Sindra.

"Am I going to be in trouble?" I ask, looking at both my Masters.

"In trouble for what? Exemplary display of courage and helping a Master defend the very foundations of this institution?" Master Uphraeus says.

"I would imagine breaking Sirrus curfew, in exchange for stopping the very man who threatened the school, may buy you a bit of grace. Not to mention the letters of commendation from two of the schools top Masters," Master Sindra says.

I'm certainly not going to investigate why my crimes stop at breaking curfew, I'll take that as a win and a 'we forgive you for being an absolute idiot' and run with it.

"Well, you might not be in trouble with the school, but as for me, you're in deep shit kid," Jessie says, with a half-smile and a couple tears in her eyes.

"Yeah, and she's in line behind us," Mat says, pointing a finger between Zach and himself.

"The fact that I'm not dead, and you guys are still here is enough of a punishment for me," I say.

Jessie punches my arm, then her Zach, and Mat laugh and hug me a bit tighter. Out of love or hatred I can't tell, but I can hardly breathe.

"Charlie, one last question," Master Uphraeus says.

"Yeah?"

"What exactly happened with you and the cornerstone? Are you…alright now?"

"You mean about?"

Master Uphraeus nods.

"It's just me. Krain was right, the cornerstone and Echo were connected in some way. I'm still not sure what happened exactly, but I do know I'll be alive for at least another year. Unless one of these three gets me killed," I say, gesturing to Jessie, Zach, and Mat.

"I'm glad to hear it, my boy. Let's give Charlie some room so he can get patched up. We've still got a month of classes left."

———

A month later, Jessie, Zach, Mat, and I graduated from Apprentices, to Protégés. A ceremony was held at each castes specific area, then a final ceremony was held where all castes witnessed the graduation of those who became Versed and were now fit to seek the title of Master if they wanted. With the end of the first semester, we all started packing our things and saying our goodbyes before it was time to move out and leave the island that we all called home for months. Everyone needed help on the last day with moving stuff. I arrived at Jessie's dorm last.

I walk up to Jessie's door and knock; her voice comes through from the other side.

"Come in!"

I open the door to see a lot of her boxes already packed. "Sorry, helping Zach took longer than expected. I thought I'd have more time," I say.

Jessie speed walks over and gives me a long hug.

"It's fine, I'm just glad I get to see you before you leave," Jessie says.

"Me too."

We linger in each other's presence for a moment before I awkwardly look around her dorm.

"Don't you have a roommate?" I ask.

The when I remember; Jessie's roommate was part of the Queen's Wraiths.

"All the Queen's Wraiths that weren't caught in the fight last month vanished. All her stuff got confiscated by the Administration a week ago," Jessie says.

"Huh, did you take anything useful before they got here?"

"Maybe a few potion ingredients here and there. I was a little nervous taking anything, seeing as though she was part of a murderous cult and all."

"Yeah, that means she had the good stuff."

"So, how does it feel not having raging psycho in your head?" Jessie asks.

"You know, I actually kind of miss him. It's weird not having him interject my thoughts every two seconds."

"*Seriously?*"

"Hey, sometimes he had some very interesting things to say. Especially about you."

"Wait, what?"

Jessie scowls at me for a moment before rolling her eyes and stacking another box.

"Are you going back home for the break?" Jessie asks.

"Nah, I don't really want to go back home."

"Well, if you need a place to stay, my parents have a guest room on Maethril. I'm sure they'd love to have you there; they've heard enough about you," Jessie says.

"That's great. I guess I owe you six now."

"Seven. I *may* have left out a few things. But! They know you helped the school recover from the damages, and that you competed in the Sorce Games as an Apprentice, and you almost won."

"I appreciate all of it, Jess, but I'm actually starting a sort of summer internship here with Master Uphraeus. I'd like to get a head start so I'm not falling behind you and the others."

"Well, if you burnout and decide you'd like a weekend to get away, the offer still stands."

Jessie finishes packing her last box.

"A weekend together? Sounds like a lot of trouble," I say, with a with a slightly nervous chuckle.

"Especially without you having Echo, there's no one to save you now," Jessie says.

"I'm perfectly capable of saving myself. If anything, Echo was holding me back."

"Sure thing, Charlie. Whatever helps you sleep at night."

I shake my head and smile as I turn to head out of the door. "I'll see you soon."

I turn to look at Jessie one last time. "Yeah, I'll see you soon."

We embrace for a hug that lasts longer than I expected, but not as long as I want.

"I should get going. I uh…I'll miss you," I say.

"Me too," Jessie says. "I mean, I'll you miss you too, not that I'll miss myself."

"Right, right. You had me worried there for a second."

The awkward silence sets in and I can't take it anymore, so I turn around and leave through the open window instead of the door. I have no idea. Don't ask. After I leave Jessie's, I take my time walking over to the Administration building, watching all of the students moving around and getting their things packed with friends or family.

Sitting at the top of the steps, where Krain and I first entered the Administration building, I look out over the school grounds and can see all sorts of mythical and majestic animals flying in to pick up the students ready to leave and get back home. Some with wings and beaks, others with scales that swim through the air, and those that you wouldn't expect to fly at all. I hear footsteps walking down the steps behind me.

"Beautiful sight, isn't it?" Master Uphraeus says.

"Yeah, I'm glad I'm staying," I say.

"Well, we won't be staying for long. I have a few errands to run, and as a start to your internship and somewhat punishment, you'll be helping me procure a few tiger-mander talons."

"Tiger-manders?! Shouldn't you get a Master to help you with something like that?"

"Well, you defeated a Master, didn't you?"

"Technically, no. It was his greed and ambition that killed him."

"You had power he wanted. I think that counts."

"Okay, and technically, I don't have that anymore."

"Technically?"

"I mean, I still have my sarcasm."

"That you do. Follow me, my boy! You're going to need a lot of gauze."

"Is the gauze for the tiger-mander, or us?"

Master Uphraeus continues through the giant doors of the Administration building.

"Or is it for me? Is it just me? Master Uphraeus?" I say following him inside.

As Master Uphraeus enters the doors, I wait back for a moment.

I open the top of my robes and stare at the symbol tattooed on my chest. It started fading in the day after I was put in the nurse's office, and stopped getting darker after a month. I don't know what it is or what it means yet, but I'm hoping I can find some answers without almost getting killed for it. Since Sirrus is docked at Eclipsys, I'm hoping my internship here with Master Uphraeus will prove helpful in my research.

Still weird, not being able to talk to Echo. That vision I saw, of the throne room still haunts me to this day. It felt real, and that woman, she said *death exists in time, but there is no time for death.* I can only imagine tha—

"Charlie, we need to get our supply list!" Master Uphraeus shouts from beyond the doors.

"Yes, Master!"

I close my robes back up and head inside after Master Uphraeus. I lost the love of my life to a cult, I made a permanent enemy, reunited with old friends and made a few new ones. Something tells me that I haven't seen the last of Laurie, or Rhody. Krain is dead, so the Queen's Wraiths are leaderless, but I'm not sure how many of them survived the attack on Sirrus. Hopefully they're all on the run, hoping to dodge any justice that should come their way. Echo said he'd been with me since I was a kid, maybe that means I'll find answers here at Eclipsys, my birthplace.

EPILOGUE

This letter is to be sent out in the event of my untimely death.

If you are receiving this letter, it means that the attack on Sirrus was unsuccessful and I have not yet found the key to utilizing the cornerstone to further our plans of resurrecting Tressia's Tomb.

Though this is a setback, it is not the end of our cause. Contingency plans are being put in place, evident by this letter. The Queen's Wraiths are strong in numbers, and our influence has been growing across the world.

It is time for our Alignment to take further action out of the shadows. In my passing, Per the chain of command, I leave Master Vokun in charge of the Western Conclave. The Eastern, Southern, and Northern conclaves will remain as they are.

Collect any survivors from Sirrus and have them recount the details. If they're still alive, Laurie Barian and Rhody Smill should be found as quickly as possible. They have key information on what we've been looking for. As I am no longer living, I cannot confirm if a student named with the gift of Echo still walks among you. If he is, he is the key to resurrecting the Tomb and only Laurie Barian, or Rhody Small can confirm this.

In the event that you find any of the three aforementioned

students, it is imperative that you notify our Alignment and the Head Masters of each conclave.

My postmortem advice to those reading this is to establish a better stronghold in Eclipsys for now. If not, then we should begin expanding our recruitment efforts and should focus on our friends in Piquer in bolstering their defenses.

Good luck to you all, and may Tressia's wisdom guide us further.

> My glory shines to the next world
> My loyalty lies in the great beyond
> My freedom will be afterlife
> My allegiance is hereafter

— BASTION KRAIN, MASTER OF
ILLUSIONS, HEAD MASTER OF THE
WESTERN COUNCIL OF THE QUEEN'S
WRAITHS

GLOSSARY

Alignment A group of sorce users who have a common goal, interest, or creed. Alignments answer to themselves as rogue factions within modern society. Since the Sorce Wars, governing forces have not been able to maintain order long enough to bring such factions to an end. Most Alignments are powerful enough to run cities, but rarely overreach to countries or continents in best interest of their survival.

Apprentice The first and lowest class of sorce user. Apprentices are beginners in their castes, little knowledge, typically lack discipline. Apprentices usually age between 20-22. An official title given by sorce institutions.

Artí [ärtē] Sorce users who prefer crafting/building artifacts that manipulate sorce for them, rather than memorizing spells or taking the strain of sorce manipulation on themselves. Well-known Artís tend to create famous artifacts capable of great feats.

D [dī] Dai. The currency used amongst sorce users which has become the most common currency around the world.

DISC Dynamic Intelligent Sorce Crystal or "DISC" is a malleable sorce crystal. Though not powerful enough to cast spells, they can store a large amount of sorce. They are also capable of small tasks such lights, alarms, projectiles, etc.

Draxolotl [dr'aksə‚lädl] Draxolotl are large creatures of the sea. Mostly living in the deep, Draxolotl are known to appear near the surface of warmer waters, especially near beaches and coastlines. Their bodies shimmer as sunlight dances around their body. The scales that cover 90% of their bodies are often used in healing ingredients and Fencer weapons for their sorce resilience.

Echo A term created by Bastion Krain to give name to the unidentifiable dark entities that consume their hosts. The origin of these sorce entities is unknown, it is unclear how or if they multiply. One thing is known for sure; the host will surely die if they cannot be separated. Also, the given name of the "echo" that lives within Charlie.

Eclipsys [ə'klipsis] The sun-kissed country that is known for its tropical atmosphere, extravagant jungles, and beautiful pyramid structures. The birthplace of Tressia, and home to the Clipsy people.

Fencer [fensər] Sorce users who prefer to forge weapons often made of materials to enhance their spells. Enchanted weapons are particularly good at one kind of spell, taking it to the most extreme version of whatever that may be. If sorce is no longer usable, or the enchanted weapon is unable to perform its spell(s), Fencers rely on their weapon's durability as a last line of defense.

Legend A title reserved for those who have achieved famous or infamous feats, acquired a near unobtainable power, or forged a dynasty. Legends are recorded as some of the most powerful sorce users throughout time. The first recorded Legend was Tressia.

Maethril A collection of islands located to the West of New Shelltar.

Master A title of respect and authority to sorce users who have achieved great manipulation prowess and knowledge.

Titles such as "Master" can only be given by another Master. Typically, this title invites challenge, therefore not many take the title without having earned it from another Master beforehand. Those who take the title before earning it are prone to being reminded by other Masters where the line is between them. Not an official title given by sorce institutions.

New Shelltar The coastal city, known for its beautiful piers and golden beaches. Many travel for the clear skies and a chance to see their white-scaled Draxolotl.

Piquer An island country known for its ales and resources of sorce minerals. Piquer has many taverns and pubs, is known for its winter festivities, and its mostly cloudy skies. The people of Piquer are often referred to as the Piquish. Piquish people commonly have deep black or bright red hair, and speak with lilting/musical intonations.

Protégé The second class of sorce users. Protégés are introduced to more advanced techniques of sorce manipulation and techniques. Protégés are expected to have an idea as to what they'd like to specialize in. Common specializations exist in all three castes though there are some that are specific to each.

Sorce [sôrs] 1. The power or essence or ability used to influence/manipulate events, outcomes, course of nature, or otherworldly aspects. Whether illusions, elements, animals, spirits, minds, or creatures, sorce is present and can be controlled through different means.

2. Sorce users who prefer to wield "sorce" (see definition above) in its most natural and raw form. Sorces can cast directly from their bodies, stressing their physical forms but creating more concentrated and powerful spells. Extremely versatile, yet limited by their own bodies. Some Sorces are known to augment or enchant their bodies in attempts to exceed their body's limitations.

Tertiary The third class of sorce users. Tertiaries enter the phase of honing their skills and mastering their specialization. For Fencers and Artís, this often means forging their own weapons or artifacts respectfully. Sorces are encouraged to improve known spells or, if they possess the knowledge, create their own.

Versed The final class of sorce users. Versed show exemplary knowledge and skill with sorce manipulation, smithing, or artificing. Versed are usually chosen by establishments based on their specializations during their final demonstrations. Versed often find jobs as Master's assistants, in hopes of gaining the title of "Master" for themselves.